To My
Favourite

Happy
Birthday

# Endlessness
# of the
# *Stars*

# Endlessness of the

## DALE BOYNTON

iUniverse, Inc.
Bloomington

# ENDLESSNESS OF THE STARS

iUniverse books may be ordered through booksellers or by contacting:

iUniverse
1663 Liberty Drive
Bloomington, IN 47403
www.iuniverse.com
1-800-Authors (1-800-288-4677)

ISBN: 978-1-4759-9130-7 (sc)
ISBN: 978-1-4759-9131-4 (hc)
ISBN: 978-1-4759-9132-1 (e)

Library of Congress Control Number: 2013908749

Printed in the United States of America.

iUniverse rev. date: 5/9/2013

To my older brother Kevin and good friend Landon, both of whom I lost in my life way to early. They are greatly missed by everyone who knew them.

# Day 1

## *Wednesday*

It is mid-afternoon in October in a small rural farming town in Saskatchewan. The K-to-12 school is about to end for the day. The school buses are lined up ready to take the kids home. The sun shines on the yellow paint as they wait there patiently for the ruckus about to erupt through the school doors. The air is filled with blowing dirt from the neighbouring fields and grain dust from the farms around the town. The bell rings to end the school day, and students of all ages rush out to the buses or their own vehicles for those old enough to drive. They're excited to get the heck out of class and go home and hang out with friends or maybe even do some homework.

Landon makes his way slowly out of the school, a black backpack slung over his right shoulder filled with his lunch bag and schoolbooks that he brings home to pretend he has intentions of doing his homework. He stops at the flagpole and slowly brings down the Canadian flag. The flag is flapping in the brisk autumn wind as he brings it down. He pulls down his Oilers hat, which is barely sitting on his head at the moment. Some of the girls who are a few years younger walk by and with a slow drawn-out sexy tone say, "Goodbye, Landon," teasing him with flirtatious smiles. They giggle to each other as they continue on.

"See ya later, girls," Landon replies, laughing along with them. He shakes his head; they are younger and he doesn't want any part of them, especially since everyone else seems to have already. The girls look back at Landon with their wanting eyes and stare at his black Hotel Coral Essex T-shirt and his cute butt in his dark blue jeans.

Michelle walks out through the high school doors, her soft brunette hair gently blowing in the autumn wind as she goes over to Landon. "You forgot your bunny hug inside, dork," she tells him as she hands him his grey Michigan Wolverines hooded sweatshirt.

"I didn't forget it," he says with laughter in his voice. "I was hoping you'd bring it to me." He shoots her a quiet smile, and she beams back at him, hoping he meant more than that. Landon finishes bringing down the flag, and as he is making a half-ass attempt to fold it back up, he can't take his eyes off Michelle's innocent and gentle blue eyes. It is no wonder guys get lost in her beauty. The two of them have been close friends even with a significant age difference for high school.

The senior class and some other students stick around in the schoolyard casually bantering about the school day, dating and sports. Once the buses have left, they decide to pull their trucks and cars up closer to the sports field by the school so the music can be heard. Some of the guys, including Landon, have changed into gym clothes. The girls are gathering around a couple of the trucks while the boys are getting organized to play a quick game of football.

"Just pick a player already, you wad," pipes up one of the guys as they wait for Johnny to make a pick.

"Shut up," Johnny shoots back.

Soon the teams are picked, and the trash-talking picks up. "Don't you think you should have picked someone who can throw a ball?" Shane, one of Landon's closest friends, jaws to Johnny while making an awkward throwing gesture with his left arm (Johnny is a lefty). Johnny just glares back at Shane and the rest of the team as they make gestures toward him and his teammates. The testosterone is high on the field, even though it is just a pickup game of football.

In the back of one of the trucks that the girls are sitting in is a cooler loaded with ice and alcohol, recently filled and brought over from the bar in town. Most of the high school kids drink and get their alcohol easily from the bar. Parents know this and accept it, just as long as the kids don't drink and drive. There's also a modified sofa in the back of the truck that some of the girls are sitting on, while the remainder sit on or stand around the tailgate. A stereo is playing "Wheat Kings" by the Tragically Hip from Gord's car among the trucks. Gord is big on his stereo and often talks about it, usually to get a few more panties at parties. These panties hang like trophies from the gearshift. The music is loud enough for the kids to hear as well as some folks in town whose homes are located near the field, but not too loud that anyone feels the need to complain.

The teams have been fairly and evenly divided up between seniors and the rest of the high school guys. Some of the players are more athletic than others, but no one team is stacked with natural athletes. In this small town, even the smaller social groups among the big ones are easily spotted, as is the case with the teams. The one team has Landon, the star athlete in the school; he is a senior and an all-around good kid who gets away with a lot but is never seen as doing wrong. For the most, part that is. The other team is headed up by Johnny, who is also a senior. He is always in Landon's shadow in sports, and when provoked he has a bit of a temper. Johnny and Landon pick the teams, with Johnny choosing first. On Johnny's team are seven guys who also have rough attitudes but still are good farm boys with occasionally scandalous personalities, including Gord and Max. Meanwhile, Landon's team consists of his friends, including Warren and Shane, who are more often than not breaking up the fights their friends start.

Also on Landon's team is Ethan, the oldest of his younger brothers. Like the rest of the family, Ethan is a gifted young athlete. While Landon takes after his mother's looks with his baby face, Ethan is more like his dad, slightly more chiselled and with a stockier build than Landon's long lean frame. The two compete with each other and against each other in almost everything they do, including sports, girls, partying and schoolwork. Well, the schoolwork is more Ethan than Landon, as Landon does just enough to get by. Both of their potentials are higher than what they are putting out as an effort, though—except on the field of play, that is.

The boys have started their game, and there is yelling and screaming from the field. It may only be a game of flag football, but country boys don't always play nice, and contact is expected, as some of them want to impress the ladies. "I am open" calls go out to Max as he runs a deep route, and "Throw the damn ball, you pussy" as Johnny is pressured by the defense.

"Oh my gawd," Max blurts out as he stops his route and begins to walk with Warren guarding him, very relaxed, "do something already before the girls realize you have a vagina."

Finally Johnny launches the ball up in the air toward Max, who now has three defenders on him. The ball is intercepted, and Landon's team takes over in their own end, near the girls. Laughter rises from the pile of people as Max and Johnny argue about the play.

"Shut up and give me the ball," Shane says as he rips the ball away from his teammates' hands and walks by the two squabbling players. "If you two ladies are done, let's play some football, or do you two need a timeout? Better yet, hug it out."

Max laughs with a smirk on his face, as if telling Shane that he got them, while Johnny just gets more frustrated with everything.

In the huddle, Landon gives each person his own route to run. They break and get set to run the play. "Hut one, hut niner, just hike the damn ball" Landon shouts out as the play starts. His teammates take off running their routes, some more intense than others. Johnny is covering his man with full intensity, like he was being scouted for the army or a college team. Landon fakes a pass to the receiver Johnny is covering. He then subtly nods his head to Warren, who is now running past Johnny and his own defensive coverage. Landon launches a throw deep and into the outstretched hands of Warren, who evades the grasp and weak tackle attempt of Johnny and strolls into the end zone for a touchdown. He spikes the ball and does some sort of shuffle while laughing. Meanwhile, Landon raises his arms for a quick moment in joy, but then turns and walks back to his end. A smirk is growing on his face and a bit of laughter comes out under his breath as he thinks about how hard some people try.

Johnny is fuming. "Where the fuck were you guys? Fuck," he yells out at his teammates.

"We were covering our man, what were you doing?" Max says with a who-gives-a-shit laugh and look on his face as the rest of the team chuckles at Johnny's frustration.

As the boys are playing, the girls are cheering from the truck and talking among themselves. Once in a while a guy or two goes over to get a beer from the cooler and change the song if it happens to be one he doesn't want to hear.

"You girls enjoying the show?" Max says as he cracks open a beer before heading back out on the field.

The girls basically ignore him and give him a casual, "Oh, for sure, so exciting" as the sarcasm drips off their comments.

The girls are talking about the guys out there and other boys from nearby towns, and the name that comes up the most is Landon's. Landon is the star athlete in the area; his dark brown hair pokes out from under his hat that he is rarely without. The girls love his deep blue eyes, his soft smile and how his top lip is almost hidden. As athletic as he is, he only takes care of his physique by playing sports. His demeanour tends to be quiet at times, but during sports he lets loose, not to mention his quick smart-ass remarks and humour he always chimes in with. However, he doesn't always let a lot of people into his private life, and in high school that is tough to do. A couple of the girls know some of Landon's personal life, but they don't talk about it, as Landon trusts them with it in a way that he doesn't trust others. He also knows a lot about them, as they find it easy to talk and open up to him with any and all issues.

"I remember back in grade 4, Landon and I shared a kiss," says one of the girls, a junior at the school.

"That doesn't really count—you were kissing everyone that year," Renee responds, and laughter bursts out from the girls.

"You weren't the only one," says Jen, a cute short blonde from Landon's class, as she takes a sip from her beer. "I was his first kiss in kindergarten," she adds with a smile, knowing that most of the girls won't even get a sniff at getting a kiss from him. It's not a secret that the kisses happened, but they just aren't a story that is always on topic. A few of the younger girls whisper among themselves—they want more details—but nothing more is said of it.

Meanwhile, Michelle just sits there wearing Landon's Michigan Wolverines bunny hug, her hands tucked up in the sleeves to keep warm from the chill in the air, her feet in sandals dangling from the tailgate of the truck. She tries to hold on to the little bit of summer before fall hits. She watches Landon play from here, sometimes looking back and smiling as the girls talk around her; she adds to the conversation from time to time, but only to be polite. Landon has no idea he is being eyed up by a young girl in grade 9 who is the epitome of the girl next door. She has innocence in her gentle blue eyes, her smile is soft and coy and could make the saddest clown smile, and her body is athletically curved. She and Landon are friends and fairly close for her being in grade 9 and him in grade 12, even in the small town where everyone knows everyone and talks to each other. The girls in the back of the truck all know of the friendship between the two, but with it being those two they don't think anything of it. Well, for the most part, that is—it is high school, and teenagers will gossip. Rumours are out there and Michelle has heard them, but she lets it all slide off her back.

Meanwhile, in the game, the teams are exchanging points and turnovers just as much as they trade barbs and trash talk. "Grow a pair!" Warren pipes up as the other team bitches about a hit that was legal and clean, but not when it happens to their player.

"This reminds me of your mom … easy," Max trash-talks as he walks by Shane, scoring to put his team up by a touchdown.

The game continues, and the guys are getting tired but no one wants to quit yet. They decide after a few more plays and now a tied game that the next touchdown will be the winner. Johnny steps back and throws up a pass for Gord, who seems wide open. Landon catches up to Gord in coverage just as the ball is arriving. He gives enough of a distraction that Gord mistimes the ball and it goes through his hands and hits him with a solid thud in the stomach.

"Use your hands to catch the pass, not your gut!" Johnny yells out in frustration at the drop and the eventual turnover of the ball to Landon's team.

Landon drops back the very next play for what the other team thinks is a deep pass. Instead, he decides to run some trickery with a hook and ladder play. He makes a quick pass 20 yards down the field to Warren, who as he is running right, and with defenders coming at him, tosses the ball back to Shane, who takes off the other way with the ball. The defenders are in tow, as are his teammates. Johnny is coming on fierce and has full intent to be vicious, as he doesn't want to lose. Shane gets surrounded by the other team but slowly trudges forward. As he is almost down, he sees Landon out of the corner of his eye. They make eye contact and the ball comes out of the crowd back and to the right to where Landon is open. He takes off with only 20 yards for a victory. The girls are cheering as they run toward the boys for the touchdown. Landon senses that Johnny is in full angry flight to tackle him. He runs and can hear the footsteps and the heavy angry breathing behind him and slightly to the left. He makes a juke to the right just as Johnny takes a deep breath and makes a diving attempt to tackle him. Landon then just strolls into the end zone with a laughing smile on his face.

The girls are cheering and laughing at the play. Landon notices them but doesn't focus on them—but there is one in the crowd of girls that he does notice.

Walking by Johnny, who is just getting up and pounding his fist into the ground in frustration, Shane puts his hand on Johnny's head and gives his hair a tussle. "Wow, that was amazing, you were about as graceful as your mom on a stripper pole," he says with a chuckle and continues on.

"Thanks for coming out, ladies, it was a nice whoopin'" Landon says to the guys as he slowly walks by them on his way back to the girls and the vehicles. He isn't being a jerk, as he says it with a stupid grin on his face. They all tell him he got lucky and that they will get him next time as they pass by. Well, all of them except Johnny. He is still huffing and puffing as he walks grumpily to grab a beer.

By now it's almost five o'clock, and the guys are all tired from the game. They're standing around all sweaty in their clothes. Some, including Landon, step behind one of the trucks to change back into their regular clothes. The smell of Axe body spray fills the air from Johnny spraying it all over himself. Landon just shakes his head watching him put on the douche bag trailer-trash-whore lure. No one is worried about who won or lost other than Johnny, who is annoyed that his team lost by a late touchdown play by Landon. The frustration shows on his face and in the tone of his voice throughout the conversation he is having around the girls.

The guys slowly make their way back to the trucks. Some hop onto the tailgates while others stand around the girls and begin to drink a few beers. Johnny hops up and sits beside Jen. She is coughs a little as a joke, as the smell of Axe is killing her. The two have a weird friendship that may or may not be based around drunken encounters. The two are not exactly dating, but everyone knows that there is stuff going on. They both talk about the encounters with their friends all the time. Everyone knows but doesn't care.

Renee and Shane are getting slightly cozy on the endgate, but only casually flirting as friends. Shane slides his hand sneakily onto her knee. She looks away while taking a swig from her beer, and then she slides his hand off her leg politely. He tries again, and before she can move it he sneaks it up further and gives her thigh a squeeze. She shoots him a glare, while he looks back with his tongue out trying to get her to laugh. The two chuckle together and pound back their beers.

Everyone but Landon is drinking. He doesn't drink because of his athletic ambitions and the scare tactics and pressure put on him by his grandparents. Some of the teens only have one or two so they can still drive home, but some are well past that. No one tries to get Landon to drink. Years back they might have, but they now know it isn't worth the time. As he stands there with his friends drinking, he just enjoys listening to them and throwing in his random comments. He never tells them that they shouldn't drink.

The conversations are getting louder, and more laughter is shared as stories are told of the past few weekends of partying. Laughter from a few of the girls can be heard miles away, as they shriek at the stories being told. Some of the stories probably shouldn't be mentioned, but they come out anyway as guys talk about their hook-ups and make fun of the girls and who they were canoodling with. Some of the girls take offense to what is being said, but for the most part everything ends with laughter. They all know who is a slight tease with guys or just a straight-up slut, but that never affects the overall friendship of the entire group. They know the guys can be pigs but for the most part have hearts of gold.

Landon is standing by the truck with his iPod in one ear playing the Tragically Hip's "Little Bones." He is holding an orange Gatorade in his right hand. A hand comes up over his shoulder and he looks at the fingers to see who it is. It's Michelle. She whispers, "You played a good game today, and you looked good out there." There is a slight sexual undertone to the end of the comment. He looks at her with some confusion written on his face; his eyes are slightly stunned but excited. He had no idea she was focused more on him than chit-chatting with the other girls. She takes off his bunny hug and hands it to him. He takes his hat off to put it back on. As he pulls it over his head, he breaths in the aroma of the bunny hug, smelling a sweet new scent that is not his. He pulls his head through the neck hole, letting the hood linger on the top of his head for a moment before he draws it all the way back to put his hat on.

"Great, now my bunny hug smells like girl," Landon says with a coy smile on his face as he looks at Michelle, who is fixing her hair after pulling off the bunny hug.

"Oh, you like it," she replies with a sweet smile on her face. She reaches into her backpack and pulls out her Adidas bunny hug to stay warm in the autumn air.

The two talk quietly underneath the noise of the sexual conversations going on and the music playing in the background. She knows Landon wouldn't want to make a big deal out of something like this, not to mention she's not up for being gossip among the seniors. Even though she is accepted among the group, sometimes age and social standing takes over in even the smallest of gatherings.

Landon takes a moment to find himself after he catches himself admiring her beautiful blue eyes. He gathers his thoughts as he speaks. "Thanks, I was awesome, wasn't I." He smiles, knowing that it is only half true, as he doesn't take it that seriously. His eyes are telling a deeper story—that he is happy that she noticed him out there.

Michelle notices his eyes; she is captivated by the look that Landon gives her. The two gaze longingly into each other's eyes, their innocence blocking any awareness of the reciprocation. Landon has perfected the turn and smile as you slowly blink, and the two part ways. This always makes Michelle's heart flutter, and he knows it. The smile comes out subtle at the corners of the mouth while the eyes smile as they open up toward Michelle as she walks away. She continues on to the other side of the truck to talk to her girlfriends, smiling back as she stands with her friends from the other side of the truck.

Warren leans over the truck-bed rail and looks at Landon, asking him quietly, "Soooo? What is going between you and Michelle?" There's a slight suspicion in his voice, but heavy on the casual ribbing between friends.

Landon just shrugs his shoulders and gives Warren a look of, *What can I say? The ladies love me.* They share a chuckle and continue listening in on the conversations around them.

Warren, along with most of the guys in the school, has a crush on the gorgeous young girl in grade 9. In a small school, it may be easier to stand out in the minds of your peers, but Michelle stands out wherever she goes. The guys all flirt and try hard at times to make a move on her, or go out of their way to be extra nice to her. She is polite and smiles at their ways but never thinks more of it. She still has trouble believing that she is as beautiful as people keep telling her. All she wants is to be beautiful in Landon's eyes.

"Hey Romeo, you gonna give Michelle a ride home today or what?" Warren asks Landon as the two get back into their previous conversation.

Landon coyly replies "Prolly?!" as he takes a glance over at Michelle, just as she brushes her brunette hair back behind her left ear as it shines in the setting sun.

★ ★ ★

The group slowly begins to disperse from the scene of the tailgate beers and weekend rumour chatter. Most the kids from out of town have to leave to help out on the family farm. In the small farming community, farming and family always come first. Tonight is one night that Landon has off from sports after school, and he doesn't want to rush home, as no sports are on for another hour or so. On his family farm he is just the gofer, running little errands and doing the shit jobs that still need to get done, like sweeping out a bin, taking fuel to the field or moving an auger in the yard. He feels the jobs he does are boring and annoying, yet he does them, as he knows they have to be done. He may not rush out to get them done like his dad or grandpa might like, but he still gets them done.

There are only a handful of kids now left listening to music at the vehicles. Landon, Michelle, Chantal and Ethan are all from outside of town, while Jen, Gord and Renee are remaining of the kids who live in town. Even the town kids are farm kids, as most have relatives in the area with a farm. There is no dividing line between the town and farm kids, as they all grew up the same way in the area, not to mention the social standings and wealth of most families are not so far apart that issues come up between kids. Some kids resent Landon and his brothers, since their family is a little better off than most, but it's usually never an issue when needing a ride home from a party or that extra buck to buy snacks at school.

Chantal and Michelle are really close friends, even though they are two years apart. Chantal is a chatterbox at times but isn't as annoying as some make her out to be. Her autumn-enriched shoulder-length red hair shines in the falling sunlight. "Ethan, you want me to drive you home?" Chantal says as she motions with her head at him toward his brother. "Because it looks like your brother is taking Michelle home." She and Ethan have been close friends from an early age, as they grew up on neighbouring farms only a few miles apart and have been classmates since kindergarten.

Ethan nods to her. "That'll do, donkey," he says in Shrek's voice with a laugh.

Landon has no complaints about this, as he is shy and tends to just let things happen around him, especially with decisions that he doesn't really want to make. The friends all say their goodbyes to each other, and jokes are made as they leave. The local kids begin to walk back to their houses.

"See you at home, Narbo," Ethan yells at Landon as they are getting in their vehicles.

Landon replies, "Yeah, yeah, shut up." He smiles at his brother from the driver's side door, which is slightly ajar. "If the parent asks, tell them I'll be home for supper."

Landon didn't have to offer Michelle a ride, but he is more than willing to take her home. For two friends to still be so awkward around each other in a possible relationship situation is amusing to their friends. Michelle is already sitting patiently in the passenger seat, her backpack at her feet. Landon finally gets into his parents' GMC Yukon, which he had to drive to school today. His car had a flat from running over a nail in the driveway last night, and he didn't want to change it this morning before heading to school. He isn't allowed to drive his parents' vehicles just for fun, but in certain circumstances they permit it. This happened to be one of those days. It has a solid sound system for a stock stereo, but not quite as good as his custom set-up in his ride.

In the vehicle, Michelle looks over at Landon, trying to get him to notice her. She is a nervous young girl with teenage love butterflies, sitting beside her crush. Her mouth moves, wanting to say something, as she tries to catch his eye and get him to look at her. This wouldn't be so hard if she only knew how nervous Landon was. He is playing it cool, but in reality he is a wreck with nervous energy. His right hand hangs over the top of the steering wheel with very little grip on the wheel. He moves his fingers to the beat of the song playing, just to let out some of the energy; rhythm isn't really a factor at this point. He wants to reach over and hold her hand but is too scared to make that first move. The prettiest girl in the school and a true friend is in his vehicle, and he is taking her home. He has driven her home many times in the past from school or parties, but he still doesn't know how to talk to her past being friends, how to tell her that he likes her. He is afraid to wreck a friendship by taking a chance with the one girl he has feelings for.

Music provides the background noise in the vehicle as the two of them joke back and forth through the awkward moments. Landon stayed up late last night burning a mix CD just in case today worked out like this. He is a hopeless romantic and a naïve teenager all at the same time, so timing is never his thing. The range of music is mostly '90s grunge with some country thrown in and some new top 40. Landon got into grunge music thanks to his uncle Matt, who grew up during that decade and was the local star back in his day.

Landon looks up to Matt for everything; he even wants to follow in his footsteps and go off to college in the states for hockey and maybe volleyball as well. Matt is now back in the area and helps out on the family farm from time to time while dating his high school sweetheart, Robyn. Landon doesn't want to come back after he graduates this spring. He wants to venture out and only come back to visit, if even then.

Michelle is also a fan of the music, as her older brother grew up in that same time period and went to school with Landon's uncle. Michelle sings softly at times with the lyrics, making it contagious for even Landon to join in. They begin to belt out the chorus to "Temptation" by the Tea Party.

Landon is focused on the road, but he steals glances at Michelle as she sits in the passenger seat. She looks so sweet and adorable in her grey Adidas bunny hug and jeans, her hair now pulled back into a ponytail. Her natural glow shines as the setting autumn sun comes through the windshield. Compared to Landon, she looks like an angel. His hair is a mess underneath his hat that is slightly tilted back on his head, not to be cool but for comfort, as his head is hot. He sits behind the wheel casually driving along all sweaty in his Michigan Wolverines bunny hug that has Michelle's sweet scent lingering in it even over his sweat, and jeans that look like he has been wearing them for a few days. Which is the case, but he will have to change them tomorrow as they got dirty from football.

He attempts to say something, but only an awkward sigh comes out as he stops his intentions before words even emerge. The silence in the vehicle is normal, but the underlying teenage drama is higher than usual today. The music fills the gap between the two, even though Michelle's hand is trying to entice Landon's right hand off the wheel to hold hers, as she has placed it on the centre console and moves her fingers gently across the edge, feeling the stitching with her fingertips. He doesn't notice her attempt to break the ice without even saying a word. Eventually, one of them will have to be brave and take a chance on what they both unknowingly want together.

Michelle beats him to the punch. She turns to him, shoots him a sweet smile with her lips as her eyes gaze at him with innocent intent, and says, "Do you think you could ever see yourself dating a girl who was in grade 9?"

Landon gives a sly smile and looks back at Michelle, replying with complete charm, "Like who?"

Michelle gives him a dumbfounded and annoyed look and punches him in the arm as she says, "Me!" She pauses for a slight moment before she realizes that she just punched him like a friend would when teasing.

"Sorry, did that hurt?" She didn't mean to be so mean and hopes that he doesn't misread the punch.

Landon slightly cringes taking the hit but laughs it off. He doesn't reply right away, which by the look on Michelle's face is not helping the nervous tension. She has just made the first move and now is wondering why it is taking so long for him to respond. He changes the song on the CD just before he slows down the vehicle to make the turn onto the gravel road to Michelle's parents' house. Silence is growing between the two, as Landon drags out the response he is rehearsing in his mind. He is doing so to make the moment awkward, but he has it in control. He can't handle awkward situations that he has no control of.

Landon drives down the gravel road a little ways and pulls over into an approach to a wheat field. The vehicle is still running, with the stereo playing Stone Temple Pilots' "Interstate Love Song" in the background. He looks nervously and honestly at Michelle as she looks back with anticipation. He takes a deep silent breath to relax before he begins to open up to Michelle. "Michelle, I would love to date you. You are the prettiest girl I will ever know. Are you sure your parents will be okay with this?"

Michelle is shocked and happy at the same time. "It will be fine, don't worry, my parents think the world of you," she assures Landon. He is worried about this because her parents are both teachers at the school.

Both of the young lovebirds are nervous and excited yet not sure who is going to make the next move. Finally Landon reaches over and takes Michelle's hand in his. She looks at him with happiness in her eyes, and he looks back with passion in his. They share a moment smiling honestly at each other as they both lean in for their first kiss. It's a deep passionate kiss; it is Michelle's first real kiss, unless you count the playground ones back in kindergarten. "The Freshman" by the Verve Pipe plays in the background on the stereo. They break away from the kiss, their eyes still closed, taking in the sensation of the moment.

"You have no idea how long I have wanted that moment with you," she tells him.

Landon just smiles as he replies, "I hope that I didn't disappoint." He pauses as he softly licks his lips, tasting the sweetness left on his lips by her lip gloss. "I would be lying if I said I hadn't wanted to do that for a while as well."

She shakes her head no and says, "It was perfect," as she smiles, still enjoying the lingering soft sensation on her lips. They look at each other with excitement and lean in to kiss again, this time with more passion. Landon holds her face with his left hand, pulling her in ever so gently and kissing her deeply. Their lips stay locked as they begin to make the kiss less churchy and more of a slow, sensual French kiss.

They pull away from each other, their faces aglow with honest young love. Landon starts the vehicle and slowly gets it back on the gravel road to Michelle's home. They are holding hands and sharing smiles and glances with each other on the way back, acting all endearing and shy. As Landon turns the Yukon into the driveway leading to the house, they meet Michelle's grandpa in his hunting gear on the quad. They smile and wave at him as he goes by.

Driving up to the house, they see her mom and dad are outside. Landon and Michelle both wonder what is up and if they should be nervous. They pull to a stop beside her parents' car; her parents are on the other side as they pull up. Michelle gets out, as does Landon after he shuts the vehicle off. Her parents greet them with polite hellos and smiles.

"So what's the occasion? We just saw Grandpa on the quad," Michelle asks.

"Oh, we are about to head over to his place to help with the deer he shot," her dad replies, "and then we are going to stay for supper. Grandma is cooking up pierogies, fresh veggies and pork chops."

"You are more than welcome to stay if you like, Landon. I'm sure there will be plenty," her mom tells him.

Landon respectfully replies, "I'll have to pass on the supper tonight, thanks anyways. Besides, I'm not very good with helping out on the skinning of animals."

They share a laugh, as they know Landon is speaking about his last attempt at skinning a deer. He got more than he bargained for when he accidentally sliced the stomach open. The thought of the stench still makes Landon want to gag.

As Michelle runs in to get changed to go over to her grandparents' place, she gives Landon a hug and thanks him for the ride. They do not kiss in front of her parents, as they are still not sure how to go about their new relationship. Landon waits outside and talks with her parents for a few minutes. They stand back, side by side against their car, while Landon leans up against the passenger side of his vehicle. They can sense that something more is going on between their daughter and the local star athlete. They play coy and hold off on the interrogation that parents do when their kids start dating.

"Thanks for bringing her home tonight," her parents mention while she is in the house. He is one of the few they do trust of the group of kids who could have brought her home.

"Oh, it wasn't a problem," he assures them and continues on with teenage awkwardness as he stammers through the choice of words. "I enjoy, I mean, I hope to drive her home."

Michelle comes back out from the house, her wavy brunette hair out of the ponytail and bouncing gently as she walks. Her bunny hug has been exchanged for a comfy layered look with a scarf. As she heads over to her parents' car, she stops by Landon, the two smiling at each other while trying to hide their excitement from her parents. She gives him a loving hug with a gentle kiss on the cheek before he gets back in the Yukon. Michelle's parents smile and wave goodbye. Michelle and Landon share a wink and a smile, hoping that her parents don't see as they are getting in their car. Landon heads out first, with Michelle and her parents leaving right behind him. As he gets to the end of the driveway, he gives a wave goodbye in the rear-view mirror before he makes a right out of the driveway heading back to the highway. Michelle and her parents make a left out of the driveway on their way to her grandparents' place.

In the car, Michelle's mom asks, "So you and Landon seem to be really close?" She turns around to look at her daughter. She already knows the answer, as she can see the smile in Michelle's eyes.

"Mom!?" Michelle replies quickly, as if to tell her to be quiet, as she doesn't want her dad to know just yet. "It's Landon. What do you think is going on?" she says with intent.

"You know, Landon is a great guy, we wouldn't hate it if he was around more," her dad pipes in from behind the wheel.

Michelle smiles but doesn't want to let on anything more at the moment. Her parents don't press the situation, but they did want to have some fun with the questioning. The three of them sit silently as they head down the dirt-road trail with the Killers' "Runaways" playing from the radio. Michelle looks out the window lost in thought as the light of the setting sun shines through the trees onto her face. She can't stop thinking of the kisses; her lips still have Landon lingering on them. She pulls out her phone from her pocket and sends Landon a quick text, what she hopes will be her first of many as boyfriend/girlfriend.

★ ★ ★

Landon turns up the CD as he drives down the gravel road. Dust is kicked up and lingers in the air, giving a slight haze in the rear-view mirror as the dwindling sunlight tries to pass through. His head nods to the song and a huge smile appears on his face. He is smiling more in this one instance than he has in probably 10 years as he thinks about Michelle and dating her. It's not that Landon isn't ever happy or never has a reason to smile, he just prefers to keep his emotions in check so that he won't get hurt or hurt others. He is playing the drums on the steering wheel as he drives—not very good, but it's good enough for him. He starts to belt out the lyrics to Eve6's "Open Road" as he turns off the gravel road and onto the highway, the dust settling as he hits the pavement. He meets a couple of cars on the highway as he heads home, and he waves to them and smiles, as he knows almost everyone in the area.

At the corner where Landon turns off the highway and back onto the gravel road to his house, there is an old cemetery that isn't used anymore and has only a couple of unkempt gravesites. As far as Landon can recall, they've never been cared for. The tombstones have started to fade and crumble over the years. The entire set-up seems out of place, as there is no church around and there are only about a dozen trees protecting it from the field of wheat that surrounds it. At the corner, he meets his uncle Matt, who is off to his home in town to visit his girlfriend, Robyn. The two have been together since high school and are an inspiration to Landon. He hopes that he and Michelle could be like them. Almost all of Landon's relatives married their high school sweetheart; if not, they have all remained married through thick and thin. Landon takes pride in knowing what makes a strong relationship and how he wants his to be.

They slow down and pull over to a stop, each on his own side of the gravel road, and talk to each other through the rolled-down windows of the vehicles. The dust is settling around them from their sudden stopping. The sun shines over Landon's shoulder as they both turn down their stereos before they talk. The sound can be faintly heard outside their vehicles, but nothing to drown out a conversation between the two.

"School is in the other direction, where might you be coming from?" Matt asks Landon with a knowing smile on his face, guessing that he was probably at Michelle's.

"Well, after school we played football." Landon pauses. "Then, if you must know, I took Michelle home."

"Oh! So as friends?" Matt slowly spits out as if to rub it in.

"It started out like that, but we may have kissed, and I asked her out." Landon doesn't talk openly with most of his family, but with Matt it's a different story.

"You mean she brought it up and you finished the thought," Matt replies. "That is awesome for you. You two have always looked good together."

Unsure how to reply to that, Landon takes in a breath of crisp autumn air. "Thanks," he says. "I am still nervous that I don't know what I'm doing."

"You have nothing to worry about, just relax and be yourself. That is who she fell for," Matt assures Landon.

Landon and his uncle talk a lot, about school, sports, and girls. Landon's first time swearing in front of a family member was his uncle; he got his first beer from his uncle and was told not to drink another one again from his uncle at the same time. The two have always been close even though there is a huge age difference. Landon always got to hear about his uncle's escapades that inspired him to do bigger and brighter things—concerts, sporting events, or the random road trips he made over the years, some that not many knew he even took.

"Well, good luck with Michelle," Matt says as they wind down the conversation.

"Thanks, say hi to Robyn for me," Landon replies.

"Will do," Matt says as they both nod to say goodbye, rolling up their windows before heading off in their own directions, both kicking up dust and rocks at the other while singing loudly with their stereos. Landon meets his neighbour in a grain truck only moments after leaving. The two wave at each other from their steering wheels with a two-finger salute.

Landon only has about a 10-kilometer drive down the gravel road to his parents' place. He passes corners and fields with farmers harvesting the year's crops. He gives a wave of a couple fingers from the steering wheel at a few, as they are near the road and can see Landon passing by the field. The dust is heavy in the air from combining going on and grain trucks on the road. Landon has his head turned looking at a deer in a field outside his driver-side window.

Thoughts of Michelle are still floating in his head; the smile hasn't left his face. He sings along with the radio, nodding his head to the beat. As he passes by a small group of trees in a field owned by his parents, he glances back with his eyes to watch the road without moving his head. Out of the corner of his eye he sees an object on the road that he wasn't expecting.

A deer has run out from the trees and is only feet away from the vehicle. Landon tries to slam on the brakes and manoeuvre so as not to hit the deer. His foot strikes the brake and he cramps the steering wheel to the right. As he does this, the deer jumps forward to go the other side of the road, getting back in his way. Landon swerves back to the left with his foot still pressing on the brake. He can't stop the vehicle in time, as he was driving over a hundred kilometres an hour. He catches a rut in the road caused by the grain trucks and heavy farm equipment driving on the soft roads. The passenger-side bumper grazes the ass end of the deer. The deer spins and lands on its side motionless, partially in the ditch and partially on the road.

Dust and rocks are being kicked up on the road, but no one is around to notice the commotion. The sun barely breaking through the dust catches Landon's eye in the mirror as he tries to gain control.

Panic is setting in, but he tries to remain calm, tries to figure out the next move like he would in a racing video game.

The vehicle is getting away from Landon after hitting the rut and the deer. He tries to regain control but it is too late. The vehicle is going into the ditch. As he goes into the ditch, he runs over some gopher mounds, and his foot bounces around, hitting the brake and the gas pedals. He tries to steer the vehicle away from the trees and not tip his parents' Yukon. He thinks he has regained the vehicle through the rough patch and tries to get back on the road. Landon tries to put the brakes on again, but this time his foot hits the brake and slips off and catches the gas, slightly speeding the vehicle up.

"Oh *fawk* …" Landon cries with a drawn-out controlled scared calmness.

Unexpectedly, the vehicle takes a big dip and lunges to the left. Landon has run over a tractor rut from earlier in the year, which was hidden from sight thanks to the tall grass in the ditch. He cannot gain control of the vehicle as it starts to go onto its side. Landon's head slams against the door and broken glass flies around as the vehicle lands on the driver side going about 60 kilometres an hour. The metal and the dirt make for an eerie unsettling noise that no one is around to hear.

The air bags go off as the vehicle slides on its side along the tree line in the ditch. Landon's hands go off the steering wheel as they flail around; his body bounces in the seat. Thankfully, he is held in by the seatbelt, but at this point he has no control and is unconscious from the hard hit to the head. The vehicles slides a good 50 feet before it comes to a stop.

Landon is bleeding from a deep gash on his head. Some glass is embedded in his skull and arms, and he has unconsciously swallowed some as well. He lies there as smoke and dust fill the air around him. The sound of metal and dirt grinding on each other has subsided. The back passenger wheel slowly spins in the settling dust and fading sunlight.

The deer has gotten up and takes off running into the trees on the other side of the road. The deer he had been looking at before the accident has taken off as well, scared by the loud noises. The wheels on the vehicle are still spinning slowly; the hood and front of the vehicle is banged up good, and the windshield is shattered but still attached to the cab. The stereo is still playing. The CD skips as it plays Our Lady Peace's "4am."

Landon is losing a lot of blood now. His leg is broken, but he feels no pain from it. The various injuries he has suffered should be forcing him to scream in pain, but he feels none of this pain, nor can he yell for help. Internal bleeding is slowly killing him, along with the head trauma. Landon has no idea that he is dying, and chances of survival at this moment are slim to none. A new noise rises up through the wreckage. It is Landon's cell phone receiving a text message. One solid beep, and that is the end of it. The song changes to Toadies' "Possum Kingdom" as Landon's life fades out.

★ ★ ★

Half an hour passes before the same neighbouring farmer Landon met on the road earlier comes back down the dirt road in his swather and sees the wreckage through his grain-dusted windshield. He quickly pulls out his cell phone and begins to dial for the ambulance; his mind is a nervous rush as he rushes over to the vehicle to see if anyone is okay. "Is everyone okay?!" he calls out. "Can you hear me?! Are you okay?!" He runs down the ditch shouting at the vehicle, which is blocking his view of Landon on the other side. The phone still pressed to his ear, he is talking with the ambulance dispatch trying to coordinate them to get out here as well as listen to them help him with the situation. Dirt is rutted up all around the vehicle, the grass is ripped up, and what isn't is laid flat in the path of the wrecked vehicle. He walks around the vehicle through the mangled ground, not hearing any response to his voice from the vehicle. He climbs onto the passenger side in the hope of being seen and heard, since he can't see through the spider-web-shattered windshield. His footing is slippery on the vehicle, but he manages to fight his way up and get balanced, still yelling for a surviving voice. The dispatcher is in his ear still trying to help him and keep him calm as he rushes to help those in the crash.

In his haste to help out any possible survivors, he doesn't recognize the vehicle. He realizes quickly that it's Landon in the driver seat, though, as he looks through the passenger window. He calls out to

Landon, but there is no response. The EMT on the phone is trying to listen to what's going on, offering help and comfort. The farmer calls out again, this time louder, to see if Landon can hear him. There is still no response.

He tells the EMT where he is, giving the exact land location. It will be another 20 minutes at least before an ambulance arrives. He asks if he should be the one to tell Landon's parents of the accident or wait until the EMTs get there. The EMT tells him if he is okay in telling them he can, but it might not be a good thing if the boy hasn't survived the crash. That decision, though, would best be made on his own.

The farmer thinks that Landon has passed away. His chest isn't moving, and he isn't reacting to anything. Tears are filling up the farmer's eyes; he is fighting through the shakes in his face and body. Because of this, he knows that he can't tell Landon's parents, even though it would be the right thing to do.

He paces nervously around the vehicle, unsure of what to do. He debates on trying to get Landon out or if that would hurt any chances of survival. The EMT does her best to keep him calm on the phone until someone arrives. The farmer's voice is emotionally distraught as he responds to the EMT, and as he talks to himself out loud in the hope of finding the right way to deal with this.

Finally the RCMP and ambulance show up, followed shortly by a tow truck. One of the police officers goes to the farmer to see if he is all right from this, the other heads down with the EMTs to the crash site. They all can tell the farmer is in shock; it is written all over his face and his tense body.

The EMT crew rush over to the wreckage and try to get to Landon. The police officer pops out the windshield and one of the EMTs manoeuvres slowly into the vehicle. Once inside the vehicle, the EMT does what she can to revive Landon, but no luck. Finally, after a few minutes of trying to revive him, the EMT realizes that Landon has passed on. She lets the other EMT on the outside know this.

They walk over to the police and the farmer and let them know that Landon has passed away. They all take a moment, as all of them feel bad for the young man who died. One of the police officers walks over to the tow truck to get the driver to move the Yukon so that they can get Landon out of there.

As they are working on this, a grain truck and a few vehicles have now come across the accident scene. All are kept a good distance away, although in the grain truck is Landon's father, Kevin. He doesn't realize that it's his vehicle because of the damage and not knowing that Landon hasn't made it home yet. "Who had the accident?" he asks the police officer who has stopped him before the scene.

The officer won't say a name but tells him that the young man in the Yukon didn't survive the crash.

Hearing that it's a Yukon and knowing that they are the only ones in the area who own one of that colour, he begins to choke up and tears fill his eyes. "Did you say Yukon?" he asks.

"Yes, a Yukon with a young man in the driver's seat," the police officer replies.

"That's my son Landon in there. Let me go. Let me go see him," Kevin says frantically as the police officer tries to hold him back.

Landon's father tries to remain calm, but his body language and facial expressions are a wreck–all; his mind is running a million miles a second. Thoughts are coming and going about Landon and the rest of the family. A small, stocky man, he is politely aggressive with the officer as he tries to get by. His face is dirty with grain dust and in shock as he tries to fight with his emotions and get by the officer in his way. The officer can sense the frustration growing with Kevin but tries to remain firm in maintaining order at the accident scene.

"Sir, you will have to wait until we get your son out of there and into the ambulance," the police officer tells him. He offers his deepest sympathy to the father. "I am sorry that your son was in the vehicle, but I am just trying to do my job."

Kevin responds while taking deep breaths of the chilling autumn air, "Thanks for your compassion, but I must go see my son." They walk over to the ambulance together, their steps quick and aggressive even though they both know it is probably too late. Kevin maintains hope that he will get a chance to save his son in some way.

As the body is wheeled past him, Landon's father collapses to his knees, his eyes full of tears for his son. He can't control his emotions anymore. His heart sinks as he understands that the worst has just happened to his family. They have lost a son and a brother. He blankly stares at the stretcher with tears in his eyes, unable to find the words to say goodbye or ask why. He tries to quickly gather himself as he sits in the ditch, his head in his hands as he rests his arms on his knees. The smell of the harvested wheat and heat from the wreck are making him uneasy in his stomach and his mind.

He reaches into his pocket and takes out his cell phone, clumsily dialing his wife with his cold shaky hands. After three rings, Landon's mom, Justine, picks up on the other end.

"Hello, Hon ..." she says and then hears a shaky scared voice, making her nervous.

"Hon, it's Landon." He pauses to gather his composure. "He had an accident." She starts to cry uncontrollably, screaming in emotional pain. "He ... he ... he didn't make it," Kevin says with scared hesitation in his voice, the words tumbling out of his mouth as his wife hears the devastating news.

She drops the phone to the kitchen floor as she stands next to the stove where she is cooking supper. She can barely gather her senses. She is a complete wreck as the tears fall fast. She picks the phone back up with her shaking hands, trying to gain control of herself in a situation over which she has lost all control. She leans back onto the kitchen counter, her legs stretched out on the floor. Her hand covers her mouth as she tries not to let her husband hear her cry. He offers comfort from the other end of the phone; he too is fighting through the emotions, but he knows he must be strong for her.

"Where is the accident?" she asks through tears with quivering, scared lips.

"It's at the corner of the three little pigs' houses and Eeyore's house," he tells her.

This is how Landon and his brothers learned which fields were which. The one field of theirs has three small buildings in it, and the one house is made of brick. It is slightly rough-looking and not liveable, but it's the best one of the three standing. Kitty-corner to that field is Eeyore's yard—it has a house that is falling down on a slant and sinking into the ground. It looks so sad as it sits tucked into the trees that surround it. Landon liked the house; he enjoyed when he and his mom would take lunch to the men in the field there.

The people in the other vehicles that were originally planning on passing by but stopped because of the crash have now all realized who is in the vehicle and have started texting and phoning everyone they can. Word of the loss travels fast in the small farming community. They call close friends of the family, and they contact the ones close to them who should know of this. Parents are on their phones talking to other parents with heartache and sadness in their tone. Kids are all texting their friends as they stop their homework or video games or TV watching. The news travels fast among the youth as well as the adults. It is all over their Facebook pages and on Twitter, with memories of Landon popping up. They are texting nonstop, trying to come to grips with the devastating news.

By the time Landon's mom arrives at the scene of the accident, the entire community has found out, although it was only a few short minutes from when she left the house. She pulls up in haste with dust flowing behind her as she brakes hard behind her husband's grain truck. She quickly jumps out of the vehicle as she puts it in park, the engine still running. She runs over to her husband who is standing by Landon on the gurney just outside the ambulance.

The two embrace, screaming in emotional pain as the tears descend from their eyes onto their shaking cheeks.

"Landon!" she screams. "My baby!" Her arms reach out from the embrace toward her son's body. Kevin tries to hold her back so she doesn't see Landon in the state he's in now. She breaks free from Kevin, shaking him off of her. She stands over her son, the tears falling from her eyes onto his lifeless face. She places her right hand on his face as she leans in. "Landon, I need you. Don't leave me. Come back," she says hastily with quivering lips.

Kevin pulls Justine back from Landon and into his embrace, as one last tear falls from her loving eyes onto his cheek. "I am here for you. I got you," he says as the two watch the EMTs place Landon into the ambulance.

★ ★ ★

Michelle receives a call from Chantal while still in her grandparents' kitchen. They have just finished supper and are in the kitchen cleaning up as the men are outside skinning the deer. She answers her phone with excitement. She was having fun with her mother and grandma, still thinking of Landon and telling Chantal that the two are now dating.

"Hey, Sexy," she says, answering the call with teenage enthusiasm.

"Hey, Michelle," Chantal says with tears falling down and a sad nervous tone to her voice. "I have some bad news." She slowly fights out the words to Michelle. "It's … it's Landon. He was in an accident."

Before Chantal can finish, Michelle is sobbing uncontrollably. "Is he okay? Please tell me he is okay," Michelle frantically says through her sobbing. Her mother is standing near her, ready to be there for support, but she doesn't want to go too soon in case of an overreaction. "Chantal. Is he okay?"

"I'm sorry. So sorry, Michelle."

The two begin to cry together as Michelle falls to the floor in shock and emotional distress. Her mom leans down to her and tries to comfort her with a loving hug. The tears are now filling her eyes as well. All three of them are overcome with emotion.

"What … what happened?" Michelle stutters out through the sobbing.

"He tried to avoid a deer and lost control of his vehicle on the gravel road," Chantal calms down enough to tell Michelle, even though her body language and tone still indicate shock. "It looked really bad from what I heard from my parents." Chantal nervously shares the little bit of detail she knows.

Michelle hangs up the phone and drops it to the floor as her eyes look frightened and heartbreaking. Her mom holds her even tighter; her whole body is shaking in her mother's loving arms. She is trying to gain control of herself, taking deep shaky breaths. Her mind is a complete mess as she tries to gather her thoughts—all of which are of Landon, school, his family, and not being able to be with Landon ever again. Every thought leads to another one, a never-ending cycle that is not helping her calm down her emotions.

"Mom," she says into her mother's shoulder. "It's Landon. He died." The tears fall even faster from her eyes.

Michelle's mother tries to stay strong for her daughter, but the tears are now falling from her eyes as well. She gives her daughter a kiss on the head, trying to be as comforting as she can. The two sit there on the floor together for the next few minutes as they try to collect themselves.

Michelle's phone is vibrating, ringing on the floor as it is being flooded by text messages—none of which she wants to read right now, if ever. She pushes the phone away. Her grandma picks it up and places it on the kitchen table.

Her grandma walks out of the kitchen and heads outside to the men, who are just about to finish up skinning the deer. She tells the two men that Michelle just got a phone call from a friend, and that Landon was in an accident and didn't make it. The men are in shock; they stop in mid-cut and just stare vacantly. They take a deep breath, gathering their thoughts.

"We just saw him," Michelle's dad says.

"How is Michelle handling it?" her grandpa asks.

"Not well, but Kate is with her," Grandma quickly replies as the three of them make their way back into the house to be there for their grieving daughter and granddaughter.

Michelle's dad is feeling the loss of Landon differently than most. He has a feeling that his daughter and Landon were dating, but he also knows that Landon was his star athlete, and he was hoping for big things. Now that will never happen for the young man, and how will he and the school move on from this loss?

★ ★ ★

Landon's parents are standing on the road watching the ambulance drive away into the setting sun. A couple of the neighbours come over with tears in their eyes, offering some comfort to the grieving parents. Kevin and Justine thank them for their support, but they are so lost in a wreck of emotion that nothing is registering with them. Kevin holds onto his wife to comfort her and for his own support as everyone slowly leaves the scene.

Kevin walks over to the farmer who found Landon first. "Thank you," he says as they embrace.

"I am so sorry for your loss. I wish I could have done more," the farmer replies quickly through nerves, as he feels guilty that he couldn't save Kevin's son.

"Don't beat yourself up over this. You have nothing to feel shame about," Kevin says as the two stand looking at each other, trying to be pillars of strength as their eyes show the emotional stress they are both under.

Soon only the police, the tow-truck driver, and Kevin and Justine are left at the scene. "Officers, is it okay if we go and grab our son's stuff from the vehicle?" Kevin calmly asks the police.

"It is okay. Just be careful, as there is glass everywhere," the officer replies with firmness in his voice.

Kevin walks over to the Yukon. He sees the blood and all the damage of the wreckage that took his son's life. He goes down on one knee, covering his eyes with his left hand as the tears fall fast, even though he was attempting to be so strong just moments ago. He looks through the tears and his fingers into the vehicle; he slowly collects his emotions and goes into the Yukon and grabs Landon's backpack from the backseat, along with his son's white Edmonton Oilers hat.

Kevin then hears a beep from the passenger side; it's a reminder from Landon's phone for the text that he missed. His father reaches over to the passenger seat and fumbles around it until he finds the cell phone. It's damaged, with a cracked screen, but it's still in its Michigan Wolverines case. Kevin can't bring himself to look at the text. He puts the cell phone in his son's backpack as he begins to walk back up the ditch to his wife, who is still standing there looking on at the ambulance way off in the distance. Nervously she looks at her husband coming from the wreckage with Landon's stuff. As she sees the backpack in his hand, she begins to cry hysterically again, falling to her knees on the gravel road.

The two of them head home to their kids to console them and make sure everything is okay. Landon's siblings have already heard the news through text messages. When they hear it from their parents, it hits them even harder. They all break down in each other's arms. Brett and

Damon are frustrated by the loss and don't want to be hugged. Kevin and Justine don't really know how to react and help, as they are still learning how to deal themselves. Kevin remains calm on the outside, but inside his emotions and frustration are building up. He tells Ethan that he is going to have to be there for his brothers more than ever now. Ethan knows that he has to be strong for his brothers, but he also is having trouble holding back his emotions.

Justine walks around the house trying to distract herself by finding stuff to rearrange or throw out. Brett has gone and locked himself in his room with his music, while Damon is exhausted and frustrated and sits on the couch with the television on to distract him. None of them want to believe that this happened. Their eyes show a different understanding, as the tears and emotions are slowly coming through.

Kevin goes over to his wife and holds her close, as he can see she is slowly losing control. As he wraps her in his strong arms, she sinks into them for comfort. She sobs uncontrollably into his body. He tries to comfort her with just the embrace at first but slowly starts to say loving words to her to help her. She finally calms down. "I want to go and see my son," she proclaims as she wipes the tears from her eyes. Her breathing is becoming more focused and wanting as she gathers herself. "I want to go to the hospital and see him." Her eyes are focused with a slight nervous tinge to them as she brushes her hair back from her face and looks her husband in the eyes.

Kevin is not sure if this is a good idea or not, but he knows this isn't the time to fight her on anything. He picks up the phone and calls his parents, who live just up the road on the old family farm. He tells them they have to come to watch the kids for a few hours as they run into town to see Landon. His mother is heartbroken on the other end of the line—she has been in tears since she heard the news. She tells him that they will be down soon.

Kevin and Justine tell their kids that their grandma and grandpa will be around to take care of them and help while the parents run to the hospital. They promise they won't be long and tell their sons not to ignore Grandma and Grandpa. They also mention that if anyone calls, let Grandma answer the phone, as it will more than likely be family members they rarely hear from trying to act like they were close. Ethan and Damon nod, knowing which ones they are speaking of, not to mention their grandma loves to talk no matter the circumstances with any family member. Even though she has her favourites, she always tries to keep in touch with as many as possible.

Kevin's parents pull in and make their way into the house. Justine and Kevin embrace them with love and emotion. Even the strong old farmer sheds a few tears and gives in to a hug as he holds his son. They share a quick conversation, but Justine and Kevin are in a hurry and say they will talk more later. As they leave the yard, Ethan greets his grandparents in the kitchen with a hug as more tears and loving words are shared. His grandma won't stop asking if he is okay and how the others are doing. He gets them up to date on how they are all dealing with it. Ethan says that he will look out for Brett, who is still in his room, but Damon is tired and frustrated and will probably be asleep soon on the couch.

Grandpa goes into the living room and sits down by a sprawled-out Damon. He tries to engage the boy in a conversation, but Damon is vague and just wants to be alone. Grandpa tries for a while to get his grandson to talk; he tries old tricks that made them laugh as young kids, but eventually he gives up and goes over to the recliner. Both of them fall asleep as the television plays in the background. Ethan goes down to check on Brett, to distract himself with video games, and to reply to the texts coming in. His grandma is already on the phone talking to more family members. She calls some and answers the phone as soon as she hangs up. Each time the story comes from her mouth, she becomes number. The tears still flow, but the words come out easier.

★ ★ ★

With news of Landon's death travelling so fast among his friends, some have decided to go and meet at Renee's place in town. The town kids are there right away, soon followed by the kids from farms in the area. The group isn't that large, but it is mainly made up of Landon's real close friends. Renee's parents are there for support, offering humour, stories and snacks for comfort. Renee's mom was the grade 1 teacher in the school; she retired just last year, but she was always Landon's favourite teacher. On their fridge is a magnet that said "#1 Teacher" with Landon's grade 1 school picture inside it. Renee's dad is telling stories of Landon from his days playing hockey, as well as any story that will bring laughter and conversation to the kids in his home.

Michelle gets a text message from Renee asking if she would want to come back into town to hang out with some close friends so that she doesn't feel alone and left out. She is unsure if she can or should go to Renee's. She is a complete wreck and not sure if she wants people to see her this way. She mentions the idea to her parents, who tell her that it's okay if she wants to be with friends right now and that they will drive her in if need be.

Michelle calls Chantal and asks, still with some nervousness in her voice, "You going into Renee's tonight?"

"I was just about to see if you wanted to catch a ride in with me, actually," Chantal quickly replies as she is getting herself ready to go.

"I'll be ready by the time you get here. We should stop and pick up Amanda on our way into town as well," Michelle anxiously says as she too is getting ready—even though for her, that means walking around looking confused and staring blankly at everything in her room.

"Sounds like a plan. See you in 20 minutes," Chantal says as the two agree on the plans and hang up. Both begin to frantically finish getting ready to leave.

Michelle texts Amanda and tells her they will be there in a half hour to go to Renee's. She gets a reply back quickly saying that she will be ready. The three girls have been close from a young age, even though they were born in three consecutive years. They have always been like sisters and the best of friends.

Renee's parents have a quaint place—it's only a trailer but has additions built on. It is a familiar and comfortable spot for Landon's friends to meet at, as they've spent many nights partying there and playing Kaiser with Renee's parents. There are hockey sticks lined up neatly against the wall as you walk into the home. Family pictures and Ukrainian designs are everywhere.

The kids have gathered in the living room, with conversations going on while *Dumb and Dumber* plays quietly on the television. It brings comical distractions to the group as they try to deal with and yet avoid the reality of the loss of Landon. Every once in a while one of the kids quotes a line before it comes up, sparking laughter from the group.

By nine o'clock that night, there are about 20 kids at Renee's. Some are in the kitchen hanging out, talking with her parents. In the living room, some are looking at yearbooks and talking about memories of their childhood at school. Laughter—as well as hysterical debating and arguing—breaks out over school pictures and stories.

"Oh my *gawd*," shrieks Jen as she turns to see her grade 4 picture and the rest of her classmates. "What was my mom thinking that day?" She tries to hide the page from the others around her. "My hair is huge!" she says in shock.

"Oh, it can't be that bad, Jen," Amanda says to be polite, without seeing the picture.

"Oh, it is. Trust me," Renee says, knowing full well that it is a bad picture and so was hers. "Mine isn't much better, if at all."

"Let us see. It can't be any worse than you look today," Shane quickly replies with a smirk on his face, knowing that he will probably get a hit on the shoulder and an angry glare from the girls.

They pass the yearbook around, letting everyone see the bad hairstyles and clothing of the era. They also take a note of Landon, whose picture shows him with a smile that shows teeth. His hair is neatly combed and no hair looks out of place in his short slightly spiked style. He is wearing a dark blue T-shirt with Brett Hull's picture on it and Brett's name written in graffiti style. He's not very fashionable, but the style fits him.

As the yearbook is passed around, they begin to talk more and more about Landon and stories from school that they thought they forgot about. "You guys remember back in grade 6 when we went through I believe it was seven teachers?" Johnny mentions with some subtle chuckling as he talks.

"How could I forget that year? The quiet area in the corner behind the bookcase, so fun," Jen says with laughter.

"Ha. Is that because you were making out with—oh, what's his name—during breaks?" Shane asks, knowing that she made out with a classmate who left after only one year at the school.

"Shut up," Jen says with some anger but still laughing. She just wants to smack him for his comment.

"Hey you guys, remember the presentations that we got to do that year? I did mine on N Sync's Justin Timberlake. Oh, JT, I thought you were soooo dreamy," Renee says laughingly.

"Didn't you girls do one on each of the band members? Who got stuck with Kirkpatrick? It couldn't have been that in-depth or good," Johnny blurts out, laughing along with the rest of the kids.

"That was Cherie. She liked his hair," Renee recalls, rolling up against Jen as they sit on the couch laughing hysterically. "Speaking of, why isn't she here?"

"Who cares? She is so bitchy, and everything has to be her way," Shane quips. "What was Landon's presentation about? Let me guess, hockey?" he asks as though he thinks he knows what the obvious answer would be.

"Actually, no, he did one on Wrestlemania, and one later in the year about ulcerative colitis. You know, the disease that his uncle Matt has," Renee says. She slowly comes out of laughing as she and the others realize that Landon isn't there to enjoy the stories. The laughter dies down but doesn't fully go away. Side conversations start up around the group; some talk about Landon and others talk about anything that will keep their minds off of the situation. Although the group is maintaining a strong demeanour so that no one feels weak, inside they are all torn up over the loss. The memories help heal, but at the same time they open up the fresh wound of an experience they wish they never had to live through.

"Hey you guys, you know what I am gonna miss the most about Landon?" Renee pipes up, getting the group's focus back on why they are there tonight. "It's his friendship and smile. He was always there but never made anything about him, just like his smile."

As she says this, she and Michelle make eye contact, and both hold back their emotions, sucking back their bottom lips to hide the sad nervous energy that wants to come out. Chantal gives Michelle a hug to comfort her as they sit side by side.

"I have to say, I am going to miss the sarcasm and his quick one-liners," Jen says as she tries to look at her friends but instead hides her face behind her hand as she rubs her head before brushing her hair back from her face. "He made his jokes as though he was making fun of himself as well as you. You never felt ridiculed."

"Will you girls stop being so sappy?" Shane says with a bit of laughter.

"Shut up, Shane," the girls quickly reply with a glare, even though they know he is trying to lighten the mood just like Landon would.

"Hey, I miss Landon too. For me, though, I have to say I am going to miss just hanging out with the guy at parties, or in the locker room and just in the hallway at school." Shane explains his feelings as generically as possible so that real emotions don't have to come out.

Renee's mom comes in and places a plate of jerky on the coffee table and two 12-packs of Dr. Pepper on the floor beside the table. They all say thanks to Renee's mom. "I couldn't help but overhear your conversations from the kitchen," her mom says. "I will never forget when Landon came into my classroom in grade 1. He was a quiet kid, not shy, just quiet. He had an old lunchbox that I am sure was his uncle's. It was He-man, I believe it was. He wasn't the smartest of you kids, but he would catch on quick. He did have issues with cursive. But when he got to gym class, boy, could he play any sport," she says, recalling the earlier days of Landon as her student.

"So you are the one to blame, I guess, for his sloppy writing," Renee tells her mom.

"I guess so, but I was still his favourite teacher, so it couldn't have been that bad," her mom quickly responds as she looks at her daughter with a smile. "Watching him and the rest of you grow up as close as you are, you are all lucky to have each other. You should never forget him or the memories of your time together." Her voice becomes motherly and comforting. She leaves the room, and in passing she gives Michelle a smile, as she can see Michelle is fighting to stay in control. She doesn't know what is going on in Michelle's mind, but she knows the girl needs comfort.

"I am gonna miss Landon taking my drunk ass home from parties. He never left a party early and always gave someone a ride home when he left," Max says as he steps away from the wall he was leaning on and makes his way over to the couch to sit with Shane and Renee.

"Oh man," Shane says in agreement as he slides over to make room for Max to squeeze onto the couch. "I don't remember all the stuff that happened in that vehicle, but man, was there ever some good times." A smile comes on his face as he thinks of Landon and the fun they had.

"Hey, you remember that night down by the river, when we left the party to go get smokes and more beer? Landon offers to drive and says that his car smells of gas since a jerrycan spilled over in the trunk. I was messed up after that ride," Max says as he gives Shane a little nudge with his shoulder. They both laugh as they remember the moment.

"All I remember from that ride is sitting in the backseat and making Landon play 'The Dance' by Garth Brooks as we belted out tunes with the stereo," Shane says, laughing with every word. "Is that the same night we stole signs and thought we were gonna get caught?"

"Yeah, I think it was that night. We drug the one sign behind the car, sparks flying down the highway. Oh, and the one we had both posts going through the side windows as we drove down to the river to toss them all over the bridge," Max utters somewhat quietly. He doesn't want Renee's parents to hear of the illegal activity. The laughter picks up as they all remember that night.

"Yeah, even worse, we thought the cops or wildlife cops were after us, but it was only Warren and Gord in Warren's truck with a spotlight following us after we dropped the signs over the bridge." Everyone laughs as Shane shakes his head at Warren and Gord as he speaks. The two of them just sit there and laugh, shrugging their shoulders as if to say *not our fault*.

The stories continue on about random events Landon was involved or not involved in. Some voices are heard more than others. Michelle's is not one of those voices. She sits there quietly with a vacant expression on her face. She wants to talk, but she can't find the words to say to the group. She will at times whisper something quick to Amanda, but nothing more than that. The stories and pictures in the yearbooks put a smile on her face and make her heart heavy. The smile is the simple and kind type, one that you use to be polite and hope no one asks you a question or wants you to say more.

The kids comfort each other with memories and laughter. The laughter relaxes them as they deal with the loss of their close friend. It isn't easy to laugh at this time, but remembering their friend with the stories makes it easier to deal with the loss. Some do better with it than others. Michelle and Renee have trouble laughing at times, but there are some stories that bring out a smile or a solid laugh.

These stories of Landon include parties and the social web at the school. His friends talk about how he would drive home the drunkest people who couldn't hold a beer anymore—or a simple conversation, for that matter. Be it a girl or guy, a close friend or someone he barely knew, he would offer a lift with few or no questions asked. Landon was always there, he was at every party, every event in the community. He never made a scene, so everyone remembered his actions. He was just there enjoying himself in the company of his friends. He was a wallflower of sorts, even as popular as he was.

Shane and Max tell stories of the many weekend nights the three of them would go from town to town hitting up parties. Landon would drive, and Max and Shane would be a wreck by the end of the night, often having hit up two or three parties. Landon always went to these parties for his friends, as he didn't care to meet drunken people who wouldn't be there for him if needed. His sarcastic comments would sometimes piss off the wrong person unintentionally; it didn't happen a lot, but it did happen enough. This is when Max would step in and make sure nothing happened to Landon. Max was solidly built as an athlete, even though most might call it Molson muscle. He was a tough guy who had a good heart. Ladies loved him for that, and he took full advantage of it. Max often had to fight someone, and he was always willing and never lost. It didn't take long for people from out of town to know not to mess with the Brookhaven three. They got the title from friends from other small towns, as they always showed up together at parties and came from the small rural town of Brookhaven. Landon was always there quietly making one-liners, with Max getting into fights if called for. As for Shane, he was the middle ground of the two. He was a skinny nerdish athlete. He talked a bit more than Landon but kept his one-liners to himself unless talking to his buddies.

Max starts to tell a story of one night when they were at this cabin at the lake. "Hey, I got a story for you," he starts off, getting everyone's attention. Everyone who has stuck around this late has now gathered in the living room, only half the original number if that. They are all sitting on the couches or leaning up against the front of the couch by the legs of their friends. Max, sitting on the couch now with Jen and Chantal on either side of him, leans forward so that everyone knows to listen to him.

"A couple summers ago, me, Shane and Landon went to this party at a cabin up the lake. We knew a girl who was going and she invited us to the party even though it wasn't her party and we maybe knew four people before we got there. It was a bunch of city kids who thought they owned everything. Well, they found out that night that we run the show at the lake."

Max looks over at Shane, who is nodding his head, knowing full well what story Max is talking about. Some of the other kids know the basics of the story but not all of it.

"We had been drinking all day as it was," Max continues, "still able to be somewhat normal, but basically three sheets to the wind as we got there." Smiles and chuckles come out from the kids in the room. They know that the stories get good when these guys get drunk.

"Landon found this cute brunette on a couch inside," Max recalls. "He chatted her up for a long time. Others would come and go from the couch and around them but they sat and chatted like old friends. Me and Shane were playing beer pong not far from them. Which we dominated!" Max says as he high-fives Shane. "Oh, and then this other chick came over and was hitting on him but he wasn't paying much attention to her. She was a drunken mess and, well, let's just say someone eventually had to take care of her," Max says as he smiles and gestures to himself with his thumb, letting everyone know it was him.

"But then the brunette's boyfriend came in the cabin—he, I guess, had been outside by the fire and never knew his girl was flirting with Landon. He was not impressed. He got all up in Landon's face, calling him so many names and making an ass of himself. Which his girlfriend didn't really like. Landon, though, just sat there with a smug look on his face and let the guy talk. You could tell he wanted to say something," Max continues on, as he now is acting out the scene with his hands and his facial expressions, occasionally standing up as he talks. "Finally the guy takes a break for a brief second of yelling at Landon, as his girlfriend stands up and tells him to calm down. Without hesitation, Landon, who was sitting calmly on the couch, looks slyly up at the guy and tells him, 'Guess I will just get my gum back later.' That confused the guy for a second. His girlfriend was chewing on a piece of gum that Landon gave her. He starts his motion to punch Landon the fuck out. Landon sat back deeper in the couch expecting a drunken swing. But the girl stopped the dude and hands Landon his pack of gum back." Max is now in full action in telling the story as everyone laughs and their minds fill with memories and the visual of Landon.

"Funny thing is, do you guys remember Landon ever chewing gum?" Max asks the group.

"Not that often, usually when bored," says Chantal.

"Didn't he have a saying that if you are chewing gum, that means you got no one to kiss?" Renee replies.

"Yeah, he did," Michelle quietly says. "His aunt told him that."

"I was ready to go over there and knock the prick out," Max adds, "but the scene died down. The couple went one way and Landon went outside with the drunk girl to the fire. Plus we were one cup away from beating those city punks in beer pong. Pretty sure it was light beer that was in the cup, unlike when we play with shots of whiskey and vodka." Max flexes his Molson muscle telling the story.

"We eventually lost Landon for a couple hours as the night went on. He was at the fire with us and others. The brunette came back and sat with Landon for a brief second, before they took off alone. As he was leaving, he told the stoner beside him that when the girl's boyfriend comes out here, give him this pack of gum. He then sat the pack of gum on the stump he was sitting on. The two then walked off, and me and Shane sat there around the fire conversing with the city folk. Shane, you eventually passed out in the front seat of Landon's ride that night," Max says, looking over at Shane with a smile on his face.

"Oh, I remember enough from that night. Especially passing out in the car and being woke up by someone," Shane replies, shaking his head and laughing.

"Yeah, you got woke up from me and that chick making love stains in the backseat. But you did get a good show. She was hot!" Max says, proud of himself for his sexual prowess. "I have no idea if Landon and the brunette ever hooked up or what. He sure as hell could have if he wanted to, but the guy wasn't one to kiss and tell. I know I sure would have taken advantage of that situation." Max sits back into the couch, placing either hand on the girl on each side of him. The girls turn and shake their head at him and remove his hand.

The conversation soon turns to a party that happened last year, filled with many events, big and small. Looking back on it now during a hard time, the memories are becoming clearer, and it hits home harder since Landon isn't around to share in the story. Everyone adds in what he or she remembers. During this story, the emotion hits all of them in their own way. Michelle even speaks up during this story, adding in bits and pieces, as it does focus on her and Landon. She still sits back on the couch, listening to the stories with the constant thought of Landon and her together. She hides the emotions that are running amok inside her mind. Her face shows little strain as the story is told, but Chantal can see that her best friend is struggling with the story.

★ ★ ★

It was at a party in November last year at Renee's place. There were close to 60 people at the party throughout the night in her small home, which has been the host to many high school parties. Michelle was in the kitchen sitting on the counter with Amanda, and they were talking to each other along with others in the room. At the kitchen table were Ethan, Shane, Renee and Landon. They were playing Kaiser and drinking the beer of choice that night. Even for underage kids in a small community where everyone knew everyone, it was never tough to get alcohol.

There were roughly another 10 or so people hanging around in the kitchen. One of them was a guy from out of town who had played hockey against Landon and the rest of the boys in town. He was trying to make nice with Michelle using all the lines he could think of. Michelle was polite and patient with the guy as they talked about music, as well as his attempts with the pickup lines. Keith Urban's "Making Memories of Us" was playing in the background.

"Hey, Baby. You just gonna sit there, or you wanna go make a memory together?" the guy said as he leaned in, trying to entice

Michelle. He was harmless, they all thought, as nothing wrong was going on and Michelle seemed to have it under control.

"No thanks. I don't want to have a memory wasted on you," Michelle politely said.

The drunk guy had no idea he was burned by her. He just kept laying on the lines and making moves on her that constantly fell short. For a girl her age, she was composed and never let others peer-pressure her into things, especially the guys who flocked to her wherever she went.

The four who were playing cards could hear the conversation going on but were so involved in their own stories and laughter that they never paid close attention. The music then switched to Nickelback's "Old Enough," loud enough from the stereo in the living room to drown out most of the extra noises.

Landon leaned over to Michelle and said, "You even old enough to be here, Missy?" The two gave each other a stupid face and stuck their tongues out at each other.

The guy was not impressed with Landon's cock-block attempt and became more and more intense with his attempt at getting some quiet time with Michelle, not to mention his wandering hands on her legs.

Amanda was sitting right next to her on the counter watching all of this and talking to Max as they stood there drinking their beer. Max was unimpressed with the guy as well, but they both knew it was under control and wouldn't let it get worse if it began to go that way.

Michelle got off the counter, walked over to the table, and leaned over Shane's shoulder to ask if he could watch out for the guy who was talking to her. Shane took a swig from his Molson and told her that he would do what he could and that she might want to let Max in on this as well, or he could if needed. She gave him a hug around the neck and walked into the living room, shortly followed by the guy, who shot a glare at Shane and Landon as he followed her. Max stood back and glared at the guy as he passed.

Shane looked over his shoulder and saw the guy follow Michelle into the living room. He turned around and tapped Max on the leg. "Hey dude, can you go in there and watch Michelle and that douche? She doesn't like him hanging on her. I'd go, but I'm playing cards."

"Yeah, no problem, I was thinking of doing that anyways. I don't really like the guy," Max replied as he picked Amanda up off the counter. They walked into the living room with his arm around Amanda's waist. Amanda placed her right hand in Max's right back pocket, giving him a little squeeze. Both had their drinks up to their mouths, taking a sip, as they entered the living room to party with the other party crowd. The kitchen area was quieter and social, as kids played cards and talked to each other as they drank their alcohol, while the living room was more boisterous with the conversations and the music playing as well as a drinking game or two taking place.

Michelle was sitting on the arm of the rocking chair that Chantal and Carmen were squeezed into, while the guy was standing close to her, lurking over her shoulder, pretending to be in the girls' conversation as well as the guys' conversation on the other side. Max brought a little kid's stool into the living room and set it down next to the chair, somewhat separating Michelle and the guy. Max sat down on the stool with Amanda sitting on the floor in front of him, resting her back on the stool between his legs.

The two quickly jumped into the conversations around them and began to laugh and carry on with their friends. When you were from the area and knew everything and everyone, it was hard not to jump into the conversations as if you were there the entire time. Max, being the smart-ass that he was, threw random comments into the conversation to annoy the girls, while Amanda was the calming influence to whatever stupid remark Max spat out as she tried to have a simple conversation with the girls.

The guy, annoyed that Max would move in like that, tapped Max on the shoulder and said, "What the fuck is your deal, man?"

Max looked up at him. "Sorry, Buddy, not playing cards, that is in the kitchen. You are more than welcome to go back in there and play."

The guy was not impressed. "If you couldn't tell, me and this pretty little thing were having a conversation before you got here."

Max looked over at Michelle. "Michelle, this guy says you were having a conversation?"

"He was having a conversation. I was just kind of there," she replied, shaking her head as she looked awkwardly at the guy.

Max turned to the guy. "Sorry, Buddy, I think that ship has sailed." He took a swig from his beer and got right back to talking to his friends, who were now ignoring the guy fuming behind them. The conversation grew into laughter and they began to clink each other's bottles in celebration of randomness. Max, being a smart-ass, tapped the top of Chantal's beer bottle, which made the beer foam up. Chantal tried to suck back the foam, but before she could get all of it, a slight mess was made on the chair and the floor. And just a very small amount landed on the guy's foot, which did not sit well with him. Up until that point, everyone seemed to be having a great time. Well, except for him, that is.

The guy chugged the remaining beer in his bottle and threw it to the floor. Everyone in the living room stopped talking and looked at the guy, who had now knocked Amanda over in an attempt to get at Max. He then picked Max up by the shirt. Not the smartest of moves by him, but he thought he knew best at that moment. The crowd slowly separated around the two of them. The crowd in the kitchen was slow to react to the events, as the sound of "Let's Get Rocked" by Def Leppard drowned out the noise, and the card game was more interesting.

Soon they as well became entertained by the ruckus in the living room. As the guy brought Max up and was about to punch him and start a fight in the living room, Max shook his head and said, "You don't want to do this, Buddy." Now the guy was pissed off and was staring down Max, while Max just looked back at him with a cocky smile and excited eyes.

The aggravated guy told Max, "Shut your pie hole." He made a quick attempt at a punch to Max's face but it missed as Max ducked away from the pathetic angry punch. The guy stumbled as he swung with the punch. Max let him stumble and find his balance in the small open space in front of the partygoers, some of whom were standing around while others remained on the couches watching it all take place.

The guy came back again at Max with another swing at his face, but this time as he missed Max grabbed the guy's arms and took him down as if he was a WWE wrestler. Max had him pinned and said, "You best just leave the party before this gets worse for you. No one wants you here. Especially Michelle." He rubbed the guy's head into the carpet as he told him this. Max then let the guy up so he could leave the party.

Michelle was standing next to Shane and Amanda as the guy got up, angry and embarrassed. He made his way out to his vehicle to leave, passing everyone who was glaring at him for making a scene at the party. Even the friends he had there were embarrassed by his actions and ignored him as he left. Michelle glared at him as he walked by while the guy glared right back at her. "You are just a fucking tease. Get over yourself, you aren't that special."

Landon took a deep breath and glanced menacingly at the guy from his chair at the kitchen table as he watched the asshole pass by before leaving to go outside. He got up from his chair where he was comfy and followed the guy outside to make sure there was no more trouble.

The guy turned around and hissed, "You are a fucking cock-block. You're lucky I don't knock you the fuck out. Asshole!"

Landon remained calm but took a deep breath standing on the porch deck in the cold November air. The others inside watched from the windows as Landon walked slowly behind as the guy headed back to his car. At the car, the guy stood behind the open driver-side door and decided that he was tough enough again to make one more comment, loud enough so that those inside could hear him: "She is a bitch and a dick tease. She can go fuck herself. You all can!"

Landon had now had enough and kicked the open driver side door into the guy. His hands stayed in his bunny hug pocket and his face didn't stray from the calmness he had from the start. The guy fell in pain to the cold ground. Landon stood over him. "If you ever—and I mean *ever*—say anything like that about Michelle or any other girl for that matter, you are going to get your ass handed to you like the little bitch that you are!"

The guy got up in a huff. "You are an ass. Watch your back, Buddy."

Landon stood there listening to the guy run his mouth and without missing a beat stood on the other side of the car door, the two separated only by the width of the open car door. "How about you just stay away from my ass. I don't swing that way. But if you do, that is great for you," Landon calmly said as the guy got back into his vehicle.

The guy gave Landon the finger before shutting the door.

"Just leave before this gets worse for you," Landon said, shaking his head at the juvenile actions of the idiot. The guy shut the car door and peeled off from the yard, kicking up rocks and hitting some of the cars as he left.

Michelle walked out from the party, made her way to Landon and stood next to him. "Thanks. You didn't have to do that, you know." They watched the dust settle in the chilly autumn night as snowflakes slowly fell upon them.

"I couldn't just sit and watch anymore," he told her. "I know Max and Shane will always have your back if stuff like this happens, but tonight I felt as though I had to do something." He paused for a second, taking in a breath of cold air. "Just make sure that Max doesn't hit on you afterward." He gave her a little shoulder nudge as the two laughed, knowing it was true. Max was a nice guy but a bit of a player in their small community.

Michelle gave him an honest and heartfelt look. "Why did you make your way outside and do what you did to that guy?"

Landon looked her in her beautiful eyes. "Well, I needed the fresh air anyways. Not to mention he was being a complete dick to you. Besides, even the nice guy has to stand up for the prettiest girl once in a while." The two shared a smile and a laugh before heading back inside. Landon placed his arm around a shivering Michelle, bringing her close to him for comfort and warmth as the two walked back to the party, where the sound of "Blow at High Dough" by the Tragically Hip was playing from the living room. Inside, beers were being downed with ease and the possibilities were endless for the night, as though the fight never happened. Well, other than the exaggerated talk of how it all went down.

The rest of the night went off without any major incidents, just a couple people not being able to handle their alcohol and throwing up in the kitchen sink and out on the deck. Renee managed to get most of the crowd out by four in the morning with the help of Max and Shane. The few who stuck around to help clean up were the usual ones—Michelle,

Chantal, Shane, Ethan, Max, Jen, and of course Landon. The guys took care of the bottles and made sure they were boxed up and any broken bottles were disposed of. Meanwhile, the girls took care of cleaning up the little messes of chips, dirt, and spilled beverages on the floor and the couches.

After the clean-up was done, Landon took Michelle home at the same time that Chantal and Ethan took off together. As they left, the remaining kids sat around the table playing drinking games and talking about the ones who just left. Those remaining knew they would be crashing on couches or a bed at some point, as none of them was capable of driving home.

Michelle and Landon walked to his vehicle that night closer than just friends, but still just friends. Landon walked Michelle like a gentleman to her side of the car, but once at her door he took it upon himself to be a smart-ass and grab some wet snow from the ground, giving her a face wash. She tried to fight it, but Landon got her a couple times. She grabbed some snow and threw it back at him but missed. The two laughed, separating to their sides of the vehicle. Michelle brushed off the snow from her jacket and out of her hair. She looked over, annoyed and laughing at Landon, who was sitting in the driver's seat as if he had no idea what happened. He had a smile on his face that made Michelle forget about the cold snow in her shirt. They took off, heading to Michelle's as "Tattoos on This Town" by Jason Aldean playing on the stereo.

The remaining kids wondered if Michelle and Landon were an item or if anything was going on romantically between the two. No one thought that anything was going on to make fun of, but it still brought up some minor gossip, with *minor* being the joke used because of Michelle's age. The girls believed that Landon was just being a nice guy to Michelle, as he always was with girls. The guys said that Landon wouldn't ask or even try anything with Michelle, even though he should.

They did however share a few laughs over Ethan and Chantal leaving together, as those two had hidden their affection for one another for so long in their friendship. No one knew if they were dating or were friends with benefits, yet at the same time no one really seemed to care. It was clear that eventually the two would be dating, if they weren't already.

★ ★ ★

As she listens to the stories, Michelle's face begins to tremble and tears start to slowly trickle down her cheeks. Unable to take it anymore, she gets up quietly from the couch and takes off to the bathroom, hoping to not make a scene. Amanda is right behind her trying to comfort her.

"What was that about, is she okay?" Max asks.

They are all showing some effects of the emotional toll this day is taking on them. No matter how strong they try to be, they still are having trouble at such a young age dealing with the loss of one of their own. They are sitting there confused until Chantal speaks up, stopping in front of her friends before heading to the bathroom. "I shouldn't be the one to say this or say anything about it, but Landon asked Michelle today when he took her home from school." Everyone is in shock, and some of the girls start to fight back tears. The guys can only muster up a collective "oh fuck." At that moment, they all realize how difficult this death is going to be on everyone. Especially Michelle.

In the bathroom, Michelle is sitting on the floor with her back against the bathtub, tissues all around her crumpled up with tears and snot. Amanda is sitting on the toilet with the seat cover down, one hand on Michelle's shoulder trying to comfort her broken-hearted best friend. Chantal is standing by the sink getting a towel wet for Michelle to wipe away her smeared makeup and to cool her down. Michelle is swaying slowly back and forth, her legs crossed in front of her and her hands pressed together and held up to cover her trembling mouth.

In her mind, she is running through the day's events with Landon. Many thoughts of what her future was to be with him and the past time they shared are melding together. The three girls comfort each other, as they are now all sitting side by side on the floor holding each other close. They don't say a lot but just sit there in the moment, taking on each other's pain in the hope that it will help the other out. Michelle's tears are slowly stopping but her eyes are still sad and lonely. Tears fall as she thinks of the kiss she shared with Landon earlier that day. Eventually, the three of them collect themselves and walk out of the bathroom and back into the living room. Their friends don't say anything in fear of more emotions spilling from any of them. They just sit there quietly alone with their own thoughts as the sound of "Youth Without Youth" by Metric plays on the stereo.

★ ★ ★

Meanwhile, Landon's uncle Matt has not heard any of the bad news as of yet. His cell phone is turned off because he and his girlfriend are at the movies. They make their way to his vehicle outside in the dark cool autumn night. Walking up, he starts the vehicle from his keys. The two of them get into the vehicle and he leans over and gives his girlfriend a loving kiss. He drives away from the cinema back to her place. She grabs their phones from the centre console; both have a dozen text messages and missed calls on them. For the two of them, it isn't out of the norm to get messages while at the movies, but never this many messages, even if it is his mom calling to ask questions about the most random of things.

She tells him about the number of messages they both have. They exchange a look of confusion, trying to figure out what would bring up that many messages in a short period. Neither one thinks the worst, but they are wondering if something bad has happened. He tells her to put on his voicemail. The first message is his mom calling to tell him that he has to be back on the farm for six in the morning. It is quickly skipped over, as he already knew that.

The next message hits them like a brick. The call is from Cindy, a neighbour of Matt's parents. In the past, Matt played sports with her sons. Both families have been close over the years. Her voice is broken and fighting emotion. "Matt, I have some bad news." The two of them look at each other ready to tear up, both fearing the worst for a family member or a close friend. "It's Landon. He has been in an accident a few miles from his place. It was a bad accident. He didn't make it." Her voice breaks up as she provides a few details about the accident. "I am so sorry for having to tell you this. I am so sorry. You better call your mom as well as Kevin and Justine. They are still at the scene but I am sure they and the kids could use your support right now."

It is nine o'clock, and many lost moments have come and gone since that message. The two of them pull over to the curb in front of Robyn's place. Tears trickle down both of their faces. Matt stumbles through questions of *why*. They hold each other close in the vehicle, trying to collect their thoughts and emotions. Through the tears and sniffles, Robyn says, "You have to call your mom right now. At least see if there is anything we should do or can do tonight. I think we should head out to the farm now."

"Thanks, Hon. You call her, I'll start driving," he replies as they both compose themselves.

Without even thinking of tomorrow, they leave for the farm, lost in a moment they can't escape from. Both of them feel awful for not answering the phone, but they also realize that it was out of their control. "I can't believe this. I just talked to him. We talked at the corner at the highway. He was coming back from Michelle's," Matt says as he drives to the farm with the darkness blanketing them.

Robyn sits in the passenger seat in emotional shock. As the two hold hands, she says, "I am so sorry, Babe." She has the feeling that he was probably the last one to talk to Landon, but at this point she doesn't want to bring that up unless he does. She knows she has to be there for him; she can tell he is already not doing well with it. His hand is shaky within hers, and he is breathing deeply trying to control his emotions. She calls his mom as they are leaving town.

It only rings once. The cell phone has been in his mother's hand for the past couple hours or so, as she calls family members and they call her. She and Robyn share a heartfelt cry and try to figure out what they can do tonight. "We are on our way to the farm right now," Robyn tells her.

"It might be best if you go to Kevin's for tonight. The kids could probably use the support. Not sure what Kevin and Justine are up to yet, but I am sure they will be back with their kids soon," Matt's mom tells Robyn, trying to be motherly and supportive for the young couple. "Make sure Matt doesn't speed on the way out here. We don't need another accident tonight."

"Don't worry, I won't speed too much," Matt assures his mom.

"Okay, see you soon. We are down here with the kids right now and will leave soon after you guys get here," his mother tells Robyn.

"Okay, sounds good. See you then," Robyn says before they hang up.

Driving to his brother's place, Matt is visibly shaken up. He often takes one hand and wipes it over his eyes for a second and then slides it over his mouth to not only wipe the tears from his face but the emotion he can feel coming over him. Robyn as well is distant in her actions as she stares out at the stars in the sky. Their thoughts are all about Landon and the family. Though they say nothing to each other during the ride, they know they are there for each other. They steal soft glances as the silence speaks for itself. The two of them can't believe what has happened tonight. There is no one else on the road, it seems, which allows the night and the depth of the loss to sink in even more. There is nothing to distract the two other than the sound of the wind as Matt speeds down the road and the sound of No Doubt's "One More Summer" plays from the stereo.

Matt breaks the silence. "It seems like only yesterday I was playing hallway hockey with Landon when he was little. I can't believe that I will never get to do that with him again, or watch him play hockey."

"I know what you mean. Landon was a special kid. But you have three other nephews who are gonna need you more than ever now," Robyn reminds Matt. The two hold hands as they near the farm.

"I know. I just hope I can be that support they need. Be that uncle for them," Matt replies while trying to compose himself with deep breathing. "I can't stop thinking about Landon. The times we woke up to watch World Junior Hockey over the Christmas break. All the times we played sports together, he always wanted to know more and to be better. He was such a good kid, why did this have to happen to him?" Matt pauses, choking on the words. "I should have warned him about the deer in the area," Matt says as a tear slowly falls onto his cheek.

Robyn reaches over and wipes it away. "Don't beat yourself up over this. You didn't know any of this would happen. You still have three nephews you can share all those moments with and more. They are going to need you, and you will need them," she says while comforting him with her hand and her soft calm voice. "I love you," she says, looking him in the eye. Both of them have tears filling up their eyes.

"I love you too," Matt says, looking back into Robyn's eyes before she leans over and kisses him on the cheek.

As they pull into his brother's place, they can see his parents' car still in the yard. The house seems still; there are no shadows moving around or any signs that someone is home other than some lights being on. They get out of the vehicle and the crisp night air has them shivering, which doesn't help their nerves before they go into the house. They are greeted outside by two of Kevin and Justine's dogs. Both are happy to see someone. They pet the dogs, trying to calm the animals down and keep them from jumping up or making too much noise. The door opens up and Matt's mom is standing there. "Thanks for coming, guys. Hurry, get inside, it is cold out there," she says as she shivers from the cold air sweeping over her feet.

They walk up the steps, their composure slowly fading. Robyn gives Matt's mom a hug as the two share tears on each other's shoulder while Matt stands back trying to keep the dogs at bay. Matt then gives his mother a huge loving embrace. He is trying to hold back his tears. "Why Landon?" Matt says into his mother's shoulder as he slowly breaks down in her arms.

"I don't know, son. I don't know," his mother says, trying to comfort her youngest son.

She tells Matt and Robyn that she and Matt's father will be going home now to try to get some rest, even though his dad has been napping in a chair in the living room for the past couple hours. "It has been a long and rough day for him. He is taking it pretty hard," she tells them as she goes into the living room to wake her husband up. He wakes up startled by his wife, and soon notices that Matt and Robyn are there now.

"Well, I guess we can go now," he says, slowly getting out of the chair as he tries to not talk about Landon at the moment.

"Have a nice nap?" Matt asks with a smirk on his face as his dad passes him at the entrance to the living room. The two share a firm handshake, one that is comforting as well as passing the torch of responsibility in the house. Nothing more is said before Matt's parents leave until they exchange goodbyes as they head out the door.

Ethan walks into the kitchen and sees Matt and Robyn sitting at the kitchen table, talking quietly and trying to brace themselves to talk to the nephews. Ethan and Matt make eye contact. The two can't help it and begin to shed tears for Landon. Matt gets up from the chair and gives Ethan a big hug. Their tears fall onto each other's shoulders. "Why, why did he have to die? This is so fucked up," Ethan says as he fights back the emotional pain that his face is clearly showing.

"I wish I knew," Matt whispers as he holds his nephew close.

The two of them remain in the embrace for a few moments, not wanting to let go and trying to regain some sort of strength. Robyn stands up and walks over to the two of them. She rubs her boyfriend's back and tries to comfort both of them. She is remaining strong for the guys, but she can feel the emotions coming on strong. With Matt and Ethan letting go of the embrace, Matt and Robyn give each other a nod of the head as if to say *thanks* and *you're welcome*. Robyn then embraces Ethan as Matt walks away to see the other nephews.

"Robyn," Ethan says quietly as they hug. "Thanks for coming out tonight."

"We are family, it isn't an option," Robyn replies, even though she isn't officially family yet. She knows that she is a part of this family, though, even if she is still just dating Matt.

Matt comes back into the kitchen where the two are just separating from the embrace. "I see that Damon had enough. He is stretched out on the couch sleeping," Matt proclaims.

"Yeah, he had hockey practice and hasn't been home long. We told him the news. Not sure if it registered or not. He has been like that on the couch since that moment," Ethan tells them.

"Well, better let him rest then," Matt replies.

"Brett is downstairs hiding in his room. He has his iPod on and isn't really talking at the moment," Ethan tells them of his youngest brother, aiming his comment particularly at Robyn. Brett has always liked hanging out with Robyn whenever the chance arises. The two have found a connection close to the one Landon and Matt had. Brett finds it easy to talk to her; the two of them have a similar sense of humour and can make each other laugh nonstop.

"How is he doing? Have you tried talking to him?" Robyn asks.

"We talked a bit," Ethan says as he goes to the fridge to grab a Dr.

Pepper. "He was very upset and took off to his room. I think he was afraid to show me that he was crying. I tried to tell him it was okay to cry."

"I should go and see how he is doing, if that is okay with you two?" Robyn says as she is already heading toward the stairs for the basement.

The guys both nod that this would be a good idea. They both take up a seat at the kitchen island on bar stools and sit there saying very little, both trying to figure out what to do. Ethan, for being only in grade 11, is very mature and is keeping it together for his brothers. They bring up memories of Landon that make them laugh as well as distract each other. They sidetrack the conversation with talk of school, girls and sports. Ethan's cell phone rings as text messages are coming in. He has ignored a lot of them tonight, but will answer this one from Renee.

★ ★ ★

Downstairs, Robyn finds Brett lying in his bed with headphones on and a pillow in his arms as he stares up at the ceiling. "Brett," she says in a drawn out, unthreatening way as she walks in. She gets no response, even though she knows that he knows she is there. She goes to tickle his feet; he is usually ticklish, but not this time. He is not in the mood. He looks at her but has no expression on his face. It's unusual to see him without his typical smile and silliness. The loss of his brother is hitting him hard. He doesn't know how to react, so he drowns his thoughts with music.

Robyn sits down on the bed beside Brett but doesn't say anything. She looks around the room with wonder and sadness while glancing at Brett now and then. Brett's music is blasting in his ears, but he is watching everything around him. He tries to remain emotionless, but he is unsuccessful. With Robyn beside him, he reaches out with his right hand and takes her hand in his. She turns to look at him, neither one saying anything. She sees the tears start to empty from Brett's sad eyes, his lip quivering. She embraces his hand tighter and gives him a sympathetic smile. She understands the pain he is going through and the struggle to deal with this. She leans over and gives him a kiss on the forehead.

Back at Renee's, some of the kids have already left for home. Only Shane, Michelle, Chantal, Jen and Warren remain at the house with Renee. The six of them are sitting in the living room talking about what they can do for Landon's family and the funeral. They try to be as mature as one can be only hours after the loss of a friend. Their emotions and minds are running a mile a minute, but they are trying their best as teenagers. They hope that they can be mature together and get through this as a close-knit group.

Renee and Shane are texting Ethan to see how he is holding up. Ethan is slow to respond, making them worry a little. Renee's mom comes into the room with tired eyes. "You kids can stay the night if you like. Just make sure you tell your parents." She then leaves the room. The kids all say goodnight to her as she leaves. They know that they should head home to be with family the rest of the night and tomorrow, as this news is not going to be easy to deal with.

They text Ethan and other friends while still discussing what to do to pay respect to Landon. "We should make a list of songs and put them on a CD to be played at the funeral. Landon told me once that he hated the music at funerals," Shane mentions as he sits on the couch half awake. "He mentioned it a couple times after family funerals he went to, even though they were his aunt and uncles, he said if he was to die he wanted music that meant something to him and those around him, not church organ music." They all agree that this would be a great idea.

"What about if we started annual tournaments in his honour? We could do volleyball, slo-pitch and hockey, with all the money going to a scholarship in Landon's memory," Michelle proposes. The group all thinks that would work and be a great thing for the community.

Renee stops the discussion of funeral ideas and asks the others if they remember back a year or two ago when they were up at the lake. She thinks it was May, a long weekend. She says she remembers Landon came and picked her and a few others up—she thinks it was Jen, Max, Colin and someone else—and they drove up there in his old 1987 Dodge Diplomat.

They all mention some epic teenage story about the Diplomat.

Mainly they remember that car for the adventures in it, or how Landon drove it like a race car and was carefree yet always careful when doing so. Warren mentions that he remembers the many long booze cruises in that car, most of which he can't *really* remember.

Renee agrees with the statements and says that is her point. "Landon was involved in a lot of our memories," she says. She doesn't recall that whole weekend because of the alcohol, but she remembers the ride with Landon and that old car. They all unintentionally take a collective deep breath as each of them thinks fondly of memories with Landon.

Hiding in the conversation, Michelle tells them she is having a real tough time with all of this. Not looking for attention, she says that this was the greatest day of her life, and now it has turned into the worst possible. Hearing all their stories only makes her heart ache more. Renee goes over to Michelle and holds her tight; both of them are tearing up. Renee tells Michelle that it will be okay and that they are all there for her.

Shane and Warren are talking to each other about the actual accident. They are talking quietly so the girls don't overhear and it makes things worse. The guys are still in shock that Landon got into an accident on a road that he and they drive basically every day. They mention that if it was a bit further down the road, he would have run into the slough that was just on the other side of the corner he didn't make it to. They are both in complete shock, as they know that Landon drives fast but has quick reflexes and remains cautious.

Noticing that Michelle is still visibly upset and isn't handling everything that well, Shane says, "It is getting late, and we should all probably get home." Warren agrees with Shane, as he is feeling a bit sleepy from a long day. Renee tells them they are welcome to stay the night at her place if they don't want to drive. Warren says for himself, but kind of speaking for the group as well, "Normally I would and I probably should, but my parents will want to see me tonight and for sure early tomorrow."

Warren looks over at Michelle, seeing if he can tell if she is ready to leave or not. Michelle has zoned out of the conversation; her mind is replaying memories of Landon, especially the ones the two shared earlier in the day. Warren taps her on the shoulder to get her attention.

She is slightly startled and tunes back into the conversation. "You want me to take you home, or you going to crash here tonight?" he asks patiently.

She looks up at him. "I would like to go home tonight. I am sure my parents would worry if I wasn't home, even if I called them."

They all start to get up to go home, moving slowly toward the door to put their shoes on. Renee gives Shane and Warren each a hug and thanks them for coming over, and tells Warren to make sure he drives safe with Michelle with him. He tells her not to worry. They both smile at each other, knowing that it is an awkward position they have put each other in. Michelle has her shoes on, and she gives Renee a huge hug. Both of them are being strong at this moment and doing their best not to cry. Small tears fall from their eyes as they release from the hug. They all say goodnight as Shane opens the door, and they make their way out to their cars.

Shane heads off in his car, followed shortly by Warren and Michelle in the truck. Michelle and Shane live in the same area, so Warren is following Shane down the highway. Shane has his stereo cranked so he doesn't have to think about anything but driving. Linkin Park's "Figure .09" is blasting from his speakers and he belts out the tunes with them. Back in Warren's vehicle, Michelle is looking out the window at the stars, quietly singing along with the music on her head. Warren doesn't have the stereo cranked, but the country station is playing Taylor Swift's "Tim McGraw." Warren gives Michelle a couple of glances now and then just to make sure she is okay.

"You okay with the song?" he asks politely as he keeps his eyes on the road. "You seem to be vacant from the conversation."

She stops singing for a second. "I am all right, but it's going to be a while before I am really feeling better or comfortable about everything," she replies as she slowly turns her head toward him, taking her focus away from the stars in the dark autumn night sky. She turns back to the window and looks out into the passing night.

"If you ever need anything, don't be afraid to ask someone. Everyone is going to be going through a lot, and everyone is going to need help," Warren tells her, glancing at her as she stares out the window, unsure if she even heard him.

She did hear him; she just didn't know how or want to answer at that moment. The conversation, as brief as it is, helps her in that moment. She just doesn't know how long this moment will last.

They both wave at Shane as he pulls off onto the gravel road heading to his place. He steps on the brakes a couple times, flashing his tail lights at them as a signal of goodnight and drive safe. Michelle thanks Warren for the offer and his kindness. She turns away from the window and slouches down into the seat, her head in her right hand as her hair falls over her face, slightly covering her eyes.

Warren looks at her, worried. "You sure everything is all right, Michelle?"

She assures him, "I just don't want to see this stretch of road from here to my place right now."

Warren is confused but knows better than to ask a question about it at this point. He makes his way down the gravel road. The ride can't end soon enough for Michelle. Every passing tree and fence post reminds her of Landon. As Warren turns down the driveway, he dims the lights so they don't shine into the house. He turns down the radio as well, so her parents aren't annoyed by the music. He pulls up to the house and parks his vehicle in the same spot Landon did earlier.

"Thanks for the ride, Warren," Michelle quietly says as she exits the vehicle in a calm haste.

Warren is quick to reply as he looks out the passenger side at Michelle, "It was not a problem. If you ever need anything, just ask." They smile at each other and give an understanding nod. "You know that everyone is here for you and each other if needed. No point trying to go this on your own," he says, trying to reassure her with some comforting words before they part ways.

"I know you guys will be, I just hope I can be there for you as well," she replies as she gives him a sombre wave goodbye and they head their separate ways.

Michelle shuts the truck door and walks to her house slowly while looking up at the stars, taking the evening air in. Warren watches her walk to the house and then backs up his truck. He begins to drive back to his place. At the end of the driveway, he turns the headlights back on bright and cranks the stereo up as Dierks Bentley's "Cab of My Truck" comes on. Warren laughs unknowingly and starts singing along.

★ ★ ★

Michelle stands at the front door, not yet going in, her head filled with emotion and fragile thoughts. She is standing facing the door imagining things she never thought she knew. Taking a deep breath, Michelle steps away from the door, brushes her hair back from her heartbroken face with her hands and walks over to the tree swing. She dumps out some ice water in the tire before she sits in it. As she sits in the tire, she can't help but think of the summer and the time she did get to spend with Landon.

She remembers the small parties she had here, Landon pushing her on this very swing, the quiet conversations they had about nothing and how they meant so much. Michelle remembers how Landon was convinced that if you listened to the Tragically Hip you could find the meaning to life and life's situations in their lyrics—at the very least, a lyric that could define a moment or emotion you were going through. He often said that the *Day for Night* album kind of defined who he was; the lyrics made him see things differently than most people.

Landon was a deep thinker, but not many people knew he had different thoughts than the community he lived in. Since he was the star athlete, he was always afraid of what people thought of the persona that was engraved into the community at a young age. He didn't want people to question where his head was at or constantly ask him if he was okay. He wasn't in a dark place, but he would go there with thoughts from time to time. Michelle found some of those moments out as they discussed some of life's bigger questions, but never too deep, just in an innocent way that touched each other as they grew closer as friends.

Michelle knew he came from a family where two of his uncles played on possibly the best senior men's league hockey team; they could play any sport easily and be one of the best around at it. His aunt was a provincial figure skater back in her day and could also pick up any sport with ease and play it well. Landon never thought twice about sports—it was his life and he loved it, but he also knew there was more to him than just a winning goal or a block in volleyball.

Landon let Michelle into his thoughts—maybe not all of them, but the ones he believed would be fun to talk to her about and some that would make her think outside the box. He never told Michelle in depth of his fears of death and the infinite nature of everything possible, but he did open up some to her about his thoughts beyond parties, the next game, grades and high school drama. She never knew of his depression. No one did, actually; she suspected it at times, but he hid it well behind many layers of reality and sarcasm.

They never talked of their feelings for each other in depth until the day of his death. They maybe hinted toward them over time but always stayed as friends instead of taking the next step. Landon liked his privacy and trusted Michelle to keep it that way, even though Chantal and Amanda knew of their talks. They just had no idea what they were about. Michelle kept that part to herself. Their friendship was quiet. People knew they were friends—everyone is friends in a small town. Some thought Landon and Michelle were dating for a while. You would never really see them alone together, but they were always near each other during social events.

Michelle swings back and forth slowly on the tire swing. She is full of the thoughts of her and Landon over the recent past. She closes her eyes and a soft smile lights her face. As the night shines on her, she begins to softly sing with poetic pauses, "I promise you, I will treat you well, my sweet angel." These lyrics come from one of Landon's favourite songs, "Possum Kingdom" by the Toadies. She stops the swing from moving and slides out from the tire slowly. Michelle looks up at the stars searching for Landon, searching for comfort and understanding. She whispers to the stars and the open night air, "I love you, and you will never be forgotten in my heart." She stands tall on her shaky legs as she blows a soft kiss into the stars and wishes Landon goodnight. A tear falls down her cheek, stopping at her lips as if it is giving them a soft kiss goodnight. The tear then falls from her lips to the ground next to the tire swing.

# Day 2

## Thursday

The sun rises on a new day, no better than the day before for those in this community. The memory of one of their own who has left them too early still lingers as they eat their breakfast and listen to the news on TV. Most are moving on with their regular lives, with harvest and going to work in the morning, some with heavier hearts than others. The school is closed for the day. It wasn't an easy decision, but the teachers thought it would be best for the students to be with family. Most days this would be great news for the kids, but not on this occasion.

It is a bit chilly outside in the morning. The overnight frost lingers on the lawns. Farmers are getting their equipment ready to go out as soon as the swathes are dry enough to combine. Parents in the community who are home with their children talk with them throughout the morning about Landon's passing. They do their best to console, as most have never dealt with the loss of someone that close to them. Some prefer silence, patience, understanding and timely conversations with their children. Others bring it right out in to the open and have a discussion whether it is needed or not. Everyone in the community deals with it in his or her own way, and some are dealing with it better than others.

The kids are still texting each other about the news, as well as passing along Facebook messages among friends who may and may not have known Landon. There is already a memoriam page set up on

Facebook for him. In less than 24 hours of his passing, there are more than a couple hundred people on the page and even more messages left. Condolences and prayers for the family seem to be the norm, but a few memories are shared as well. It keeps Landon's memory alive even if it is a fleeting notion of nostalgia.

In Brett's bedroom, he and Robyn are lying on top of the covers of his bed. Brett is curled right up next to Robyn as she lies there with an arm over him. They stayed up for a while last night and talked about anything and everything, but not for too long, as Brett finally gave in to the tired in his eyes, as did Robyn. She was going to leave during the night but decided not to, as she knew Brett needed her more than Matt did. In Ethan's room next to them, Matt is sleeping on Ethan's bed. Ethan is sleeping on the pull-out couch in the common area downstairs. He tends to sleep there most nights because he stays up playing video games or watching TV until the wee hours of the morning. He is used to the awkwardness of the mattress in the pull-out.

Upstairs, Kevin and Justine are making breakfast. They arrived home at around two in the morning, a lot later than they anticipated. There was nothing for them really to do at the hospital, after saying a few last words to their eldest son. They spoke with a counsellor at the hospital to figure out what they had to do, as this was never something they had thought of dealing with as parents. They talked about their raw feelings at the moment. During the conversations with the counsellor and between themselves on the way home, they never placed blame on anyone, especially themselves and Landon. They know that they have to put on a brave face while still letting the emotions show, but where is that line? The counsellor discussed their other children with them, as to how they would be reacting to this. Justine and Kevin weren't really sure last night how each of their boys would react to the passing of their oldest brother over time. They knew that no matter what, they would be there for their sons in whatever way they needed, and the support group around them was strong enough to help them all move on.

Justine is standing by the stove; there are pans on the burners warming up, each getting ready for a different breakfast food. Kevin is standing at the window looking out into the yard. He knows that going to the field to harvest today isn't going to happen, but it would be a good distraction for him. Down the road from their place he can see his parents' place, and he can see the movement of a vehicle down on their farm.

"We are getting company for breakfast," Kevin mentions to his wife as he watches the vehicle head down the road toward them.

"Oh should I stop now and just let your mom take over?" Justine says in jest, as it is a running joke between them that his mom always wants to be the one cooking for the family. They share a sharp quick chuckle in the moment, but it doesn't last, as they both go back to their distractions of cooking and looking out the window at the farm and what should be done.

Kevin walks over to his wife and gives her a little tickle and squeeze on her waist. She smirks and gives him a look of disdain. "Not now," she says. "Not the time." He tickles a bit more and then walks away, and she shakes a spatula in his direction, both hiding their grief in their soft laughter. They feel bad for laughing at this time, but they are trying to find ways to get to the norm, and they know that any form of comfort at the moment is a good thing. Kevin was never one to show his emotions, and he tries to lighten the mood so he won't be seen with tears on his cheek. Landon was the same way, always trying to bring laughter to the sad, awkward and painful situations life put in front of him. This is the norm for most of the men in the family, as they grew up with firm father figures who didn't show much emotion.

Damon has now awakened from his sleep on the couch, not the one he first fell asleep on last night—he got up and changed to the larger one not long after his parents came home. Now he can't sleep through the noise of his parents. The smell of pancakes and bacon is easy to wake up to.

"Good morning!" Justine greets him as he strolls slowly into the kitchen. "Why did you sleep on the couch last night?"

He sits down at the kitchen table, rests his head on his crossed arms and mumbles, "I dunno, just tired."

His mom can't hear him over the crackling on the stove and his arms covering his mouth. "What?" she asks as she looks at him, confused by his groggy speech.

He lifts up his head a bit. "I just fell asleep there yesterday and was too lazy to go to my room."

"How are you doing, you want to talk about yesterday?" she asks as she cracks some eggs into a pan.

He shakes his head, slightly annoyed. "I'm okay, but I don't want to deal or talk about it right now." He pauses and looks at her, still slightly asleep. "But if I do, I will come to you," he says as they both look at each other.

A small smile appears on his mother's face. She is happy to be there for her son, and that he would go to her. It is a happy and sad moment at the same time.

In the driveway, Damon's grandma and grandpa pull in. Kevin goes outside to greet them. His mom can't control her tears as soon as she sees her son and can see one of her grandkids through the kitchen windows. Kevin goes over to her door and opens it for her.

"So sorry, this shouldn't have happened. I am so sorry." She gives Kevin a big hug.

"It's okay. Everything will be okay. Not sure how, but we will be fine," he says, trying to reassure her.

Kevin and his dad aren't big talkers, but as his dad comes over and gives him a hug and tells him he is sorry, a few tears come from the old farmer's eyes. Kevin is all cried out at the moment. He has too much in his mind to feel like crying. They separate and all head to the house. Justine gives a sad yet polite wave at them from the stove as they are walking in. She is trying to remain calm but knows the feelings will hit hard soon.

Damon mumbles to his mom, "Grandma better not make me cry." Justine shoots him a glaring look as if to tell him he better not make a scene. She is in no mood for something like that at this time. Damon is trying to be a smart-ass as usual, but it's not good timing.

The front door opens as Grandma and Grandpa walk in, offering a strong presence and sad eyes. "Thanks for coming this morning and for last night as well," Justine says as they are taking off their jackets and making themselves at home.

Grandpa walks over to Damon at the table and puts his hand on the boy's head, as if he was going to comfort it, but begins to mess up his hair instead. Grandpa asks how Damon is doing while trying not to show the heartache in his voice. Damon shakes his head to get his hair back in his preferred bedhead style. "I'd rather not talk about it, Grandpa. I don't really know what to be thinking. I am just hungry right now."

Grandma walks over to Justine, and they exchange a tearful hug, overcome with emotion. Kevin walks in from outside where he has been turning on the fans in the grain bins. He silently shuts the door behind him. He sees his mother and his wife both crying and holding each other. "I am guessing you two spilled some milk," he says with a dry charm. Damon looks up, shaking his head, and gives a laugh of disbelief at his dad making a joke.

Damon's grandpa sits at the table and says, "If you spilled the milk, might as well clean it up, crying won't clean it up." The other four chuckle to themselves. It slowly grows to a good full-hearted laugh. It is a good release for everyone, as they had been running around with only despair and loss on their mind. Grandpa didn't catch on to the humour, which was of the norm.

★ ★ ★

Downstairs, Matt is lying in the bed trying to figure out if he is half awake or half asleep. His eyes are confused, not knowing if light is good or bad at this time of the morning. The noise from upstairs makes him realize that it is probably as good a time as any to get up. He slowly rolls out of bed and rubs his face with his hands, trying to shake the sleep out, yawning the entire time. He looks around the bedroom, almost forgetting where he slept last night. His mind is still confused from last night's news and the compressed timeline he rushed into. He gets up from the bed still fully clothed in last night's attire and strolls over to the door to make his way upstairs.

Robyn is on the other side of the door just about to open it, and they startle each other. She just woke up as well; she left Brett sleeping on his bed, but she's sure he will be up soon. They give each other a soft and quick morning kiss.

"How was Brett doing last night? I looked in at one point but the both of you were fast asleep on the bed," Matt asks quietly, not wanting to wake Brett or make a big scene from a small conversation.

"Brett was sad and heartbroken. We talked a bit about death and Landon's passing, but for the most part we just laid there silently looking at the ceiling," she tells him as she tries to focus on waking up. Side by side, with their arms wrapped around each other, they walk toward the stairs to head up to the kitchen. They look over at Ethan, who is sleeping on the pull-out; he has his clothes on from the night before and a Hockey Canada fleece spread across part of his body. "Should we wake him?" Robyn asks.

"Nah, let's leave him sleep. He will be up soon enough," Matt replies.

Robyn is in front of Matt as they walk up the stairs together, and she reaches back with her hands, palms up, as if she is offering loving guidance as the two go up to his family. Without looking, Matt reaches out and holds on to her hands. Walking up the stairs they hear voices, the soft sound of the radio turned on for farm reports, and bacon and sausage crackling in the frying pan.

Kevin notices them walking up the stairs. "Good morning," he says. "Glad to see that the two of you finally woke up. Damon has been waiting to eat."

"Well, I thought the food would be better here this morning than at Robyn's place," Matt replies before he is up to the top of the steps.

Robyn turns and gives him a little poke in the stomach.

"Thanks Robyn, he needed that," his mother says.

Robyn walks over to Justine to give her a hug. They look at each other, heartbreakingly fighting back the tears. "Justine, do you need any help with breakfast?" Robyn asks as the two let go from the embrace.

Matt walks over to his mom and dad, gives his mom a quick hug, and says good morning to both of them. Kevin and Matt share a moment of sorrow as they look at each other from across the table. Neither one will talk about it in front of people; they will at some point, but they will not go out of their way to plan it. The men in the family are like this. They try to keep their emotions in check and only talk about feelings when it's needed. Matt has always tried to figure out why but never got anything more than that the family is set in the old ways, and it gets passed down through the generations. Slowly it is fading within the men, but not his dad. Matt can't remember the last time he heard his father tell his mother he loved her or said thanks for anything. Togetherness with this family is for weddings, funerals, and whenever turkey is served with the fancy knives and forks.

Robyn makes her way to the table. As she walks by Kevin, she gives him a hug from behind. Damon is sitting between Matt and Kevin, and they are annoying him by grabbing at his knees or poking at his sides, trying to get a rise out of him. He is still a bit sleepy. Robyn walks over to Matt's mom and gives her a hug good morning. She pulls up a chair and sits between Matt and his mom.

"Why are you two picking on him?" she comments as the two brothers pester Damon at the table.

Matt has Damon squirming by squeezing his knee, and replies quickly, "We aren't picking on him, we are just waking him up."

Damon is fighting it, laughing with each annoying tickle and grab at his knee. Finally he gets up from his chair, almost falling over as he shakes himself a bit to get the ticklish feeling out. "Mom, call me when breakfast is ready," he tells his mother as he shakes his head, giving his dad and uncle a look of annoyance and walking away.

Matt's mom looks at the two of them. "Are you two happy? You made Damon mad."

Matt and Kevin look at each as if to blame each other, but from the background Damon pipes up, "I'm not mad, I just don't want to deal with those two when I am tired and they know it." Everyone but his grandma and grandpa gets a chuckle out of it. His grandpa doesn't even know what all the fuss is about, as he is only getting part of the conversation thanks to his bad hearing and a bad hearing aid.

From the stove where Justine is cooking breakfast a timer beeps. She forgot that she set it a while ago. "Kevin, can you go down and wake up Ethan and Brett?"

From the staircase, a mumble comes saying, "I'm up, no need to wake me. You guys are too loud to stay asleep." Ethan walks up the remaining few steps and looks over to see who all is there. "Is this everyone? Sure sounded like a lot more from downstairs." He walks over to the fridge as his mom gives him a quick hug and kiss on the forehead.

"Why would you think that?" Justine asks as she continues to flip pancakes. "Were you expecting more people this morning?"

As he opens the fridge, grabbing the orange juice, Ethan replies, "No, you guys just make a lot of noise."

"That was Damon squealing like a li'l schoolgirl," Kevin replies as he looks into the living room at his son, who is back sprawled out on the couch.

A loud grumble comes from the couch as Damon speaks up, but clearly not to everyone. "Maybe if you and Matt weren't being dicks and annoying me."

Ethan looks at them as he takes a swig of orange juice from the carton and shakes his head.

"Don't you want a glass for the orange juice?" his grandma asks, wishing that her grandkids would be more polite when she is around but also knowing it more than likely won't happen.

Ethan replies as the carton is barely away from his lips, "No thanks, I'm good. I just wanted a sip." He takes another quick swig from the carton before putting it back in the fridge. He walks over to his mom and stands beside her, looking at all the breakfast food she is preparing. "So, what's for breakfast?"

She looks at him and tells him with a bit of humour, as she tries not to get mad, "Well, for you, there is a plate of make-it-yourself and a warm glass of don't-start-with-me-this-morning." He laughs at her and gives her a quick embrace. The two of them smile at each other, trying to hold back the emotion. Ethan is just pretending to be his older brother with his mother, and she knows it. Landon used to always ask his mother that on weekends when she would cook a big breakfast for all of them.

Robyn asks, "You want me to go get Brett up for breakfast?" She is feeling a bit awkward sitting at the table with the family.

Kevin pipes up, knowing that he was asked not long ago to do that, "Yeah, you should go and do that. He will sleep all day if you don't."

"Didn't I ask you to go and do that?" Justine looks at her husband with a slight anger in her eyes.

"I think his chair is tied to his ass," Matt quickly replies so that the mood doesn't get too serious. They all know that now is not the time for petty arguments and disagreements.

Robyn heads downstairs to wake Brett up; as she heads down the steps she tries not to trip over the cat, Ovie, who has found a good place to sleep on the steps. She gives the furball a quick pet with her foot as she steps over him. She makes her way over to Brett's room and knocks on the door; there is no response. She opens the door and sees Brett lying on the bed with his earphones on and his music just blasting from them. She can clearly hear "The Pretender" by Foo Fighters coming from his headphones.

Robyn goes over to him and plucks the earphone from his right ear. "Might as well get up, everyone else is up and breakfast is ready," she tells him as she reaches her right hand out to help him out of bed.

He looks up at her with some sadness left on his face from the night before and quietly asks, "Did you say anything to anyone about me crying last night, or anything that was said?" He didn't want to seem like a little child to his family. He wanted to be counted on and not be a burden.

"I would never say anything, and I promise I won't tell anyone," she says, reassuring him that his secret is safe with her.

He sits up in his bed. "Thanks for being there for me last night. I needed that."

Robyn reaches out with both hands. "So, you ready to go and eat? Everyone is waiting."

He looks at her and then at her hands. "Thanks, but I can manage on my own." The two of them laugh and head upstairs, not holding hands but walking close beside each other.

★ ★ ★

Justine has finished making breakfast, and she mentions to everyone, "Breakfast is ready, come and get it."

Ethan and his grandpa head on up first to the counter and stove where all the fixings for a great breakfast are arranged. Damon is standing up against the side of the fridge just waiting his turn as his grandpa passes by and says, "Come on, Damon, better get in there before it's all gone."

Damon looks annoyed, as he is only standing a few feet away from the food. He gives a little frustrated shrug and says, "I will get food soon enough. I think there will be enough to go around." His mother shoots him a look telling him not to start with the attitude today. They both know that his grandpa is always like that, and it gets annoying.

They all eventually makes their way up and go through the routine of filling a plate, adding hash browns, scrambled eggs with jalapeños and mushrooms, pancakes, bacon and breakfast sausages as well as toast. On the table is a large ketchup bottle, salt and pepper, as well as maple syrup. Kevin, Matt and the boys all cover their plates of food with syrup and ketchup. Ketchup is almost its own food group in this family. They don't eat it by itself, but it goes with every food.

Damon, Matt and Robyn sit at the island in the kitchen, while the others are at the table. At end of the table is Grandpa, to his left is his wife, and on his right is Ethan. Brett is sitting at the other end with his mom on his left and his dad on his right. Conversation at the table is nothing more than asking someone to pass the ketchup. The mood is confusing for everyone in the room. Matt and Robyn give each other a look, trying to figure out if they should say something or not. They decide to wait and see if anyone else makes conversation.

Brett looks out the window and watches the dogs play outside as he chews on a mouthful of eggs and hash browns. While in mid-chew, he asks in an honest manner, "Do you think Fred and Barney know that Landon died yesterday?"

Everyone thinks for a second and look at Brett, confused and not sure what to reply. Kevin gives an awkward chuckle at his son's comment and pats him on the head. "I am sure that Ovie passed along the news." Everyone begins to chuckle awkwardly, Brett and his dad laughing the loudest. It was an unexpected comment from their youngest son that broke the silence. A few tears trickle from Justine and Robyn as they laugh at the joke and the thought of Landon flickering in their mind.

Matt, sitting at the island, turns around with food in his mouth and replies, "I'm not sure Ovie passed on the message, since he speaks *meow* not *woof*." The laughter continues on for a few more minutes as everyone revels in the momentary humour and tries to not think of the death of a loved one. They know there will be enough time to do that. They all know that if Landon was here, he would have made the joke. He loved the little jokes even if not everyone caught them.

Ovie has now made his way into the kitchen and is walking under the table through the maze of legs looking for attention, as he heard his named mentioned. He eventually walks over to Matt, reaches up and paws at Matt's hip. Matt looks at Ovie and teases him with some ketchup that got on his finger before putting it on Ovie's nose. He then picks the cat up and continues to eat his breakfast with the cat on his lap.

The phone rings from the living room. "I can't believe it took this long this morning for phone calls," Kevin mentions as he stuffs his face with a forkful of food, hoping his wife or mother will go and answer it.

★ ★ ★

Everyone is finishing up eating breakfast and placing the dirty dishes in the sink. They all take off to do their own thing. Justine and Kevin stay near the phones. Grandpa is in the living room sleeping in the recliner with the Weather Channel on, while his wife is on her cell phone talking to more family members and friends, letting them know what happened and trying to give them some idea of when the funeral will be. Justine is on the house phone calling her family, who won't be able to make it to the funeral since they live in Australia. Both Kevin and Justine talk to her parents; while one is on the phone with them, the other is talking to whoever is calling on their cell phone because they can't get through on the house phone.

Matt is downstairs in the living room with Robyn and the boys. He is texting his friends who are asking him about the accident, as well as calling a few of his close friends who'd known Landon from birth. Landon was born the year Kevin coached Matt and his Atom Hockey team. Kevin brought them all blue gum cigars at the tournament that same weekend. The tournament was two days after Landon's birth; it was in the same city as the hospital, so Kevin was able to come and coach it. Hockey and most sports in this family are what binds them, so it was never an issue.

Robyn finishes talking to her boss about the news and telling him she won't be in today. She sits in a beanbag chair in the downstairs living room and calls her parents, trying not to cry as she talks to them. The boys have the Xbox 360 on; Brett and Damon are playing the latest edition of *EA Sports NHL* while texting their friends at the same time. All of their school friends and those they know through sports are contacting them, offering condolences and apologies.

Downstairs in his room, Ethan is on his cell phone talking to Chantal. She called him to see how he was doing. Chantal and Ethan have always had a weird friendship; they used to think they were dating when they were very young and playing in the living room when their parents would visit. As they got older, they grew apart. In school, Ethan was always the cool kid, as he was a sports star like his older brother, while Chantal was a bit more awkward and not socially accepted all the time. Now that they are both in high school they've started to be friends again. Even though it's a small school, it is still easy to not be friends with everyone.

That is, unless you were Landon; he talked to everyone, made fun of lots of people but was always in among the various groups. He talked to the smart kids like he was a nerd himself, cracking jokes on Shakespeare and discussing where technology was heading. He would hang out with the older crowd and was accepted, as he knew his place, yet he made time to hang with the younger ones and was able to act immature. The girls talked to him like he was one of the girls, the guys talked to him like one of the boys. He could fake interest in any conversation and hold his own, so you felt empowered by what you were saying to him. He didn't know much if anything about cars, mascara, computer parts or writing an essay, but he would listen and banter back and forth anyway.

The small-town school was kindergarten to grade 12. The high school kids didn't always hang out with the little ones, but Landon would make time once in a while to go and play hallway hockey with them. He was always around, and he never asked anyone to remember him for being there. The younger kids always looked up to him, and they liked it when he hung out with them. The teachers loved having him around too. It was like an extra set of eyes supervising, but at the same time, he would always allow the young kids to say or do things that the teachers wouldn't, from casual swear words to running in the classroom if a girl was chasing one of the boys trying to kiss him.

Chantal and Ethan never dated and weren't in the same social group, but they have always stayed friends in their own random way. Chantal begins to tell Ethan what they talked about at Renee's last night and how everyone is very sad about the loss. She is still having trouble talking about it. She mumbles, and her tone is nervous as she speaks. Ethan mentions to her that he has received many texts and calls this morning and last night from some who were there as well as many more who have heard through social media.

"You wanna go grab a coffee in town this afternoon?" he asks with a sombre tone in his voice, hoping that she will say yes to his heartbroken request.

"I would love to, but I was going to go hang out with Michelle today," she replies with empathy, as she is torn between her two closest friends.

"Why not ask her if she wants to go?" Ethan mentions with some hope for comfort from their company.

"I'm sure that would be fine with her," Chantal answers. Her voice shakes, as she is nervous and excited. The two finish up the conversation and say their goodbyes so they can go get ready to go into town. Chantal still has to talk to Michelle and tell her of the change of plans.

Chantal starts to dial Michelle's number as soon as she hangs up from Ethan. Finally, after a few rings, Michelle picks up her cell phone. The two of them exchange greetings, both trying to be uplifting but with sadness in their voice. Michelle hasn't talked to anyone since arriving back at her place last night, not including when her mom came and asked her if she was okay and she said she just wanted to be alone for a while.

"How are you holding up today?" Chantal asks as she tries to be supportive. She knows Michelle was hit hard yesterday, as they all were.

"Some moments are better than others," Michelle tells her. She is lying on her bed looking at an old yearbook. "I keep thinking of him. I don't hate that part. It is just enjoying the memories and then remembering he is no longer with us."

"Be strong," Chantal tells her as she stands in the bathroom fixing her hair, getting ready to leave with Ethan. "This won't be easy, but I am here if you need to talk. Speaking of which, Ethan asked if the two of us would go for coffee with him this afternoon."

"Thanks for the invite, but I don't know if I can handle seeing Landon's brother right now."

"Come on, Michelle, you can't hide forever. Besides, it would help all of us to be together right now." Chantal tries to convince her but doesn't push it. Finally, after a few minutes of talking, Michelle gives in and decides to go with Ethan and Chantal into town. They both hang up and head off to shower to get ready.

★ ★ ★

Matt and Robyn are preparing to head back to Robyn's place to rest and get some stuff done while they can. They are downstairs saying goodbye to the boys. "I might stop in later tonight, but I'm not sure. I will be in town this afternoon," Ethan tells them as they exchange a hug before leaving.

"You guys are always welcome any time, just call first," Matt replies. His voice helps comfort and reassure them that everything will be okay. He and Robyn then begin to head upstairs where the rest of the family is sitting around the kitchen table going over some pictures.

Matt takes a deep breath and asks, "What are you guys looking at? Don't the memories from the pictures hurt a bit too much right now?"

No one answers Matt's questions, and they continue to look at the pictures and share stories of those moments. Robyn walks over and looks at an album over Justine's shoulder. "I remember that day up at lake. That was when Landon, Ethan and Matt started a water fight with the neighbours and it got a bit out of hand."

Matt replies without hesitation as he slowly walks over to the table, grabbing a pancake from the counter, "I remember that, but I recall it a bit differently. Wasn't it Robyn who tried to soak Matt and Landon, and her terrible water-gun skills missed and soaked the neighbours unexpectedly?"

Robyn gives him a cute shut-up face. "Oh, be quiet."

Laughter starts to fill the house once again, but it slowly fades away as they continue looking through pictures. The stories become grander and more heartfelt, bringing laughter and tears and some things that at times can't be defined individually.

Ethan makes his way up to the family at the kitchen table, showered and dressed. "I am going into to town with Michelle and Chantal for coffee," he says as he stands by his mother, who is lost in the pictures with her own memories of her son.

"Okay, just be careful and be back at a decent hour, or call us if you have other plans after that," his father says, looking at him with worry. He knows his son needs time with friends right now.

"I will," Ethan tells them as he gives his mom a hug and kiss and heads out to his car.

"We should head out as well," Matt mentions to Robyn as he slides his hand around her back, placing it on her hip.

"Why are you leaving? You should stay and help out," his mom says as she looks up from the pictures at her youngest son.

"There is too much going on right now. I need some space. Plus, we have stuff to take care of at Robyn's place," Matt tells her as he looks at his family in their moment of joy and grief, putting themselves through the memories. Robyn gives Justine and Matt's mother a hug and a kiss goodbye. Matt gives his brother a solid hug, as they know they are only a phone call away. Matt stands at the door with his shoes and jacket on, waiting patiently for Robyn to pull herself away from his family and the pictures. He waves and speaks up over the conversation at the table and the local radio station's news report. "We will be back out tomorrow sometime." His voice is firm as Robyn finally steps away and walks over to the door. She gives a wave goodbye and they head out the door to their vehicle.

Kevin and Justine are sitting at the table with Kevin's mom and dad, still looking over old pictures, talking of memories not just of Landon. Kevin and his dad are discussing farming and adding little bits to the nostalgic conversation the women are having. Kevin is thinking of getting back into the field tomorrow or Sunday. They only have a week or so left of harvest depending on the weather, and he doesn't want to leave anything out there like they had to do the year before.

"Don't rush out to the field and have something go wrong," his dad tells him with old farm wisdom as he sits in the chair at the table with his arms crossed. "Go out on Sunday. We can get the farmhand to get stuff ready for then. The four of us should go into town and take care of funeral arrangements." He is trying to be the elder statesman of the family but at the same time wants to guide and be there for his son in the way he knows he can.

The women, who are looking at pictures of Landon, turn the conversation to funeral arrangements as well. Justine looks up from the pages of pictures in the album. She looks at the other three at the table and without hesitation in her voice but hopeful enquiry asks, "Do you think the town would let them hold the funeral in the rink? The church won't hold everyone. Besides, where else would Landon want it to be?" The local Lutheran church holds just over a hundred people upstairs and then a few more dozen downstairs, which is usually left for snacks and Sunday school classes.

Grandma nods her head in agreement. "That would be a great idea. I don't see it being a problem with anyone."

"That would work fine, we will look into it," Kevin says with confidence as he takes in his wife's suggestion. He reaches out and holds her hand over a picture on the table of Landon as a kid playing on the outdoor rink.

As they are discussing memories and funeral plans, Damon strolls into the kitchen. "What are you guys up to?" he asks to be polite.

"Just looking at some old pictures," his mother tells him. "You should check out some of these shots of you and the other rug rats."

Damon walks over to the fridge and grabs the same orange juice that had been swigged from before. His grandma looks at him and says, "You know, Ethan drank out of that. You should really put it in a glass."

Damon lifts up the carton and starts to drink from it with a smirk on his face. As he puts the carton back into the fridge, he says to his grandma, "It's okay, Grandma, we're related." The humour from him is much needed, as the conversations had been turning memories into tears.

The men at the table have grown distant in the talk among the pictures. Even the discussion of hunting, farming and the weather has slowed down for the men, as they just sit there unsure of what to say or do. They support their loved ones from a distance, even though they are close to each other at the kitchen table.

Justine grabs her son by the wrist with a soft grip as he is passing by. Her eyes move slowly away from the memories on the table and into Damon's tired eyes. "What is your little brother up to? Is he is doing okay?" she asks quietly with some soft nervousness in her voice.

Damon stands there for a second as his mother looks up at him, waiting for the answer she wants to come from his mouth. He glances down at the pictures and slowly walks away from his mother's grip and sits down on his grandma's lap. "Brett is fine. He is playing video games and texting his friends," he says reassuringly as he looks at the pictures and tries to ignore his dad and grandpa's talk about farming and the weather. He wonders to himself if he is going to leave here to be something more than a farmer. Memories of his brother play in his head as he looks over the pictures.

Damon feels bad for his brother, who would have gotten away from being a farmer after high school and gone on to be an athlete, or at the very least gotten away from here. Leaving by death is the saddest way to get away. As he wonders if he will get that chance, he sees a picture of him and his brothers out on the backyard rink up at his grandma and grandpa's when they were really young. He looks up from the pictures, realizing that he is supposed to have hockey practice tonight. He looks at his parents, confused. "So am I going to hockey practice tonight or not?"

His parents give each other a look, realizing that they forgot all about it, which at this time is understandable. Their minds are filled with the loss of their son, and mixed in with the struggles of being strong parents and the day to day life on the farm, it isn't easy for them.

Damon sees the look of confusion and loss of time in their facial expressions, and he tells them with confidence, "It's okay if I won't be. It is only a couple hours away."

His grandpa speaks up, trying to gain control of the situation for his son and daughter-in-law. With a strong presence in his voice, he says, "Your grandma and I can take you into practice, if that is okay."

Damon, growing frustrated with the ongoing confusion and the lack of decision, says, "I don't care if I go or not. I just want to know if I am going or not."

"You sure you're up for seeing everyone right now?" his mother asks nervously, more so for herself, as she is unsure if she can handle seeing others.

Damon tells them with teenage frustration in his tone, "Well, I am going to have to sooner or later." He takes a calming breath, trying to not piss off his parents or say something he would regret. After a few moments of pondering and nothing being said other than what Damon can tell by looks passed around the table, they finally give the okay for him to go with his grandpa and grandma to hockey practice. He gets up from his grandma's knee slightly frustrated with the whole process and heads downstairs to get all of his gear ready to go and maybe try to take a little nap.

He meets Brett on the stairs and gives him a look of *good luck dealing with them.* He then pretends to pull the hood over his brother's head to be funny. Normally Brett would squirm or get mad at his brother, but he barely even notices the attempt to be annoying. Brett heads up to talk to his parents. He has been playing video games nonstop since breakfast, not to mention talking to friends who keep talking about Landon. This was not helping him be distracted by the video games and music. Brett slowly walks over to the table with one earphone in his right ear and the other hanging down by his neck. Music can be faintly heard coming from the hanging earphone.

"Mom," Brett asks in a monotonous voice that goes with his dejected appearance. "Would it be okay if I go over to Josh's and hang out with him for a while?" He pauses for a brief second as he looks over the leftovers from breakfast. "I am bored here, and I want to be with friends for a while. I can't stop thinking of Landon," he says nonchalantly, hoping that they only pick up on the wanting to be with friends and not his troubles. He wants someone to listen to him but is unsure how to do that with his parents at the moment.

Kevin says as he holds his wife's hand, "Yeah, that should be okay. Grandma and Grandpa can take you over on their way to Damon's practice."

Grandma, trying to be loving and reassuring but sounding more annoying to Brett than anything, tells him, "We can drop you off and pick you up after practice." Brett had already gathered that would be how it worked, but he nods his head and smiles politely for his grandparents. He then walks over to the island and grabs a piece of toast and throws some eggs on it. He puts the hanging earpiece into his ear and heads downstairs to play video games. The sound of "Only" by Nine Inch Nails fills his mind as he slowly walks away, dragging his feet and taking a bite out of his snack.

★ ★ ★

Ethan and Chantal are sitting in the front seat of his car as they drive over to pick up Michelle. They are sharing stories and laughs, trying not to talk about too much of the stuff that is scaring them at the moment. They pull up to Michelle's house. Ethan turns the car off, and he and Chantal walk up to the house. Chantal knocks on the door. They wait a second and then hear a faint voice from inside welcoming them in.

Ethan opens the door and Chantal walks in followed by Ethan, who takes a look back as he hears a dog rushing happily toward the house. He lets the dog inside and pets it as he stands inside the house waiting for Michelle. They can hear footsteps running down the stairs in the house and a few people talking. The two of them take off their shoes and walk from the entrance into the main part of the house.

Michelle's mom is in the kitchen doing some baking. She turns and sees the two kids. "Hi, kids!" she says with unexpected excitement. "Michelle is around, just not sure if she is ready though."

Michelle's father walks up from the basement, and he gives Ethan a nod as they each give a simple smile. He walks over to Ethan and gives the boy a hug and, with a polite comforting tone, asks, "How are you and your family doing? We are so sorry to hear of your loss."

Ethan, standing in front of Michelle's parents, looks at them nervous and scared, but he shows little in his demeanour and voice. "Okay, I guess. I think it is still hitting us."

Michelle's mom washes her hands, walks over to Ethan and gives him a motherly embrace. "If you ever need anything, we are always here for you," she tells him in a comforting voice. As they end the hug, Michelle's mom reaches out and holds Chantal's hand. "Thanks for being such a good friend for Ethan and Michelle. They are really lucky."

Seeing Michelle at the top of the stairs, Ethan gives her a smile. "You ready to go?"

Michelle stands there with a puzzled look on her face; she froze when she saw Ethan standing there. She thought it would be okay, but for a split second she thought he was Landon. She knows that she can't be doing this to herself, so she gives her head a shake and pretends that she is looking in her purse to see if she has everything. She looks up with a smile. "Yeah, I am good to go," she says as she walks down the stairs. She gives her mom and dad a quick goodbye kiss, and the three heartbroken teens head out to Ethan's car. Michelle's parents say goodbye to all of them and tell them not to be too late, or to call if they are going to be. Ethan turns around as he is putting on his shoes and thanks Michelle's parents for everything.

The three of them hop into Ethan's car, Michelle in the backseat, Chantal in the front passenger seat, and Ethan in the driver's seat. They take off for town, heading down the driveway and out onto the gravel road. Ethan is fiddling around with his iPod, trying to find something that he wants to hear. Michelle and Chantal are sharing a conversation about school and the volleyball season. When Ethan can't settle on the right song, Michelle takes the iPod and says, "How about you drive and I will find a song." He shoots her a look as if to say *it's my car, let me control the music, but you win, just don't pick something stupid*. She gives him a smirk and a silly look. The three of them laugh as they continue on to town.

Michelle is going through the iPod trying to find a good song to set the mood. The three of them are discussing the past, random memories of friends and events, mainly those involving Landon. Michelle finally settles on Webb Wilder's "Human Cannonball," a favourite of Landon's and of pretty much all the kids they are friends with. Ethan looks into the rear-view mirror at Michelle and gives her an approving nod at the song selection. He turns the stereo up a little and the three of them sing along and laugh at each other. They continue this as they head into town, with Michelle making every song selection.

They finally arrive at the coffee shop, Jack's Bean Stop. The town isn't big enough for a Starbucks or even a Second Cup franchise. This place is more artsy and not so pretentious as those you find in the big cities. It has the best sandwiches in town, and the waitress who works there is the reason the guys usually go there, and not for the sandwich or coffee.

Walking into Jack's Bean Stop, they notice that there is an older couple sitting next to the window and a middle-aged woman sitting at a table alone reading a book. The three of them head up to place an order. As the owner walks in from the back area, he sees that it's Ethan and his friends. "Their order is on me today, Lauren," he tells the waitress.

Ethan looks over at him and gives a smile and a nod. "Thanks, but you don't have to do that for us."

The owner smiles back. "Don't argue, but don't expect it all the time."

Ethan and the owner laugh awkwardly at the comment. The two walk toward each other and meet in a huge hug. They share comforting words as a few tears fall slowly from their eyes. They both take a moment before turning around to Ethan's friends. The owner is a real good family friend; he used to play hockey with Ethan's dad many years ago and was in his wedding party. "How is the family doing? If your family needs anything, just ask," he tells Ethan as he places a firm hand on the boy's shoulder, offering comfort.

The girls grab their coffee and Ethan's as well and head over to the couches. They exchange pleasantries with the owner as they pass by. "Well, I will let you go hang out with your friends. Just remember, if you ever need anything, just ask," he tells Ethan as the two shake hands.

"Thanks," Ethan replies calmly as he turns and walks to his friends, who are already sitting on the couches drinking their coffees.

They start to discuss memories of Landon. They didn't mean for the topic to come up; it started innocently, just talking about school and high school life in general. All of them are stressed and trying to deal with it, and some are doing better than others.

Ethan is trying to show strength and comfort with his posture and relaxed tone of voice, even though running around in his mind is a variety of memories and *what ifs*. He is sad and dejected but doesn't want to give in to those feelings. He feels the pain of losing his best friend and older brother. He knows that he will cry, and he won't think of it as a sign of weakness around his two friends—one of whom, Chantal, he hopes to finally ask out. The loss of his brother has made him realize you can't take moments for granted.

Chantal is bubbly and excited, acting as though nothing has changed or affected her. Her eyes, if you really look, tell a different story. The memories are filling up right behind them and are about to run over and out in tears, but she holds them back with deflecting conversational banter.

Michelle is nervously sitting on the couch unable to get really comfortable and relaxed—not fidgeting, but instead just changing body position with every sip of coffee. Her tone and actions don't show despair and heartbreak. She hides that with soft laughter and smiles that are attached to the stories shared and the memories in her mind. Michelle is caught somewhere in between the happy memories she thinks of and the pain of missing Landon. Smiles don't come easy, but they don't hurt her either. She knows she will have to get past these emotions, but when? That is the struggle she hates.

Michelle is sharing a story of a couple years ago when she was away at the lake with her family and Landon brought Chantal and Amanda up to see her for the day. The girls start laughing as they remember the craziness of that day and how Landon basically slept out on the dock all day and then that night almost burned his sandals on the firepit.

Ethan looks at them with a confused look on his face. "How long ago was this? Where the hell was I?" he asks with a surprised tone, as he doesn't recall that road trip in his stories.

Chantal looks at him over her coffee cup. "It was two summers ago. I am pretty sure you might have been away at hockey camp or something sporty."

Ethan remains confused but realizes that there are many stories that he doesn't know of his brother. The three of them continue to share stories with laughter and some tears of happiness and sadness as they drink their coffees on the couches at the back of the coffee house.

During all of this, Michelle pauses and begins to softly sing along with the music in the coffee shop. Her friends look at her confused, as she had been silent the past few minutes. Then they realize she is singing along with Alanis Morissette's "Guardian" being played in the shop. They join in, softly singing the words they know. Ethan sings more softly than the girls and knows even fewer of the words; it's the chorus he focuses on. Chantal reaches over and holds on to Michelle's hand and the two share a soft smile as they sing along.

Chantal is enjoying the music and the change of conversation, as the lyrics haven't fully reached her yet. Michelle's voice becomes cracked and softer as every word coming from her mouth is releasing more emotion than any conversation of a memory was doing. Ethan begins to finally realize the depth of the song. His eyes are overcome with emotion, and tears slowly fall onto his cheek. He tries to hide them from the girls, but they notice. They give him a smile, as tears are slowly falling from their eyes too as they sing. Chantal reaches over with her other hand and holds on to Ethan's hand. The two share a smile, comforting each other as if to say thank you.

The three of them sit there as the song ends, the emotion hitting them. Chantal and Michelle give each other a deep loving embrace as they try to compose themselves and yet let the emotion of the moment happen.

★ ★ ★

After a few coffees and laughs, the three teens decide that it would be best to make their way back home. Ethan knows his family is probably waiting for him and will probably want to talk and see how he is doing. Chantal knows she has to get home or else her family will be wondering what she is up to with Ethan for this long. Even though they know she and Ethan have been close friends since a young age and Michelle is here too, her parents are overprotective at times. Michelle, who is happy to be out of the house and away from the thoughts that kept her up all night, knows she should get home as well before her parents start to worry more about her. She hasn't really talked to her family about the whole situation but knows the conversations will be coming soon. They leave town with Ethan driving and the girls talking over the music playing or singing along with it as they head home.

During the ride back, Michelle thinks to herself of all the little things that have been happening to her and around her since Landon's passing. She remembers things the two would do together as friends and how much she will miss those moments. Michelle is struggling now and then with the loss, putting on a brave face when the subject comes up. She can tell the other two think she is so strong and such an inspiration, as she seems to be moving on with grace and patience. They never notice the signs that something more may be going on inside, as they are both lost in their own issues. She knows that once she gets home, she is going to be alone with her thoughts and will be battling many sad and confusing feelings.

Before the passing, she was often out at the parties on the weekends with everyone else. She participated in most social activities in and out of school, but now she feels out of place. Inside her mind she is with her thoughts; she is very distant from most of the things going around her. The brave face and smile don't allow others to know that about her. No one knows the struggle she is truly going through. The ride home with her friends is awkward for everyone, but they try to smile and joke when it's needed. None of them wants to always be serious about the situation. It's not what Landon would have wanted of them. The awkward jokes and laughter among friends make it easier for everyone when they talk of Landon, especially for Michelle.

Michelle drifts in and out of the conversations and into her own quick memories of Landon. She remembers the past few Christmas holidays, spending most of her days away from school at the local ski hill, which is very close to her place, or at the local hockey rink to figure skate or watch the guys play shinny. She remembers sitting at the hill with her friends sipping on hot chocolate or a latte, her iPod playing through one earphone in her ear, the other hanging down the side of her jacket. The music was often a playlist that Landon made for her or songs that Landon brought to her attention. Most had meanings to them or were just good fun songs that were great to pump you up when playing a sport.

She thinks back to all the lessons she taught, mainly to young kids. She always wanted to teach Landon how to snowboard, but he never would go out on the hill. He barely even went to the hill. She laughs to herself as she recalls that he always thought he wasn't a part of that scene—even though he wore the clothing, talked the slang and knew most of the people there. It didn't hurt his excuses that he was always away with hockey, it seemed. Michelle sits in the backseat sunken back in the corner against the door as she looks out the window searching the stars for answers.

She continues down memory lane, thinking of Landon playing hockey and the joy it brought him. He always said that hockey was number one in his life. Michelle believed it, but she also wanted to be his number one. She chokes up a little, but her friends don't notice over the music. Besides, she is hiding from her friends' view in the vehicle. She remembers how she would set up playlists for Landon for road trips in hockey or just because she felt like it. A song comes on the radio that quickly takes Michelle back to those set lists. With quiet tears in her eyes, she looks out the window and softly sings along with Haim's "Don't Save Me."

She thinks of being at the rink watching Landon play hockey as she sat in the stands under a blanket with a girlfriend. Her friend focused on random social events and talking about everything, but Michelle remembers watching Landon every time he was on the ice, even some of the goals he scored and how he would rarely celebrate after a goal. He was never about a single moment of a goal—it was always big picture, championships.

Michelle joins in conversations with Ethan and Chantal from the backseat and shares in their stories, occasionally letting them into her thoughts on the deeper subjects running through her brain—the ones she thought would just be her own, the ones that kept her awake last night and woke her up when she did fall asleep. The music is playing softly in the background and slowly dictates the tone of the conversation, going from the Nearly Deads' "Never Look Back" to We Are the Fallen's "Bury Me Alive" to Stonesour's "Zzyzx Rd." They try to offer

Michelle help as much as they can, while helping themselves. She will only let them into her thoughts as much as she can handle; she remains vague and distant in her offerings but stays a part of the conversations. She doesn't want them to think she is depressed or suicidal.

She *is* depressed, though, as anyone in her situation would be at this point. She is finding ways to manage it that work for her early on and hopefully in the future. Music plays a big part in helping her, as well as solitude and wrestling and confronting her own thoughts in her head. Chantal has noticed that Michelle never loses a smile on her pretty face, but the one that can grab attention from a mile away is rarely seen because the secret behind her sweetest smile is gone. Chantal doesn't know how to help her best friend find it again. She doesn't pry into Michelle's life but always tries to pick her spirit up and bring her into all conversations.

Ethan and Chantal are remaining strong for Michelle with comforting words and happy memories. They are both fighting their own demons dealing with the loss, but talking about it with Michelle is helping them in their own ways, even if they don't know it. They think they are being the strong ones helping her, when really they are helping themselves. The openness and honesty in the conversations is opening up their minds to new thoughts and memories that are helping them reflect and deal with Landon's death.

The ride seems to take forever with all the thoughts in their minds. It does however get easier, or at least it seems that way from the outside as they look to each other for strength. Inside, though, they are all fighting back. The music opens wounds and memories of Landon as well as brings out new conversations to pass the time on the way home. Silence is at times needed for the three to reflect in their own way, with only the music as a guide.

At one point, the conversation turns to Michelle and how some of the guys have acted toward her. They all know that some guys are only being extra nice in case they would be the one to catch her in the moment she fell. Even though she won't be falling for them, it is the vulnerability that they want to seize. She knows this is the case, but she won't let that happen.

The conversation continues on without her and soon drifts off into another random story to lighten the mood. The kids don't want to be sad or depressed and know that they need to smile and laugh, and the music reflects that as Corb Lund's "Hair in My Eyes Like a Highland Steer" plays from the stereo, making the kids' country roots show through. They all sing along with the song, which leads them into laughter and stories of happier times—parties and high school life. Michelle sits in the backseat adding to the conversation at times and singing quietly with the music when she's not lost in her thoughts.

Finally they get off the highway and onto the dirt road down to Michelle's. Ethan pulls into the yard and drives up slowly to drop Michelle off at her house. The three of them exchange goodbyes and thanks as Michelle gives Chantal an awkward hug from the backseat. She then quickly exits the vehicle and walks quietly into the house. Her mom is sitting in the living room reading a book, waiting to talk with Michelle and see if all is okay with her, her friends and Landon's family.

Michelle joins her mom on the couch in the upstairs living room; she sits relaxed and leaning toward her mother slightly as her mom sits casually facing her daughter. Michelle tells her mom all she knows about what's going on and how she is feeling. Her mom is aware that she's not doing great but knows Michelle is strong for her age and just needs some guidance now and then. Michelle tells her mom stories about Landon and his family that were shared today by Ethan, making the two of them laugh through the sad times.

Her mom offers up as much motherly advice as she can think of to help Michelle out. She shares how she felt losing close friends as she grew up, although none of that happened when she was as young as Michelle. The effect the loss of a loved one has on someone never changes; it always hurts and always will. It is all in how you grow from it and never let that person out of your thoughts and heart.

Eventually the two of them run out of energy, but they enjoy the moment they shared. After a loving mother-daughter hug on the couch, they thank each other for the talk. These moments don't come around a lot for Michelle and her mom anymore; they are usually shorter and less fulfilling. They both know that they have to do this more often.

★ ★ ★

Late at night, when Michelle makes her way up to her room for bed, she plugs her iPod into the stereo and plays music softly so not to wake anyone up. She flops onto her bed and relaxes into the messy covers to the sound of the Wilkinsons' "You Heal Me." As she lies there, she suddenly gets the urge to write her feelings, as the music inspires her thoughts. Michelle slowly finds solitude and hope in her new passion for writing poetry, as it gives her an outlet for her pain and the dreams she wants to live. She finds an unexpected voice in her poetry, her inspiration coming from the music and her late-night thoughts.

> Is it asking too much
> To hold you within my arms
> I know the timing has never been right
> And all the words I say
> Come out the wrong way
> Like when the sun comes up
> Before you are ready for a new day
> It's hard to let go
> When you've been tossed away
> The waves never reach the shore
> Like waiting for a knock on my door
> Don't want to pressure you
> But I need an answer soon
> I don't want to be left with rusted shame
> With no one left to blame
> I want to move slow
> Just you and me forever.

Michelle is getting sleepy after a long day with her thoughts and the time spent with her family and friends. She finally drifts off to sleep after a few final moments of thinking of Landon and her own existence. She tries to remember the good times and the possibilities for her new future. The stereo plays quietly into the night as she sleeps. Michelle begins to dream of a time lost somewhere in her past, but she's actually just lost in her own imagination. She dreams of a party where everything seemed perfect, even if it was just for one night. Even if the dream never really happened to Michelle, she believes in it while in the moment of the dream.

*It's the New Year's party at Brittney's house the year before. Michelle shows up with Carmen and Amanda. By 10 that night the house is filled with roughly 60 underage kids and some who are barely legal drinking age, all of them drinking and enjoying the night. The music is playing at a solid decibel level for a teenage party downstairs where the pool table is, along with older couches that may have been a part of a few teenage make-out sessions. Most of the crowd is the usual group at the parties from the area and they seem to be located around the couches laughing and doing shots as they wait for the New Year to arrive. The crowd is a mixture of a couple towns but you had to be invited by Brittney to get in the door, as she didn't want her parents' house messed up like it has been in the past by some assholes who only go to parties to be assholes. Landon shows up late to the party and Shane is with him. Plenty of time to find Michelle for the New Year's kiss they have both hinted at the past little while.*

*Landon walks around upstairs and visits with those up there, having a drink or two with them before heading toward the music and the rest of the party crowd downstairs. Shane meanwhile heads straight downstairs to get his drink on and mingle. Amanda meets Shane at the top of the stairs, and she gives him a huge hug and slaps his ass as she walks away. Shane laughs and starts to walk down the stairs.*

*At the bottom of the stairs, Max and Ethan are standing against the railing drinking away, pretending to be security, often yelling across the crowd as the night goes on for someone to clean up a spill or not to get pizza on the pool table. Shane gets right behind the two, taps them on the shoulder and tells them with a disguised voice, "Fuck you." Max turns around ready to drop the asshole on the stairs, only to find out that it is Shane. He laughs and welcomes Shane to the party. Ethan hands him a beer, and the three of them clank bottles and drink up.*

*Michelle is sitting on the couch and can see Shane at the stairs with Max and Ethan; she shoots a shy smile at him. Shane smiles back and the two share a chuckle from half a room apart. Michelle speaks above the banter around her and the music in the background, trying to get Shane's attention. "You come with Landon?"*

He raises his beer, pointing upstairs with it, and yells back, "Yup. He is upstairs right now mingling with those folks." Michelle nods with a smile as she accepts the news with anticipation. The butterflies hit her stomach and sink her back in the couch as she tries to not get too excited.

Meanwhile, upstairs, Amanda makes her way out of the washroom and notices Landon in the kitchen talking to a couple of people. Amanda makes her way over to Landon and gives him a hug. "So … have you seen Michelle yet?"

Landon shoots her a sarcastic look, wanting to say something smart-ass but holding back as she stands there flaunting her body to the guys upstairs. "I just got here. I haven't seen anyone yet. I have just been chilling with the guys here in the kitchen." His voice softens as he leans in to ask her a private question. "Has Michelle been waiting around just for me?"

Amanda smiles and leans in, whispering to him, "She may have mentioned your name once or twice. You should go find her." The two teenagers share a laugh, knowing that Amanda is just trying to make Landon feel awkward.

Landon gives her a look so as to not make this awkward for Michelle and himself and responds, "Don't tell Michelle that I am here just yet."

Amanda gives him a look as she takes a drink from her alcoholic beverage. "I won't. Don't you worry." She then slowly walks away, making sure the guys notice her as she leaves, making her way back downstairs to the rest of the party. She turns back at the top of the stairs and asks him, "Are you at least going to make your way down shortly?"

Landon looks over at her from the kitchen table as he sits with the guys who are talking hockey and previous drunken debauchery. "Yeah, I will be there shortly. Don't you worry."

The two smile as she heads down the stairs, calling out to the crowd with a drunken "Woooo, party!"

This gets a louder response from Ethan at the bottom of the stairs as he screams, "Lindsay Lohan!"

The three guys are still standing away from the main group, protecting the passageway to and from the basement. Ethan confides as they all stand there trying to look impressive, "I don't know what to do with Chantal." Putting some distance in his questioning so that the guys don't make fun of him, he goes on, "I mean, we are really good friends, but I am not sure how to take the next step or if I should risk the friendship."

Ethan stands there looking across the room at Chantal, who is talking to some friends near the pool table. Max asks him sheepishly, "Have you kissed her yet?" He knows full well Ethan has, he just wants to be a bit of a dick.

Ethan gives him a glance of annoyance, knowing they know he has, and says, "Yes we have, dumbass. A couple times."

Max takes a swig from his Molson and asks with annoying persistence, "So you have kissed her? Which lips?"

Shane laughs to the point where he has to sit on the stairs as he tries to not spit up his beer. Ethan gives Max a friendly punch to the gut, as he knows he is just being a dick, and looks at him with a smile on his face. "Well, I haven't returned the favour, if that is what you are asking." This stops Max from asking the next question as the two nod and clank bottles, knowing what Ethan is truly saying.

"So is she any good at it? I think she would put on a brave face and make way too much noise for not knowing what to do." Shane is trying to drink his beer on the stairs but can't get a sip in from all the laughing.

Amanda walks by with a confused look on her face, as she isn't aware of the comical conversation between the teenage boys. Se asks with way too much excitement and confusion, "What's so funny?"

Max tells her with a straight face as the other guys laugh around him, "Oh, you know." He looks Amanda over from bottom to top, focusing on her breasts.

Amanda shakes Shane's head with her hand, messing his hair up, and walks past. "I shouldn't have asked."

Max blurts out as she walks away, "Maybe I can share it with her later? It is New Year's, after all."

Amanda turns around and shoots him a look to shut him down.

The guys laugh it up and walk over to the pool table, poking fun at Ethan as they do. Chantal makes her way over to Ethan, stumbling over her drunken feet; she is a bit of a lightweight when it comes to drinking. The guys laugh at Chantal and the state that she is in so early in the night. She laughs with them but tells them with a bit a of a slur to her speech to "shut up" as she stumbles slightly, manages not to spill her mixed drink, and plops herself onto a chair that is already taken by Carmen. The girls laugh it off as the guys just shake their heads at the drunk girls.

The music is being controlled by many people during the party; currently, the sound of the night is '80s hair metal, as the kids have been going through a phase for it. FireHouse's "Oughta Be a Law" plays from the stereo. The mingling continues between the sexes as the single guys and girls try to find someone to kiss at midnight. The girls are all playing coy to the guys' advances but teasing them into wanting more. The girls who are hitting on the guys they want to make out with at New Year's are being shut down by all the guys; they know the girls will be back later, as they won't want to be the only girl at the party not to get that New Year's kiss. The slutty girls, though, don't let up, trying to make advances on the guys well past kissing and long before the New Year is rung in.

As the midnight hour gets closer, with only about 10 minutes before the New Year is rung in, Michelle walks over and starts to talk to Landon over by the bar. The two of them haven't been avoiding each other, but both have stayed apart from the other so as not to make a scene. They always make eye contact and share private smiles from across the room. Brittney and Max walk away from the two and make their way to the main group to count down the New Year. There are a few people around but not in arm's length of the potential high school sweethearts. A few people from the crowd watch the action of Michelle and Landon from a distance, mainly so they can have something to gossip about at school or on Facebook, but they try not to be too obvious. Michelle and Landon stand facing each other, sharing laughs and stories back and forth, both flirting with each other but still nervous about what to do next, if anything. This is the first time the two have even been around each other and able to talk, as both have been mingling with others at the party.

Landon mixes a paralyser for Michelle, as that is her drink of choice for the night. They know people are looking at them, and they know that every move they make together is gossiped about even when it is something as insignificant as talking at the lockers at school. They stand there chatting as Ethan and Chantal make their way over near them. The four of them exchange a smile and nod in approval of the night's good times. Ethan looks at Landon and asks with anticipation in his voice, "When are you planning on leaving?"

Landon gives him a shrug, not knowing when he is leaving, but he gives a subtle head bob toward Michelle, telling his brother that it will probably depend on her. Landon then tells his brother, as the girls are in their own discussion of party gossip, "You should just spend the night here. I don't think you should be driving, nor should she."

Ethan smiles and leans in to tell his brother with some excitement in his voice, "Brittney has a room for me already and Chantal. I'll be fine." The two brothers share a bro hug as the girls are chatting nonstop like little schoolgirls, not paying attention to the guys next to them. Landon looks at them and shakes his head, giving a polite laugh, knowing that their gossip is juvenile.

The crowd is gathered around in the basement near the television where they are watching the countdown draw near. The crowd of teenagers starts to count down with the television for the New Year: "Ten, nine, eight, seven, six, five, four, three, two, one." As they get closer to the end, it gets louder and louder, eventually erupting in a boisterous "Happy New Year!" with confetti tossed in the air and noisemakers going off as the teenagers kiss their partner for the night. Some are dating, some are together just for the night, while others like Landon and Michelle could be starting a beautiful relationship. Landon and Michelle embrace in a sweet romantic kiss among the others that night who are making out. The sound of "Still Life With Cooley" by Better than Ezra plays as they ring in the New Year, filling the air with a calming excitement among the confetti and noisemakers too annoying to want to remember. Michelle and Landon stand among the crowd looking at each other, unsure of what just happened but knowing full well it was meant to be. Their faces are both full of life as they smile together, still in a loving teenage embrace as Landon holds Michelle around the waist, holding her close, keeping her close. They slowly separate and stand there holding hands like fresh-faced partners.

As they are standing there looking into each other's eyes, holding hands, the two smile and laugh at the simplicity of the moment that is bigger than both of them know in the high school landscape. They walk away from the crowd, heading slowly upstairs, still holding hands, passing by Chantal and Ethan, Shane, Brittney, Max and Carmen. All of them tease the couple and smile with approval as the two pass by. Landon and Michelle laugh along with them as they go upstairs to talk.

On their way up the stairs, Michelle has a moment of clarity that she wishes would have never come to her, especially not on a night like tonight. Michelle is nervous that tonight might be her first time, and she doesn't know what to tell Landon. She doesn't even know if she wants to have sex or not. She maintains her composure as she and Landon head upstairs to be alone. There is a lone couch up there in the living room and very little background noise. The two of them seem to be lost in their own newly created world as they sit down to talk.

They sit side by side on the couch, their bodies turned to each other, both *gazing into each other's eyes. Michelle can't take the silence anymore. "You don't know how happy I am that you kissed me," she says, and continues talking about her thoughts of what may happen tonight. She rambles on, and Landon sits there and listens.*

*Finally, he reaches out and touches her hand. "I didn't kiss you to get in your pants. I did it to share my life with you. You should stop listening to everyone else's ideas."*

*Michelle looks at him stunned and her voice cracks. "You mean you really like me, it isn't all about sex?"*

*Landon takes a moment and looks into Michelle's eyes and tells her with calmness in his voice, "I have real feelings for you, but I was always scared to lose our friendship if we rushed into a relationship."*

*Michelle, with emotional fluctuation in her voice, replies as she looks at Landon with anticipation on her face waiting for the next kiss, "Thank you for taking my feelings into consideration and our friendship before acting."*

*Landon looks her in her eyes and assures her with confidence, "You will always be everything to me."*

*The two have put their drinks to the side and are sitting on the couch, with Michelle's right shoulder in Landon's left armpit as they hold each other close. The two share stories and talk about their feelings toward each other and politely discuss what they should do next. Both think they should get the rumour mill going and make an early exit from the party. People are slowly starting to leave and wave and say goodbye to the two upstairs, but the party is still going strong downstairs with the music, pool and alcohol. Michelle shows little to no sign in her eyes that she had been crying happy tears moments earlier.*

*Landon, on the spur of the moment, sits up straight on the couch and slaps her on the leg teasingly. "You should grab your jacket and go and say goodnight to those you want to let know you are leaving."*

*Surprised by the sudden slap and the comment made, she asks him, "What should I tell them if they ask why I am leaving so early?"*

*"Just tell them that I am taking you home."*

*Michelle looks at him, confused, as it seems to be too simple of a plan to leave a party that way.*

*Landon runs outside to warm up the vehicle, as the winter night is cold in Saskatchewan. Michelle runs downstairs and starts to say her goodbyes to her friends. Landon gets in the vehicle and sits slightly shivering in the driver's seat* about to start the car up. After it starts, he quickly runs back inside through the snow, as he is out there without a jacket on, just his bunny hug to protect him from the cold winter air. He shakes off the snow from around his feet as he takes off his shoes and walks downstairs. He says his goodbyes to his friends as he meets up with Michelle so they can head off on the surprise trip.

The two take off together into the cold winter night as a light snowfall descends onto the already snow-blanketed countryside. Michelle is confused and excited as to what the surprise will be, while Landon sits in the driver's seat with his eyes focused on the road. She tries over and over to get him to spill the surprise, but no luck. He just keeps smiling and giving her a soft innocent look that helps her believe it will be worth it.

Michelle tries to find a decent song on the iPod for them to listen to on the drive. She finally settles on SheDaisy's "A Night to Remember." The moon shines bright through the falling snow as they drive along the gravel road. The headlights brighten well into the distance, showing every snowflake falling to the wintery ground. The two sit in a comfortable silence among the songs from the stereo as they drive to a place only Landon knows they are heading, but one where they have shared many moments in the past.

After several minutes of driving on the gravel roads in the snowy conditions, they pull up to the secret destination. Michelle looks out the window and sees through the falling snow and into the darkness a place that she has seen many times in her mind. She stares out the window trying to gather composure; her eyes tear up with happy and sad tears, and she speaks softly at the window words meant for Landon. "You didn't have to bring me here to make me happy."

Landon reaches over and holds Michelle's left hand. "I didn't bring you here just for that. I brought us here to celebrate a new year. I wanted to be alone with you without any distractions." He looks at her and gives her a slight nod as if to ask if she is ready to go outside.

She turns to him with a tear running down her cheek and a smile on her face. "Yes, I am ready."

The two walk through a foot of snow to a secluded area among the trees, atop the river valley. Landon is leading the way so that Michelle can walk in his footprints so her feet don't get covered too badly in snow. There is enough light from the moon and stars for them to see clearly. They arrive at a secluded bench in a small opening that was left over from an old party spot by the high school kids. There they can see a long way, even to the lights from Michelle's home.

For a few moments they remain silent to the world, feeling every small shiver in their body, every snowflake fall on them, every breath they take as they watch their breath in the cold air. Landon holds Michelle close to him, sharing the shivers and warmth.

The two exchange a moment as they look into each other's eyes, smiling softly as a slight wind touches their face with guidance and a shivering love. They look up into the dark starry night through the falling snow, silently thanking it for joining their evening together. Sitting on the bench wrapped up in a heavy blanket, they watch the stars in a silent embrace. Landon, looking up at the stars, asks with a peaceful tone, "Have you ever thought about the lyrics to the Tragically Hip's songs?"

Michelle looks at him confused, as she wasn't expecting something to be said at that moment, especially that, and tells him with confusion in her voice, "I haven't gone into them in great detail, but I do enjoy them."

Landon, still looking up at the stars, mentions with a soft mystery in his voice, "I think you can find all of life's meaning and hidden messages in songs, especially their songs." With a stillness and quiet conviction, he admits, "Not all the songs fit the moment, but the moments always fit. It is just in how you see things then and now." He pauses and looks away from the stars and into Michelle's beautiful blue eyes, sparkling in the winter night. "Just like tonight, there were moments that a song could have played to set the scene as if it was our very own movie, while other moments only needed a single line of the lyrics to be right, if only heard in your own head."

The two sit there and gaze into the night sky at the bright lights of the stars above, pondering the endlessness of the stars. "My mom used to tell me when I was younger that when someone passes away, they become a new star in the sky. One day I want to be the brightest star out there," Landon tells her as he holds her hand tight. They slowly shift their eyes from the stars into each other's eyes. As they share the love and sadness in their eyes, a cold tear falls from Michelle's. Landon reaches over and calmly wipes it away with his hand.

As they are about to leave, Michelle grabs Landon's hand, stopping him in his tracks. He turns around to see Michelle smiling at him. "Thanks for taking me here and being there for me as a true friend." He pulls her toward him and plants a deep passionate kiss on her chilled lips, warming them up with his own. They kiss in the cold winter night for what seems to be an eternity but is really only a few seconds. The snow falls gently upon them.

*Back in the warmth of the vehicle, the two begin to laugh as they realize that on the stereo is Gloriana elegantly singing "(Kissed You) Good Night." They begin to sing along as they head off into the night. During the trip back to Michelle's, the two sing along with the songs and laugh a lot at each other. The snow has finally stopped falling in the night and the darkness surrounds the vehicle as they head down the gravel road.*

Michelle wakes up from her dream as the cold autumn air passes over her body in bed. The doors to her bedroom balcony have blown open in the night, as she forgot to close them tight before going to bed, allowing for the cold air to come in. The bedding is tossed all over, and she lies there in her pyjamas wishing that what she just dreamed was real.

Slowly she gets out of bed and makes her way over to shut the doors. As she does, the last little bit of the night's cold autumn breeze passes by her, giving her shivers throughout her body. She stops and realizes that the song playing quietly from her stereo is "Fully Completely" by the Tragically Hip. She stands there and looks out the windows of the balcony doors with innocence on her face. Slowly she realizes the dream was real enough for her as she finds comfort in the night's stars. She smiles at them, hoping that Landon can see that she is going to be okay. "Thank you," she says softly into the night as she kisses her fingers and presses them up against the glass, before she makes her way back to her bed so she can try to get some sleep.

Alone in her room with her thoughts and the background music from her stereo fading in and out of her mind, she considers her own depression, death, and all the what ifs that one shouldn't put oneself through. She is vulnerable to these thoughts at any time during the day, but tonight alone in her room she wrestles with them even more. She can't escape them. She tries distracting herself by writing poetry or wasting time online. She needs someone there for her but she doesn't want to bother anyone, especially at this hour of the night. She knows she has to be there for herself eventually. No better time to start than now, she figures, but how she hasn't figured out yet.

She thinks of texting or even calling Chantal, but it is late and she doesn't want to bother her friend. She could talk to her parents, but even that seems too much of a hassle to go through, as she thinks they would always be watching her and protecting her. She doesn't want to burden them any more than they already put on themselves as parents.

She knows that she has to tell them, or someone, about her thoughts, but how far could she go in explaining the thoughts to others before they start to question her and think she is suicidal? Michelle is far from suicidal, but she has become so afraid of death and the unknown that she tries to drown her thoughts with music in her headphones and written words on paper. She sits on her bed, her back against the headboard and a notepad in her lap. She begins to write poetry and random rants just to let them out, without even realizing how late it's becoming. The crisp dark autumn night is slowly becoming a crisp damp autumn morning. She hides these poems among her books on a shelf in her room so that no one will see them, at least not yet, if ever. She then lays her head on her pillow and covers up with her blanket as she slowly drifts off to sleep again. She is going to be awake within only a few hours of going back to sleep, but she knows staying up isn't going to help her and she needs her rest.

Her bed is a mess from the tossing and turning in her sleep. She falls back into another dream separate from the previous one, but it still makes her restless in her sleep. Her music stays on quietly as she sleeps. Outside her window, the stars fade in and out of brightness as light clouds fill the night sky. One lone star remains bright through it all, seemingly watching over Michelle through everything that gets in the way.

# Day 3

## *Friday*

Matt leaves Robyn's place in the morning to head out to the farm to help his brother in the wake of the passing of Landon. Robyn kisses Matt goodbye. She is heading off to work for the day as well, and then eventually to the farm afterward.

When Matt arrives at the farm, Kevin is already out in the yard working on machinery, prepping it for the day's harvest. The work and familiarity help distract him from his feelings of losing his oldest son, but once in a while, he thinks of Landon and has to take a second from greasing the machine.

Matt is ready to get out there on the combine and get to work. He greets his brother with a subtle head nod, which is reciprocated by Kevin. Matt checks on the grain trucks for fuel and making sure they are running fine, and then he heads over to fill up the fuel truck from a gas tank in the yard. Normally, Matt and Kevin have constant petty arguments on the farm, over how one drives the combine or fixes things during a breakdown. Since the passing of Landon, they have put the little issues aside for the sake of the family. Matt and Kevin keep the farm arguments to just that and don't let it pass over into family life. The two have always been close, even though the age gap is more than 10 years. At times, though, you would wonder how close they are with the constant teasing and heckling that goes on.

The conversations at mealtime are kept to weather, farming and sports. That is, unless the women get a word in and the conversation turns to how the tractor looks in the sun or what happened on their soap opera or what they are canning from the garden. The men oblige the women in their conversations, as it eases the mood, even though they hate when the conversation is about some nonsense on TV.

The men in the family don't lack emotions, but they prefer to keep them in check and more often than not just let it out in anger or intensity. Sports and hunting are their main outlets; never does it go domestic. They are patient men but have demons inside, and their parents never really explained to them that it is okay to deal with feelings in other ways than yelling. So it has been gradually passed on from generation to generation unintentionally.

After harvest that night, Matt stays out at the farm as Robyn comes out after work in town. Matt and Kevin's parents are also visiting from just up the road. The discussions between the men are of farming and hunting. Kevin and his dad are the main talkers in the conversation, while Matt just sits back and tosses his comments out if needed. Matt knows not to get too involved with farming conversations between Kevin and their father. It tends to get out of hand when the younger generation tries to explain their ways to the elder statesman of the family farm. Even though the farm is their father's and most of the land and equipment is his, he isn't involved with all the day-to-day farming decisions the way that he once was.

His decisions and ideas are always heard, since he has over 50 years of working on the farm. Kevin, however, takes off on his own way from time to time, and this pisses his father off. Matt stays away when he knows this is going on; he wants no part of that battle. These conversations on farming are a solid distraction for the men in the wake of the past few days, even though it seems at times it may drive the family apart before they deal with the passing of Landon. Frustration grows among the men, but they all keep it inside and never truly bring out the real issues of why they are angry as they try to deal with the loss.

Meanwhile, the women are in another room talking about their television shows and funeral plans. They talk about the soaps that they barely get to see anymore because of work and running around. Robyn mentions how she has lost touch with the soaps for a while now and has moved on to just trying to catch an Oprah episode every now and then. Justine casually brings up the topic of the funeral and where they are with the plans—a topic their mother-in-law is interested in, as her husband and herself will be putting up a good chunk of the money for the funeral. Kevin and Justine keep saying that they don't want the financial help, but they know that arguing over the money with Kevin's parents is never going to work.

Justine assures her mother-in-law that they are picking within a budget, but she also knows that if something is slightly out of their budget they are going for it and that they want the funeral to be a simple yet glorious one to remember their beloved son. She conveys to the other women that it is the one event you never want to plan, especially for a child, so it will be done with Landon in mind—what he would want around him—which is the reason why it is at the hockey rink and not the church.

Matt has stepped away from the manly conversations in the living room. He needs another drink and to escape the stories of hunting and farming for a while. He enters the room with the women chatting and enjoying a drink while laughing over pictures. Matt sits down beside his potential future wife and gives her a love poke with one of his fingers to her side, which makes Robyn shimmy in her seat a little as it tickles her. He does this a lot to her; she is okay with it, but wishes he wouldn't do it as much. His mother gives him an annoyed look. "When are you guys going to stop doing that to your better halves?"

Matt puts his glass to his lips and before taking a drink, he says, "I will stop when she stops squirming when I do it." He takes a sip, and as he puts the glass on the table, he pokes her again in the side and she squirms some more. She gives him a *you're going to get it* look with her eyes even though she has a smirk of a smile on her pretty face.

They continue the conversation about the funeral plans. They discuss the details of time and who has what parts to do at the funeral. This discussion goes on for a few hours. Eventually, Kevin and his dad make their way into the kitchen and sit at the table, adding to the conversation. The talk is heavy on the funeral and sharing stories of past family events—weddings, funerals, reunions, Christmas dinners. They share laughs and drinks well into the night.

Eventually, Matt and Kevin's mom and dad head on home, as they are up well past their bedtime; they tend to be in bed long before midnight and up before the sun. Both are slightly intoxicated for them. They haven't been this drunk, if you want to call it that, in more than five years. Before they leave, they exchange goodnights and hugs as they slowly and gracefully leave the house. Their father does the driving, even though he has had the most to drink. He always drives short trips to and from people's houses. Long trips, on the other hand, he changes off with his wife, driving early on and she drives most of the way.

The remaining four adults stay up for a while telling stories and playing the card game Kaiser in teams of men against women. They didn't start playing cards until after midnight. The four of them are well into their second and final game of the night. The men aren't willing to admit defeat, always bidding crazy and making their bids just big enough to keep the game going. The conversations are light, fully distracting them from their personal grief. They all know that Landon would have loved to be around and play a game or two or just watch them play. They know that Landon wouldn't want them to be sad all the time, just to keep him in their mind and think of him fondly, but not to dwell on what could have been.

★ ★ ★

It has been two days since Landon's passing, and many of the local kids have gathered at what they called the pre-grad site, which is some farmland with bushes and trees surrounding a wide-open area perfect for high school parties. They have a bonfire party to honour and remember Landon and to just gather and enjoy their time together. Many kids show up from around the area, including those who Landon played sports with over the years in the neighbouring towns and those who knew him from watching him play sports. He was never the most social kid, nor was he the one they all would remember from the previous night. But to them, he was more than just a memory of a fading night before.

Many people show up who are just friends of friends who knew Landon and want to be there for the night. One of the vehicles is used as a stereo for the evening, with tunes played throughout the night setting the mood unintentionally. This helps memories come out among friends and creates new ones. Teenagers share moments alone as they get to know each other like two young lovers would, along with the occasional heated debate and fight between young drunk friends over something as mindless as old sports battles or ex-girlfriends.

The party gets so big that a second bonfire is started—a smaller, more important one to those around it. Around this fire are Landon's closest friends. Renee and Ethan get the fire going, and Michelle and Gord are next to help bring some wood over. Shane, Warren, Chantal, Johnny and Max soon follow, bringing over a couple lawn chairs and stumps to sit on. They sit around and talk among themselves and watch the larger bonfire and those having a good time in memory of Landon or simply because they've consumed a little too much alcohol.

After a while, a few more people who knew Landon fairly well over the years show up and join the smaller fire. Carmen and Brittney along with Nathan and Kyle arrive soon after and share laughs and stories of Landon, as they knew him from the sports he played. Carmen and Brittney are both dating guys on the hockey team that Landon played on, and he became good friends with them; they could talk to him about anything and he would listen and never say a word. Nathan was Landon's line mate in hockey and also played shortstop on the same ball team as Landon. Kyle was Landon's social leader when he went to their town to party it up and had many untold stories of those nights. They shared some great moments in sports as well, be it against one another when younger or on the same team as they got older.

This group shares stories and laughs all night long as they drink and enjoy the night. Others come by and try to convince them to join the others, while some come over and try to make everyone more energetic, but those around this smaller fire are happy with how they are. The group is content enjoying the fire and the company they have without all the drama that is going on around them. They laugh both sarcastically and honestly as events unfold at the other bonfire, but for the most part they are focused on themselves and their memories of their lost friend.

The night grows long and the cold air is coming in faster than the fire can keep up with on this October night. The larger fire is getting smaller and smaller as the night goes on, as does the gathering of friends around it. Soon the only fire left is the small one with only Landon's closest friends. Some of them are drunker than others. Some are barely hanging on to the last yawn before they fall asleep but don't want to give in as they want to be with their friends.

Ethan, Shane and Gord get up and begin to put out the fire and start their vehicles. Kyle and Nathan get up to leave, and they go around giving each member of the group a hug and thanking them all for everything. They take off for home. Nathan had been drinking, but he stopped many hours ago. He had his fun and knew it wouldn't be right to drive home fully intoxicated. They know to stick to the back roads, as do most of the kids in the area after a night of partying.

Gord, while walking back from his vehicle, says over the remaining vehicle engines, "I can take Renee home, she lives next to me in town, and I might as well drop off Johnny and Max as well, as neither is in any condition to drive."

Shane and Warren are slowly packing things up from the fire and cleaning up. Both ask Michelle if she needs a ride home, but she smiles at them as she sits on the stump watching the fire. "No, that's okay. Ethan and Chantal are giving me a ride."

Carmen and Brittney are trying to figure out if they should drive home tonight. Neither one is drunk, but they don't know if they should chance it. Ethan looks at them from across the hood of their car. "You can stay at my place if you don't want to drive back tonight. It might be hectic tomorrow, but I'm sure that it would be okay."

They talk openly aloud about the idea of staying or going. Eventually Carmen decides, "I think we will drive back home tonight, but thanks for the offer."

Ethan understands. He gives them a big hug and thanks them for coming out tonight. Almost all of the partygoers have gotten into their rides and started to leave the smoldering fires behind while taking memories of the night with them as they drive down the dirt road to their homes.

Ethan, Michelle and Chantal are still standing around the little bit of fire that is remaining. None of them is saying anything, just staring at the fire as it slowly burns out in the chilly autumn night. As they stand around, a faint sound of music comes from Ethan's vehicle. On the stereo they can faintly hear the Tragically Hip's "Grace, Too." The three of them start to walk back to the car smiling with a few tears in their eyes. Ethan looks up at the stars as he stops at the hood of his car. The girls stop and look up as well. They say goodnight to Landon quietly to themselves as they look up at the night's lights.

Ethan and Chantal take Michelle home. It may be a bit out of their way, but there is no issue or wavering on the decision. Michelle sits in the backseat listening to the music quietly filling the background as she looks out into the night sky. Her mind is filled with memories and lost moments that will never be the same without Landon. The two friends in the front seat talk quietly back and forth about the night as well as where they are as friends. Michelle watches on from the backseat, her eyes and ears not focused on the situation going on up front, but she has an idea from her peripheral hearing of what is going on. She is however focused on the moment she is sharing alone with the night sky. Lady Antebellum's "Need You Now" plays from the radio and offers up more and different meanings to each of the teenagers on this drive tonight.

After dropping Michelle off at her house, Ethan and Chantal make their way back down the same way Landon took his last ride. They stop at the scene of the accident and get out of the vehicle and stand holding each other close. The two of them say nothing in words, but their growing affection for each other says even more. They stare off into the track marks in the ditch and into the night sky, trying to gain an understanding and hoping to find a way to deal, alone and together. The two slowly leave the scene as they both share a quiet prayer in Landon's memory before leaving.

★ ★ ★

Shortly after the card game is finally over—one in which the women win—a vehicle pulls into the yard. It's Ethan and Chantal arriving home from the bush party in memory of Landon. Both of them are slightly intoxicated. They walk into the house and Chantal pulls up a chair to the table. Ethan grabs Chantal a beer and one for himself, along with some leftovers that he puts in the microwave to heat up. The six of them stay up for a few more hours, enjoying the company and conversations and a few more wobbly pops. The adults tease the two teenagers about being more than "just friends." Ethan and Chantal take it in stride, as they know no harm is meant by it.

"How was the party tonight?" Justine asks the two teenagers. "Were there a lot of good memories shared of Landon?"

"It was a good turnout, many people we didn't expect to see there from other towns," Ethan tells the group. "Brittney and Carmen showed up, and they convinced most of Landon's friends from around the area to show up."

"There were a lot of stories shared about Landon and just high school memories in general around the fires tonight," Chantal adds.

"Did everyone stay responsible and not drink and drive?" Robyn asks.

"I think a few drove drunk but I'm not really sure. Most of us went to a separate fire and hung out there, as the rest stayed at the large fire and did their own thing," Ethan tells them.

"So there were some fights, is what you're saying?" Matt comments.

"Why would you think that?" Ethan quickly replies.

"I'm not that far from my bush party days. I know what goes on," Matt replies as he grins at Ethan.

"Yeah, there were some incidents, but nothing too crazy," Ethan says quietly, hoping that the subject dies off.

"You weren't involved in any, were you?" Kevin asks with a stern tone.

"No, he wasn't. He stayed away. Our entire group did, actually," Chantal says, trying to calm the conversation down.

"Well, I think I have had my fun for the night. I think I should get some sleep," Kevin says as he stands up and gives a salute goodnight, tipping his hat to everyone at the table.

The rest agree that it's about that time to turn in and start fresh tomorrow. It has been a long day for all of them in their own way. They all slowly make their way off to bed. Matt and Robyn will spend the night in Landon's old bedroom, while Chantal and Ethan will be together in his bedroom. Ethan and Matt are the last to leave.

"Don't rush anything, make sure you are doing this for the right reason," Matt quietly tells Ethan as the two sit at the table alone.

"What are you talking about?" Ethan asks, confused by his uncle's comment, as it comes out of silence.

Matt looks at him as his eyes tell a story that he knows what is going on. "Look, I know you two are good friends, and maybe even dating. Just don't rush the relationship. For that matter, don't rush past the innocence and honesty and go straight for the physical."

"Don't worry. I don't think she will let me rush anything even if I wanted to," Ethan replies with teenage angst. The two sit there in silence as they finish their drinks. Ethan is the first to get up from the table, leaving Matt to finish up on his own.

Matt sits there listening to the silence in the house. His mind drifts off to simpler times with his family. He wonders to himself how and when things will get back to normal and all the subtext going on will subside. He takes a last sip from his drink and walks off to bed, shutting off the remaining lights that are on as he leaves the room and heads downstairs.

★ ★ ★

In Landon's room, Matt and Robyn sit on the edge of the bed, looking around at how it is still basically the same as it was the day he passed away. As they sit there, Matt slowly reaches over and softly holds on to Robyn's hand. The two look at each other and slightly bite their lips with sadness, each trying to encourage a smile for the other.

Books are neatly organized on Landon's desk and bookshelf, and the posters of Hollywood starlets and sports stars are still hanging on his wall. The clock on his wall is stuck on 1:37. Landon set it for that time but never turned it on. It was his homage to the movie *Empire Records*. That way, no matter when he looked at it, whether he was happy or sad, it was always an excellent time.

Landon's school backpack is propped up against the closet door slightly unzipped, and a few notebooks are visible. Robyn grabs a notebook with scribbles and doodles all over it from the desk. Their is no hint of what the subject is on the cover, unless there is a direct correlation between the Hip, STP, Edmonton Oilers, 1:37, the Michigan

Wolverines' logo, random swirls, and some games of Xs and Os to that of a class and subject.

Looking inside the notebook, they find that it is not for a subject and barely has anything to do with school. The first page has some pictures of movie stars and Transformers glued onto the page, depicting a war. On the next page his name is printed small on the top line, and below it is a list—one of many they will find in the book. This list is what some would call a bucket list or a to-do list, depending on their age. On it, Landon has little details, big plans, random events and possible future endeavours. It shows that Landon had his life somewhat mapped out, or at least he had some plans as to what he wanted. They didn't know how recent this list was, if it was made just before his untimely death or well in advance.

1. Graduate.
2. Stay healthy.
3. Ask Michelle out.
4. Travel the world; visit Stonehenge, Australia, Great Wall of China.
5. Watch a college football game at the Big House in Ann Arbor.
6. Go to college and get a degree in something that will make me happy.
7. See the Hip in concert as much as possible.
8. Get Oilers season tickets.
9. Go camping with friends more often.
10. Learn French better and learn other languages, at least the basics.
11. Make it as far as I can in hockey and volleyball.
12. Own my own business.
13. Tell my parents I love them.
14. Tell my parents to fuck off.
15. Take more pictures.
16. Write a book.
17. Have a Vegas story or two.
18. Own my own home with a sports-themed basement.

19. Coach high school sports.
20. Get lost in a corn maze.
21. Be a better brother.
22. Go to as many major sporting events as possible.
23. Win provincials in hockey and volleyball.
24. Invent something obvious.
25. Be myself and be happy.

Matt and Robyn read over the list a few times before moving on, often giggling and pointing to each other about different points. Matt wonders if Kevin and Justine even know of this. He should take this up in the morning for them to look over. The next few pages are lists of Landon's favourite things: sport teams ranked in their own sports and overall, and favourite movies, songs, bands or singers, actors and actresses; the actresses are also broke into another top list as to which would be best to bang if given the chance, with reasons why. This list, as weird as it is, is not only hilarious for the obvious reasons but because of the comedic explanations for why the women are ranked as they are. There are also plays drawn up for volleyball, made for specific players on his high school team. Landon knew the tendencies of his teammates better than they probably did.

*Sports Teams.*
1. Michigan Wolverines
2. Edmonton Oilers
3. Edmonton Eskimos
4. Dallas Cowboys
5. Seattle Mariners
6. Louisville Cardinals
7. St. Louis Blues
8. Toronto Blue Jays
9. Chicago Cubs
10. Hamilton Tiger Cats.

Honourable mention goes to Saskatchewan Rough Riders not by choice, but only when playing any team that will help the Esks playoff position. Montreal Expos and Hartford Whalers have both moved to new cities, but the retro logos are sweet.

*NHL ideas*

Allow for hand passes in all zones; closing of the hand on the puck to make a pass in any zone is not allowed.

Goals scored by kicking with intent are allowed.

A player deliberately playing the puck over his shoulders with a high stick, not involved in a scoring deflection, results in a delay of game penalty.

Goalie crease should be extended to reach the trapezoid behind the net, inside the new area the ice is in blue paint. Inside the paint the goalie can't be interfered with; outside he is treated as a player and contact can be made.

Take away the centre line. Icings only happen if shot down from your own end.

Face-offs in the neutral zone only take place at centre ice. The other dots in the neutral zone are no longer there.

*NCAA College Football ideas*

Tournament using Bowl games as locations for each game. An NIT-type tournament can also be created for the next 32 teams in the rankings. The bigger Bowl games are used as the later games with one National Championship Game that is played at a different site every year. These games can be played on Saturdays, with the NIT games on Thursdays and Fridays. Games would start mid-December and run for the next five weeks. Bowl money is based on rankings going into the game. More money given to the higher seed, and each round the bowl money goes up.

Landon also had lyrics to songs along with doodles of random things. They find the poetry mixed in with all of this, most of it is adolescent and hit and miss. They knew Landon liked to write, but to what extent they did not know.

*Those Eyes*
Every time I look into those eyes,
I never see what I saw before.
Light reflects
The perfection within.
I believe in time we will see
Who holds the truth,
Seeing what is behind those eyes.
Those dreams at night
Are reality not yet unattained.
Once stripped down,
On your hands and knees,
You will find your truth
Inside those eyes.

There are more poems in the back of the notebook, but Matt and Robyn don't go into reading them. They're both tired and have gone through enough emotions for the night.

# Day 4

## Saturday

The next morning, the adults wake up feeling the effects of last night's late-night drinking. Breakfast is on the go by the time Matt and Robyn make their way up from Landon's bedroom. Justine is slaving away over the stove as the smell of bacon and eggs fills the air. The kids are slowly waking up from their sleep and making their way to the kitchen. Ethan and Chantal are the last to show up at the kitchen table.

"Sorry we're late," Chantal says apologetically, rubbing sleep from her eyes.

Ethan, not fazed by being the last up and in the kitchen, complains, "What, no pancakes?" His comment is made in jest, as everyone is sitting around the table barely alive from the previous night's activities. Ethan doesn't even want to be up yet, but Chantal made him get up with her when she woke up to the sound of footsteps above the bedroom and the smell of bacon on the stovetop. The family eats breakfast, with Kevin and Robyn both asking for meds with their food. Tylenol and Rolaids are needed the most.

As breakfast finishes, Ethan's brothers take off in their own directions to get on with their day of lounging around on the couch. Chantal and Robyn help Justine clean up the breakfast mess. Matt runs downstairs and brings up the notebook they found last night.

"Have you guys looked through any of Landon's stuff yet?" he asks those still left in the kitchen as he puts the notebook on the table and takes a seat.

"Other than trying to clean up his room a bit, no. The pain is too much at the moment," Justine admits.

"I've borrowed a shirt, but that's about it," Ethan says as he rests his head on his crossed arms on the table. For the most part, the bedroom has been an unspoken off-limits area to common activities.

"Well, last night when we went to bed, we noticed some notebooks and decided to look into one," Matt tells them as he flips through the pages quickly. "It is basically random lists, thoughts and poems Landon made."

He stops flipping through the pages and slides it over to Kevin and Justine for them to look at. Even with the effects of last night buzzing in their heads, their thoughts and emotions are clear when thinking of Landon. His memory is never forgotten but rarely talked about in the way this notebook will inspire memories and conversation. This is a great way for the family to remember more of Landon and to think of where he could have been later in life.

Justine places the book in front of her, reading out the pages, Kevin right by her side comforting her with his hand on her leg. Matt and Robyn sit across from them at the table, laughing and crying and enjoying the memories they all are sharing. Chantal, who is listening keenly to the words on the pages, sends Michelle a text message and tells her to make her way over. She never gives a reason, just tells her friend to get here as soon as she can.

Michelle responds quickly, saying she has no way of getting there since she can't drive and Shane is probably in no shape to drive this morning. Her parents are off on some nature walk somewhere. Ethan sends her a text saying that he will run over and pick her up. Chantal decides to stick around and listen to the stories with the family as Ethan heads over to pick up Michelle.

Ethan drives fast on the gravel roads on the way to Michelle's. As he gets close to the section of road where Landon lost his life, he slows down a little and gives a sad nod of respect to the memory of his brother. Shortly after as he passes through, he speeds back up and continues on his way. The sound of "Weatherman" by Dead Sara blasts from the stereo. Ethan is singing along with the song, the raw emotion coming out of him as he unleashes the frustration and tension that have been building up since his brother's passing.

He makes it to Michelle's in a very short time. When he arrives, Michelle is sitting outside with her dog, waiting for him. Michelle looks like she didn't get much sleep last night, but she's put on her brave face and some subtle makeup for the visit to Landon's family's home.

"So why am I coming over to your place this early today?" she asks Ethan as they leave the yard. "Chantal made it seem like an emergency."

"Well, the family is going through some of Landon's things, and we thought it would be nice to have you there with us," he tells her as he takes a quick look into her tired eyes.

She is shocked by the morning's events and isn't sure if she will be able to go through with this, but at the same time she's excited, with questions she wants to find answers to with whatever Landon may have left behind. She turns up the stereo as the Tragically Hip's "Yawning or Snarling" comes on, and the two of them sit in silence listening to the song as they ponder the thoughts in their own heads. Ethan is thinking of Chantal and Landon, while Michelle is trying to calm her nerves as she thinks of his family. The two arrive back at Ethan's place in good time, so much so that those at the house barely knew he was gone.

The family welcomes Michelle into the home as she sits down at the kitchen table where the family is going through the notebook. Robyn gives Michelle a quick rundown as to what is in the book, but says she can look over it more personally afterward if she wants to see it for herself.

Currently they are on some of the lists Landon made over time. They find humour and understanding in the lists of random things, some glorifying, others just for shits and giggles. The lists are full of celebrities, people he has met, athletes, and other random people and things.

*The people that annoy the fuck out of me …*

1.  Lindsay Lohan—time to call it a career and retire to your trailer … park.

2. Don Cherry—the game has changed, I respect your ideals on player protection but that is it, oh, and learn how to pronounce a name properly, that shtick is overplayed. Just like your rock 'em sock 'em videos, which we all can make or see ourselves on YouTube.
3. Kardashians—I think my pen threw up just writing your name down.
4. Sean Avery—if you believe that you were Elisha Cuthbert's first get over yourself, you will always be the sloppy seconds. Oh, nice glasses and scarf.
5. Tony Romo—so you are the QB of America's team. Thank gawd I am in Canada, sadly I still cheer for the Cowboys.
6. Spencer Pratt—Oh, my pen just threw up again, and I think it shit itself as well, this guy seems to have that effect on everything.
7. The cast of *Jersey Shore*—GTL, more like STFU.
8. Nicki Minaj—You have a career thanks to your ass, not sure what is worse that or your songs.
9. Paris Hilton—It is not even 2007, and you still annoy me.
10. Donald Trump—Get a haircut and get a real job. Vince McMahon says it best: *You're fired!!!!*

*Five People Invited for Last Meal*

1. Sandra Bullock
2. Mean Gene Okerlund, Chris Jericho, Christy Hemme, Katie Holmes
3. Tom Hanks, Gord Downie, J. K. Rowling, Zooey Deschanel, Kevin Smith
4. Kate Middleton, Seth McFarlane, Katy Perry, Howard Stern, Jennifer Aniston
5. Tina Fey, Paul McCartney, Jay-Z, David Letterman, Brad Paisley

They all sit around laughing over these lists and others, agreeing and adding hysterical comments to the ones Landon has made. They aren't shocked by the opinions Landon wrote down, as he mentioned them on more than one occasion. He was always annoyed with radio play and music television, and he would go on rants at parties and after watching celebrity news online and on television.

*Favourite Songs*

1. So Hard Done By—Tragically Hip
2. Still Life With Cooley—Better Than Ezra
3. Human Cannonball—Webb Wilder
4. Possum Kingdom—Toadies
5. The Freshman—Verve Pipe
6. The Way It Is—The Sheepdogs
7. You and I—Lady Gaga
8. Weatherman—Dead Sara
9. Vasoline—Stone Temple Pilots
10. Springsteen—Eric Church

Kevin leaves the conversation after a while to go and take care of some farm work up at his dad's place. He gives his wife a quick kiss goodbye before he leaves. Matt steps away as well and retires into the living room to have a nap, as the night before was longer than he was expecting. The younger brothers, Damon and Brett, left the kitchen table long ago after eating breakfast. They make the occasional appearance at the table to see what the laughter is about or just out of boredom, but for the most part they've been in front of a television and texting with friends.

After a while, Robyn follows her man into the living room and lies down on the couch with him to nap. Matt makes some room for her but barely enough. Robyn makes it work as she slowly moves her butt more and more into his body, pressing him up against the back of the couch. Justine makes fun of her for going for a nap and trying to make room on the couch for the two of them but knows she will be going for one shortly as well.

The three teenagers are left at the table talking and looking over the notebook. Ethan and Chantal decide that they want to go for a walk and visit the animals outside, not to mention talk about what is going on between them. They are polite and Chantal asks, "Michelle, do you want to go with us?" Even though they would rather be alone, they know Michelle may not want to be by herself. Michelle, though, is reading the notebook and is lost in it. She barely hears what was said but mumbles, "I'll be okay."

The two young lovebirds head out into the yard for a walk, while Michelle sits at the table and continues to lose herself in the book. She looks up from the book and asks Justine, who is sitting in the living room, "Justine, is it okay if I go and read this in Landon's room?" She pauses for a second. "I promise not to make a mess, and if you don't want me in there, I understand."

Justine looks into the kitchen at Michelle, who is now standing at the entrance between the kitchen and the living room. "You sure can, take all the time you need down there."

Michelle is about to walk away with the notebook in her hand when Justine tells her, "If you want, you can stay for dinner. Just make sure to let your parents know what your plans are."

Michelle walks over to Justine and gives her a big hug and says thank you. Justine's face fills with emotion, but she stays strong and gives a happy smile to Michelle, as Michelle smiles back. Justine always wanted a daughter; even though she loves her sons, she would have really liked to have mother-daughter talks. Michelle might be the closest she gets to those moments. Sadly, it has to come at such a heartbreaking time.

Michelle heads downstairs to Landon's room, passing Brett and Damon in the downstairs living room where they are playing hallway hockey with a mini-stick and a taped-up sock ball. "Try not to break anything," she tells them, as she knows that boys tend to find something to break, be it themselves or the furniture.

"Oh, we won't," Damon says with a grin as he tries to score on Brett. "Are you going into Landon's room?"

Michelle looks back at him and tells him with a sombre smile on her face, "Yes."

Damon smiles back at her with comfort and support; he then body-checks his brother, stealing the sock ball and hitting his brother in the face with a quick wrist shot. Michelle watches to see if Brett is okay, which he is; the shot stung a little but it didn't go in. So play must go on, and it does for the boys. The shots get harder and more direct after that.

Michelle makes her way to the bedroom and can still hear the thuds of the taped-up sock ball hitting the wall and the two kids laughing and commentating on their game as they go.

She reaches for the doorknob and holds it for a short moment, taking in what she is about to do before she slowly opens the door to her deceased boyfriend's bedroom. Michelle enters the room with timid anticipation and scared excitement as to what she may see and what memories and thoughts will fill her head. She forgot how the room smelled of hockey and a random assortment of air fresheners. Landon had at least two or three scents of air fresheners in the room to cover up the smell of hockey. She walks over to the bed and sets the book down on it before walking over to the closet and bookshelf.

Michelle is filled with anxious trepidation as she goes through Landon's clothes. She touches each one as she goes past it with a delicate passion, remembering the times when Landon wore each item—some monumental memories and some just random moments in her life and Landon's. She holds in her emotions, not letting one tear drop as her face shows only the emptiness of the hope of what could have been. She is not sad from remembering Landon in the jeans that made his ass look great, or the T-shirts that he seemed to wear all the time. She did find one T-shirt that caught her eye, and she had to take it out and sit down with it. The shirt was of a grey Michigan Wolverines logo over a basketball that she got for him as a birthday present last year. He wore it every day for gym and school sports practices.

She remembers watching him in the shirt during many practices, as her dad was his coach. She would go in early with her dad to watch the practices and stay after school to watch them as well, even though her mom, who worked in the library at the school, could have brought her in or taken her home. She watched not just because she had a huge crush on Landon but because she was a fan of the sports and an athlete herself … although she seemed to only watch Landon while the guys practiced. She folds the shirt back up and sets it down on the chair at the computer instead of placing it back in the closet with the rest.

On Landon's desk she sees his iPod stereo. She takes her iPod out of her pocket and connects it to the stereo. She presses play and the music begins to play softly, filling the room with innocence and nostalgia of better days and what could have been. Michelle sits down on the bed, her feet covered up by a Roots pillow, the notebook lying open beside her and the sound of the Tragically Hip's "The Depression Suite" playing on.

She sits there and stares at the walls, wondering what they would say if they could tell her stories of Landon. The memories that only Landon and these four walls shared are the ones that Michelle and the rest won't get to know or understand through words and their own memories. As sad as Michelle is with the thoughts of missing Landon, she feels comfortable in this moment.

The walls of his room are dark in Oilers blue and covered with a variety of pictures and posters. She finds herself staring at pictures of all their friends that border a small poster of Stonehenge. While looking at these pictures and the poster, she starts to wonder if Landon was telling his story through these pictures. It is as though Landon wanted to experience more than just what was thought possible, and he wanted his friends to be there when he did. The pictures surrounding the poster show him and his friends at parties, him in his hockey gear with teammates, pictures of the school and the farm.

Landon was as honest and true a friend as they come. He knew where he came from and that there was more to life than what was immediately in front of him—that you could believe in more than what was in the good book and what your parents put around you. Michelle, lost in thought with the pictures, wonders what she has left for others in her life. She knows that she has been a good girl and knows she has made her mistakes, big and small, but what will she want from her life and for others to remember her for? How would Landon have remembered her if it was the other way around?

Matchbox Twenty's song "The Difference" changes the mood and breaks Michelle away from her thoughts, which have been lost in the pictures. She picks up the notebook and begins to read the poetic words Landon wrote, the heartbreaking ones and the joyful ones. She never really knew he was a poet. She knew that he liked to write from time to time, but always thought it was just a fun little distraction from the day to day. She never knew that his words came from his heart and could fill and break others' hearts as they read them. Michelle knew Landon was okay in English, but now she could see he wanted to be a writer, and that, if he put as much effort into his schoolwork as he had in the poems, he might have gotten better grades.

Michelle doesn't realize that the poetry came easy to him, that these were just words that exorcised some of the thoughts that scared him, and that expressing his feelings may have comforted him in his young life. He wrote poems about love, friendship, growing up and getting out of there. He tackled religion and death as well as the simple things we take for granted like breakfast and the Sears Christmas catalogue. None of the poems was a literary masterpiece, but they touched Michelle, and as long as the words have meaning for someone, that is all that Landon wanted. Even though when he wrote those words, he never wanted others to know of them.

Heartache sweeps over Michelle as she reads a poem that she finds a personal connection with. The poem is called "Fairy Tale." As she reads the words, she drifts into mindless thoughts of precious tranquility. She doesn't know who Landon wrote this about or if he wrote it about anyone special at all, but that is not her concern at the moment. She only feels a connection to the words and the feelings she still has for life and the memory of Landon.

My house may look candy coated
Led to by a yellow brick road
Where the sun never goes down
And the flowers sing in unison
You stumbled into my life
Barely knowing who you were
You fell asleep for a kiss from a prince
But you can't turn back the time we missed
Fallen from your mighty perch
Everybody gathers around your golden hair
Holding on to a forgotten piece of innocence
But the king's men can't put you together
As your great prince once did
Chasing each other up the hill
Fetching more than we can tell

You stumbled down losing your glass slipper
I broke my crown never finding you again
I hold your glass slipper 'til this day
Wishing on the memory it holds within
For just one more day to be with you.

Michelle loses herself in these poems, finding her mind expanding past what she was taught in school and what her parents brought her up on. She was finding her own way through the words of her friend in his passing. She began to realize that life isn't always as you see it, and that sometimes you have to think outside of the box, even in the simplest ways.

She reads on as Richard Ashcroft's "A Song for the Lovers" plays from her iPod. The next poem Michelle reads is "Last Match," a poem that shows Landon's thoughts of death and dealing with the struggles of getting through life if he can't get out. Michelle knows that Landon wasn't one to talk of death, as it scared him—but she also knew that he wasn't afraid to look at how others live their lives and the reality of how it could end up being if things don't change.

Take another photograph
The picture may not last
The memories will grow in time
As the colours will fade
Before it hits the floor
As I watch it all go up
The pain seems to follow
My tears dry up
Just as the last match flickers out
There is no better time
Than your last goodbye
As I told you once before
Don't shut me out
My foot is caught in the door
As I watch it all go up
The pain seems to follow

My tears dry up
Just as the last match flickers out
Looking at the memories
Good becomes the bad
That slowly fades into ugly days
Just when your eyes are closed
The daydream keeps you awake
Might as well fall to sleep
And end it all before it is too late.


Michelle sees Damon standing at the doorway to Landon's bedroom. He hasn't been standing there long—just long enough to smirk at her and ask, "Are you all right?" with youthful confusion in his voice. "You should change the music. It is kind of mellow and sad, you might want to put on something better."

Michelle looks at him with understanding and thankfulness in her face and tells him, "I am okay. I like the music, but I will change it just for you."

Damon is about to walk away, but Michelle asks, "You want to come in and talk for a bit?"

He sluggishly heads back in and sits on the edge of the bed next to Michelle's feet as she sits up against the wall with her legs stretched out. Damon turns back and looks at Michelle, wondering what she will talk to him about. Michelle smiles at Damon as she changes the music to "Downtown" by Eve 6.

She begins by asking, "What do you remember of your brother, or what will you miss of Landon the most?"

Damon, looking around the room trying to act like he doesn't really care or want to be there, tells her, "I try not to think of Landon too much. I know that may seem wrong, but I don't want to be sad, and missing him does that." He pauses for a second as Michelle tries to comfort him by placing a hand on his back. "Although, anytime I play hockey, his memory will come up." He collects his thoughts and gets his emotions in check before continuing on to tell her, "It's not just ice hockey, it is the games of hallway hockey up at Grandma's, floor hockey in their basement, watching 'Hockey Night in Canada' on Saturdays before he would head out to parties."

There is a brief silence between the two, as both of them remember their hockey moments with Landon. Damon continues, "Those are going to be the tough times for me, but I know that Landon doesn't want me to be sad doing what I love and loved doing with my older brother, even if he can never do them again."

He is choking up and trying to be manly about it, as he really doesn't want to cry in front of Michelle. She moves up to Damon and gives him a hug. "I miss him every day as well," she says, trying to offer some encouragement. "In time, everything will be okay—and happiness isn't a bad thing just because he is no longer here. He would want us to be happy in our lives. That doesn't mean you have to be afraid to cry."

Damon looks at Michelle as the two sit close together and asks her, "Will you ever love someone like you did Landon?"

It's a deeper question than Michelle was expecting from her young friend. She looks at him and tells him with a slight tremble in her voice, "I wasn't expecting that question from you. I have been fighting with the thought already. It seems wrong of me to think of myself with someone else, especially this soon."

Damon tells her with youthful confidence as he comforts her with his hand on her leg, "It is okay to be in love with someone else even if the one you first loved isn't able to love you back. No one is going to think you stopped loving Landon. You will probably always love him. That doesn't mean you can't move on to a new love at some point in your life, sooner or later."

Michelle stares at him, shocked at his honesty and helpfulness, and asks, "Since when have you been so wise at such young age?"

Damon looks at her with a smirk on his face, showing off his charm. "It is all part of the package. I am more than just a pretty face." He gives her a nudge with his arm to lighten the mood as they both feel the emotional power of the moment.

Michelle wonders to herself for a moment as she sits beside her friend, both looking up at the wall where Landon's medals hang and his trophies are lined up on a shelf. Michelle tells Damon, "I am a little confused about love and moving on from Landon. I won't be jumping into a relationship any time soon, and as for falling in love, that may take some time. I just don't want Landon to be a high school memory or a memory that holds me back."

The feeling of being alone scares her, though, and she doesn't want to let go of the comfort that Landon gave her even when he isn't around. It is something you can't get from friends, even though they care and are there for each other. She knows that staying with the memory for too long could be the wrong thing to do, but she is afraid to break someone's heart or, worse, have her heart broken by someone before high school is done.

Damon looks at her, slightly shaking his head in questioning. "Stop worrying about the little things right now. Just enjoy your life. That is what Landon would want." He pauses and makes his way over to Landon's awards. "I want to play more hockey than ever, even more than I did with Landon. You should do the same thing with your life. He was my brother and always will be, just as he was your first boyfriend. Don't stop letting love in, afraid it will let Landon's out."

He places his hand on the medallion for Landon's MVP of the league last year. He looks at it with peaceful resolution before looking back at Michelle. She is sitting on the edge of the bed, lost in thought as she stares at the trophies. "You should let love in," he tells her. "No one will hate you for it, and if they do, they don't really know you. Do what makes you happy. I am."

"Thanks, young Yoda," Michelle says, appreciating their little chat. The two smile and continue on with their afternoon.

Michelle turns the song on the iPod to Train's "Meet Virginia." She sits back and waits for Damon to say something, as she knows he isn't far away from the bedroom door. Damon walks back into the bedroom and gives Michelle a look and shakes his head with a smile on his face. He goes and shuffles through the songs on the iPod. "This is a better song," he says as he finds the one he wants. The two smile and laugh as he walks out with Nelly featuring Tim McGraw singing, "Over and Over," his head bobbing to the music matching his wannabe gangster swagger.

Michelle is laughing hysterically on the bed, hiding her face in a pillow, trying to silence her laughs. Damon stops at the doorway and gives her a mock-angry push back with his face and chest and smiles as he continues on. Michelle continues laughing as the song plays on. She can barely think; she needed this laughing fit, as she hasn't laughed this hard in a long time. It helps her get her mind right and makes her forget about the tears and pain. She knows that no matter what, she has to find humour and good in all situations, no matter how much they hurt her.

★ ★ ★

Ethan and Chantal make their way back inside after a long outdoor walk in which the two of them talked intimately and honestly with one another. They shared thoughts and feelings on their relationship and where it's going. Both teens are scared of their future, not knowing what it holds for them together and apart. Chantal is happy to have Ethan around for at least one more year of high school; she just hopes that she doesn't lose him before then. She wants to be with him for as long as they can make it, but she knows that after high school they may end up going different directions. Ethan is in love with Chantal but he is afraid to tell her. He just doesn't know if it is high school love or the real thing, especially after the passing of his brother. He enjoys her and all that she is; he just doesn't know if it will work outside of the small town life they live right now. He wants to explore the world and is unsure if it would be best to do that alone or with someone.

Neither one is thinking of breaking up with the other, but they both have issues on how they should move past friendship into a real relationship. They don't want to ruin a friendship by rushing something because it seems comfortable in a time of need. They discussed all of this during their walk around the farm in the brisk autumn air. They just want to be there together for each other, as friends, but they know they aren't dating anyone else or thinking of it. They want to think and believe they are in love but are unsure of how to make it work, being such long-time friends. Then again, how do teenagers who barely know the world outside of their own experience know what love is anyway?

They notice that inside the house it is fairly silent, other than a faint thump of music and sound effects from the television downstairs.

Damon and Brett are playing *Call of Duty* on Xbox 360 and talking smack to each other and other players online. They pay no attention to Ethan and Chantal as they walk by on their way to the bedrooms just down the hall. Ethan and Chantal continue on toward the sound of the music, and they find Michelle sitting on the bed, her back up against the wall, her eyes happy as she stares off at Landon's pictures and sports memorabilia.

Michelle sees Chantal and Ethan in the doorway and smiles. "How was your walk?" she asks as Jack Johnson's "Do You Remember" plays from the iPod. Chantal makes her way over to Michelle on the bed and the two sing together, smiling the entire time. Ethan stands in the doorway smiling at the two idiot girls on the bed. The song ends, and Ethan can't wait to say something. "You two are weird," he says as he shakes his head and sits on the computer chair next to the bed.

Chantal asks Michelle, "How have you been? Have you been sitting in here the entire time?"

Michelle smiles and softly speaks up over the pillow she has between her knees and chest. "Yes, I have been down in the room basically the entire time, and I am doing all right."

Ethan gives her a look as he spins himself in the chair and asks, "Have you been smoking something?" as he mimics puffing on a joint.

She laughs and tells him, "If only. No better time to start than now, right?" There's an obvious joking tone in her voice.

"Have you heard from Shane today?" Chantal asks.

"He texted a little while ago, but I haven't texted back. He said he was a bit ill from last night still."

Ethan swivels around on the chair. "What a pussy. He barely drank last night."

Chantal gives him a look as though he shouldn't have said that and needs to be quiet. Michelle laughs at the comment but knows Ethan meant no harm in ripping on their friend and trying to help change the subject.

Chantal and Michelle carry on a conversation, discussing gossip from the last little while as Michelle has been kept out of the loop from some friends. Ethan isn't trying to pay any attention as he plays around on the iPod, trying to find something that he wants to listen to, something that would annoy the girls. He eventually finds a song: "The Last Saskatchewan River Pirate" by Captain Tractor. The girls quickly tell him to change it before they get up and make him change it. He tells them to calm down, gets up and does a silly little jig, making them laugh even though they're still annoyed at the choice of music. As the three of them sing the chorus together, they can hear from the living room Damon and Brett singing the entire song as loud as they can. The three in the bedroom are dancing together and laughing out loud until the song ends. "Let's hear it again!!" Ethan proclaims, knowing it will annoy the girls.

"Fuck that!" Chantal says.

"Not if you know what's good for you," Michelle adds as both glare at him to change the song.

Michelle looks at her watch. "I think I should be heading home. Ethan, you think you can give me a ride?" The three of them realize that they have wasted an entire morning in the bedroom telling stories and trying to move on, with no one really bothering them other than a few text messages.

"Yeah, I can give you a ride," Ethan replies as he sits at the desk looking through his brother's stuff.

Chantal chimes in on the notion of leaving. "I should probably make my way home as well. The parents are probably already annoyed that I haven't been home much."

The three of them make their way up from the basement into the kitchen, where Justine is one of the only ones up and in the house. She has just started making cookies. Justine sees the teens come from downstairs as she stands at the kitchen table working on the cookies. "So where are you three off to?"

"I am going to head home. My parents probably want me home by now. I must say, the cookies smell delicious," Chantal tells Justine.

"Thanks, Chantal," Justine replies.

"Thanks for having me over and letting me see Landon's room," Michelle tells Justine. "I too must be going home—schoolwork, and I'm sure my parents would like me home."

"Anytime, Michelle, you need anything, you are always welcome here," Justine tells her with comfort in her voice.

The three begin to put on their shoes and jackets, about to leave. "Where are you off to, Ethan?" Justine asks her son.

"Oh, I'm going to take the girls home. I won't be long," Ethan replies as he stands between Chantal and Michelle at the front-door entranceway.

★ ★ ★

That afternoon, Justine and Kevin head into town to the funeral home to arrange for the funeral and other formalities. The two of them are staying calm and focused on deciding on a casket for their son as well as his final resting place. They are sitting in the office at the funeral home talking with the funeral director; the talk is subdued and kept to the task at hand.

The conversation finally gets to the burial service. The funeral director asks where this will take place, and as Kevin says, "He will be buried at the cemetery near the Lutheran church in the community," Justine begins to break down in her chair. The tears are flowing nonstop from her distraught and emotional eyes. She crumples over, her hands covering her face, her body trembling as she sits in the chair wrestling with the emotional wave that just hit her.

Kevin gets out of his chair and goes over and gives his wife a warm loving embrace in the hope of comforting her and calming her down. His emotions are slowly unravelling as well. Tears fall from his face, but he tries to be the strong one for his wife.

"I can't do this. Why did he have to leave us? I, I can't do this," Justine says, stumbling through her words as she trembles with raw emotion, the tears filling her eyes before falling down her face. She fights away from Kevin's embrace and goes and stands at the door. Her glazed eyes staring at the floor, her right hand reaches for the doorknob to leave the room as her left hand covers her mouth to hold back some emotion.

Kevin stays by the chair looking at his wife, not sure how to comfort her. He wants to go and embrace her, but he doesn't want to pressure her in any way.

"I just ..." she begins to say as she tries to break away from the emotional pain. She takes a deep breath and brings both of her hands up to cover her mouth; she brings them close to her face to muffle her words. "Fuuuuuuuuuuuck!" she yells into her hands to relieve some of the pressure of the moment in the hope of gaining control. She stands there for a moment before wiping the tears away from her eyes and turning around.

Kevin, still in the same position as he was when she got up, now rises and offers his hand for guidance as she slowly makes her way back to her chair. The two share a glance that they are thankful for the other but both know it is going to be a lot tougher than they have been letting on. They sit back down in their chairs and begin to listen again to the funeral director finalizing the details. While the funeral director tries to help them with their emotions and the details of their son's funeral, the couple holds hands across the space between the chairs.

They decide on a nice black coffin, with white and blue linens lining the inside. The headstone will be a dark grey stone with his name and jersey number engraved on it like it would be on the back of a jersey. Underneath that will be his birth date and the day he passed away. That will all be sitting on a stone with "Number 16 in your programs. Number 1 in our hearts" engraved on the top edge.

They thank the funeral director for all his time and support. "I apologize for the breakdown earlier," Justine says as they are leaving.

"Don't feel bad, it is natural to feel the pain like that. Don't be afraid to ask for help and anything else you may need from your family and friends," he replies as he walks them out of his office. The men shake hands just before they leave. While walking out, Kevin walks with his right arm around Justine's waist, holding her close. Her head rests on his chest.

★ ★ ★

When they get back to the farm, there is another vehicle in the yard. Kevin's sister, Jaclyn, with her husband, Liam, and their two preteen kids, Ty and Devry, have arrived earlier than expected. Liam and Jaclyn are sitting in the living room upstairs with Ethan and Damon. Their voices and laughter can be heard clearly across the house. Kevin walks slowly behind his wife. Justine moves slowly as well, bracing for the emotions when they see Jaclyn and Liam.

As they enter the living room, Jaclyn sees them and quickly gets up, her laughter with the kids changing to sympathy and tears. The two women embrace in a loving hug, each comforting the other as the tears begin to fall. Justine did not want to shed more tears today, but the emotion sweeps over her seeing more family.

Liam gets off the couch as he hands the photo album over to Damon and goes over to shake Kevin's hand and offer his condolences. The two men stand there holding in any emotion. Liam knows that Kevin is not one to show a lot of emotion—unless he is cheering for the Montreal Canadiens in the playoffs.

Jaclyn and Justine back away with tears in their eyes. "I am so sorry. He was too young," Jaclyn says as she stumbles through the words coming from her shaking body. The four of them stand there in silence, surrounded by the faint sound of the television in the background. The boys sit there texting their friends, trying to stay away from the tear-jerking parents and their conversation. Kevin and Jaclyn embrace in a loving brother-sister moment. Jaclyn tries to offer comfort, but it is her older brother who comforts her as she cries in his arms. Liam and Justine embrace, offering comfort as well, but it feels more like a *thank you for being there* hug. The two smile awkwardly through the heartbreaking feelings as they step away from the embrace.

Justine sits down on the couch next to Ethan, and Liam goes back to sitting next to Damon. After they finish their embrace, Jaclyn goes and sits down on the other side of Ethan, while Kevin takes a seat in a chair on the other side of the room.

Downstairs, Brett, Ty and Devry are watching a movie and annoying each other with jokes and tickling like kids. They've already shed enough tears and asked enough questions, so getting a chance to hang out with family and just be kids is much needed. They still have wonder and confusion in their heads, but they would rather not worry about the questions for now.

"Anyone want something to drink?" Kevin asks. "Beer, Liam? You ladies want Bailey's and coffee?"

"I'll have a beer if you are," Liam replies.

"We will go and make our own, thanks though," Justine tells her husband.

Kevin walks into the kitchen to grab the beers from the fridge. He pauses at the fridge as he sees a picture of his kids posing in their hockey jerseys. He smiles at the sight, fighting back the tears as the memories come to him. He doesn't let a single tear fall, but he begins to realize even more so that he may not always be this strong. He grabs the beers and cracks them open, tossing the caps on the counter as he walks away and back into the living room. He hands a beer to Liam and then goes back to sitting in the chair away from the group.

"So how did the funeral arrangements go today?" Jaclyn asks politely as she sips her Bailey's and coffee.

"It wasn't too bad, but I broke down in his office. It wasn't my finest hour," Justine says, almost embarrassed to tell her family.

"It can't be easy for either of you two or the kids," Jaclyn replies as she places her hand gently on Ethan's leg and gives it a comforting squeeze.

"At times you are just too busy to let the emotions get to you, and you try to keep busy so they can't, but as soon as you take a breath and think of Landon or a memory strolls into your thoughts of him, you just lose it," Justine tells her as she quickly speaks on the subject in hopes that it will fade away without too much more conversation.

"Some of my friends and myself were thinking that at the funeral, we could make a music playlist on an iPod and play that at the funeral. You know, instead of that boring funeral old-person music that gets played and puts everyone to sleep," Ethan chimes in, hoping to pick up the mood on such a sombre topic.

"That would be a great idea," Kevin says from his chair. "I can't stand that church organ music at funerals," he adds.

"Yeah, I don't see any problem in that," Justine adds to the sentiment as she sits back in the couch and sips on her drink.

"Sweet. We will get right on it. I will tell my peeps it is a go," Ethan says as he gets up and heads out of the room, Damon slowly tagging along behind him, both of them texting.

The men leave the room not long after the boys and head out to the garage to look over the guns and trucks, grabbing a couple cold ones as they head out, leaving the women to talk as they look over the photos and see their children coming and going from the room. Devry comes up from downstairs and sits with her mom and looks over the photo albums with them. She's tired of the boys farting and playing video games.

Even though she's the youngest of all the kids, Devry understands a lot of what is going on. She and Landon were close; he always made sure she wasn't left out, being the only girl. He also protected her from the boys' teasing. Ethan was also this way with her, and now he would have to do it all on his own, without his big brother being the one.

As she looks at the pictures with her mother and aunt, Devry asks questions about almost every picture. "When was this?" "Was I there?" "What is he wearing?" she asks as the pages turn. Her mom and aunt offer answers both honest and comical, depending on the picture and the question asked. They share laughs and memories as they look at the pictures, every page a new story, every picture another smile. The girls all remain calm, with no emotions overflowing.

Ethan, in passing by, looks over at Devry on the couch in the living room and sticks out his tongue. She sticks hers back out at him. This is something they have done for as long as both can remember. It is their way of saying hi. It was also something she did with Landon, as he was the one who started it one day at the lake. She never knew why, it just stuck with her and him. Ethan picked up on it and followed suit not long after. Now for them it is their special reminder of Landon, without even saying a word.

"So you guys decided that Wednesday would be the best day for the funeral? Are you sure about that?" Jaclyn asks Justine as the two sip their drinks in the living room.

"Well, we debated on that for a while, but days before or after would make it just as awkward. Besides, we must celebrate his life that day," Justine replies. "Why not do it on his birthday?" Her lips begin to tremble at the word *birthday*. She had thought of it before and she knew the pain would be there no matter what, but finally saying it to another family member makes it seem more real than she can handle.

Both of them have tears in their eyes, not wanting to look at the other, knowing it will only open more floodgates for the tears. They reach for each other and embrace in a comforting hug, even though both of them are just as fragile as the other in that moment.

Ethan overhears his mom from the kitchen where he is watching television. "I don't think it is a great idea," he chimes in, disgruntled by the date of the funeral landing on his brother's birthday.

"I am not going to argue about this right now with you," Justine says through her tears and frustration.

"Look, I just don't think it feels right, but I understand," he replies, his eyes never leaving the television screen as he watches a college football game. Ethan actually thinks it's a nice way to honour Landon, but it is going to make the day so much tougher for everyone. Wednesday would have been Landon's 18th birthday.

"Mom, can you two stop crying?" Devry says as she sits with the women. "Landon wouldn't want you to be crying on his birthday," she adds as she gives each of them a hug and walks back downstairs to be with the boys and their juvenile distractions. Ethan and Devry stick their tongues out at each other as she passes by; both of them smile and continue on with what they are doing.

★ ★ ★

Michelle is up in her room, sitting on her bed with her back up against the wall, her iPod playing music in the background and her bed littered with random things that remind her of Landon. It's another late night filled with memories and heartbreak. She has the valentine he gave her just this past February, a cute cartoon with "u + me = 4ever" written under two awkward-looking teenagers trying to kiss. She stares at it with questions in her eyes. A smile slowly emerges from her withdrawn expression as she remembers the good times. It quivers as she knows those moments will never come again.

She slides over to the edge of the bed; her feet grazing the floor below her, she swings her legs slowly as she stares out her patio doors into the night sky. The soft sound of "See You in the Spring" by the Court Yard Hounds blankets the room with hope and heartache. Her face becomes sadder with every word sung as she thinks more and more about Landon and wishes he was here to comfort her. She stands up and is about to walk over to the patio doors to get some fresh air and be alone with nature, but before she takes a full step to the patio, she turns to the bedroom door and thinks of locking it. Something she never does.

She decides against locking the door and heads outside onto her balcony. She opens the door and the cool autumn air hits her like a slap in the face. Her sad face cringes as she tries to fight through the initial cold sensation, shaking it through and out of her body. She leans forward against the railing and looks out into the yard, the stars shining some light through the clouds. The wind gently blows through the trees like teenage whispers. As she stands there trying to stay warm in her pyjama pants and bunny hug, she drifts off into thoughts she never had before.

These thoughts are far from her norm, and they scare her. She has been thinking of death and losing a loved one and wishing he was still around for her. Now, however, she drifts from life without Landon and how everyone is missing him to *What if I died? How would I die? Is it better to die young or grow old? What about suicide? What is on the other side? Is there another side?* As she is thinking these thoughts, some sneak out into the air as she quietly voices them just to make sure they are real.

She takes her eyes off the sky and looks down at her arm on the railing and realizes she had been scratching her wrist pretty hard with her nails, making a solid red line. She startles herself and backs away from the railing, looking at her hands as they shake with nerves. "I don't want to die," she whispers to herself as she tries to get out of the weird mindset she is experiencing. She quickly changes the song mood on the iPod to Selena Gomez's "Love You Like a Love Song." The music immediately brings a smile to her face as she tries to dance and sing along.

While slow dancing with herself on the patio, she smiles with the stars as she realizes that this is how she should remember Landon. "It's hard not to miss you," she whispers into the wind. "I wish you were still here." Her voice cracks as her emotions are coming out. She is fighting back the tears in the hope of staying strong, even if it is just for herself and the stars in the sky. She stares off into the night sky, her heart racing, tears falling from her face, yet she finds solace in the darkness that surrounds her. She smiles as she finds a star shimmering in the night sky. She wipes the tears from her face with the sleeve of the bunny hug that her hands are now tucked up into. She takes a deep breath and without hesitation, she whispers to the star, "Thanks."

She turns around and slowly walks back inside as the stars shine bright behind her. She shuts the patio doors and slowly closes the curtain over them. She stands there for a moment, her hand pressed up against the curtain-covered door.

Michelle turns the music on her iPod down so the sound of "Face to Face" by Dead Sara faintly fills the air in her room as she takes off her bunny hug and climbs into bed. She pulls the covers over her body and lays her head gently on her pillow. As she lies there with the blanket pulled up tight to her chin, her body tucked into a fetal position, her eyes remain open. A lone tear falls and trickles down her face. She closes her eyes as the tear comes to a stop on her upper lip.

# Days

*Sunday*

Not every day is an easy one for Matt and Robyn, even with all the love they have for one another. Even during the hard times they are going through with the loss of Landon, they can't stop their lives and forget about their own future together. They have a strong relationship built on honesty and communication, but they still struggle to make everything work. Others think it is perfect from the outside looking in, but both of them know it isn't always easy.

They have done their best to help Kevin and Justine and their kids if needed, be it talking to them over the phone or coming out to the farm and hanging out. Matt and Robyn have also welcomed some of Landon's close friends into their home since Landon's passing. It's usually only Michelle, Shane and Chantal, who often come with Ethan. Robyn has talked to Michelle lots after the passing of Landon, about life and love and how to move on from this. Robyn shares her own high school experiences with Michelle in the hope that it will help Michelle get through everything. Robyn also lost a friend when she was younger in school. Robyn and Matt talk at great length about life and death and the memories they have of Landon, hoping to find comfort in their own realm of understanding. It's not a subject either one likes to bring up, but they are never shy about talking about him when it does.

They go to church this morning, something they don't usually do. Even though Matt is confirmed as a Lutheran and Robyn is open-minded, they can't handle the bullshit that is fed to them during and after the service. The preacher notices that they are there and keeps bringing up their loss in the hope of guilting them and the rest in attendance into believing that with strong faith, Landon will not be forgotten and will be welcomed up in heaven.

The fact that the preacher uses Landon's passing to further his sermon and collection plate annoys the Matt and Robyn. They don't storm out; instead, they sit there and try to understand why others find comfort and sadness in the loss of someone else. To them, it is one thing to honour and pay their respects to a fallen loved one at a funeral and with friends and family, but it is a whole other thing when the church uses the loss to promote the ways of the Bible and how it is God's choice and that everything happens for a reason through Him.

As Matt and Robyn are leaving, some churchgoers come up and talk to them about Landon and how they knew him and that they were greatly saddened by his passing. Matt and Robyn take all of it in, but neither one really believes the church or those in attendance. Some of the people there have known one or both of them for a long time but still try to act all holier than thou. The condescending nature of the service is unexpected, especially as people who they kind of know try to act as though they have been and always will be there for them.

They stay polite to everyone and talk about Landon openly. Eventually, the preacher makes his way over to talk to the two of them. They are standing outside the church on the steps, sharing a quiet comical conversation. The priest introduces himself and says, "I am sorry for your loss. Landon was a great kid. He is in a better place now with the Lord."

Matt hesitates in response. His face expresses the comment he wishes he could make: *Oh, fuck that.* Robyn acts as the buffer, saying "thanks" as she steps slightly in front of her man to take the focus off him. "Thanks for your words and the sermon we were welcomed into."

Matt is still miffed at the way the priest continues on about the Lord and how He is with Landon and taking care of him. Matt and Robyn both look at each other, knowing that they better be polite and leave soon before something is said that shouldn't be said.

"Thanks again," Robyn tells the preacher, "but we should be on our way."

As they are walking away from the gathering to their car, Matt, still frustrated by the preacher, tells Robyn, "I so wanted to punch the fucking preacher when he started talking to us, but I knew better."

Robyn just smiles and tells him, "Oh, but that wouldn't have been in God's plans." The two laugh quietly as they leave in their vehicle.

★ ★ ★

Sunday night gets hectic around the farm. Out-of-province family members as well as many of those coming from many miles away within the province are starting to gather. Some are renting hotel rooms in a nearby town, some are staying with other family members in the area, and some are staying on one of the farms, either Kevin's family farm or his mom and dad's farm.

Family members who never even call under ordinary circumstances are showing up for the funeral, talking to everyone about Landon and glorifying the role they played in his life. Really, Landon hadn't seen or heard from some of them in five years; he understood it and hadn't cared if he ever saw or spoke to most of them again. He always thought that it was sad when family members showed up for the big moments and never kept in touch otherwise. Christmas, funerals and births always got to Landon, as people to him were fake around those moments.

Matt and Robyn are going back and forth between their families and sharing time with both of them, trying to deal with the loss. They should be able to escape questions about a wedding at this sad time, but even now some family members want to know when they are going to get married. Matt and Robyn aren't even thinking about that right now. It doesn't seem like it's the time to be talking about their future plans, as if to flaunt their joy at a time of sadness. They quickly distract relatives from the topic.

The rifts between family members come up a lot after the family's loss. Calls are still coming in from close and distant relatives trying to get info on who is home and what the plans are for the funeral. This is to see who they have to avoid and who has to put on pleasantly annoyed faces when they see family they rarely talk to—or care to talk to, for that matter.

Matt and Kevin's parents are the only ones in the family who make it a point to visit and communicate with all the splintered factions. Even they, however, have their favourite and not-so-favourite relatives. All in attendance are there not only to pay respect to Landon but also to fulfill a need to make it known that they are important to the family.

Landon had favourite aunts and uncles as well as cousins; not all can be there on this day. Some are already said to be with Landon in the next life. Landon's grandparents are stubborn yet open people—just how open depends on the moment. They don't hold grudges against family members, but they did talk a lot about them if something happened within the family. In this moment of despair and heartache, they take it upon themselves to keep everyone under control and happy. It is their moment to be in control of the chaos, something that has been missing in the family tree for a long time.

Justine and Kevin seemed to not miss a beat in life as they socialize with friends and family on the phone or in person as people show up at the farm. They want to enjoy life and remember Landon for the life he lived. At the same time, all the activity allows them to forget about the pain until they are alone. They need the support and love of those close to them to make it through these tough times. Their smile and spirit seem as strong as ever, but behind closed doors and when alone, each finds a moment to break down and try to reflect.

The past few nights they have ended up in a comforting yet sad embrace in bed as one of them breaks down from a random thought of Landon and the idea of never being able to see him again creeps into their heads. The two loving parents talk late into the night even though exhausted from the day. They comfort each other with words, but the physical embrace when alone is fading without either of them knowing it or wanting to bring it up in conversation.

Last night they laid in bed talking quietly about Landon and each other. They bickered for no reason, and offered no compassion for their partner or remorse for their words, some more hurtful than others. They both just needed to let out some emotion that wasn't tears. They know neither one meant too much of the anger expressed in the situation. Still, some of it lingers within them as they go about their day.

As the day goes on, they exchange conversations about Landon with friends and family. They remain strong in appearance among those around, often joining in the laughter and even shedding tears of joy from some of the stories shared of Landon. That afternoon, as they have family and friends over, both Kevin and Justine hit the bottle a bit more than normal. No one notices, as it blends in with the rest of the people. However, for them it is a new coping mechanism, one that they don't know they're clinging to. They both keep it hidden from each other as they know it is wrong, while still suspecting something of the sort from the other.

Ethan, Damon and Brett are dealing with the loss of their brother as best they can. Damon and Brett avoid the topic as much as possible, but if it is brought up in a situation they are comfortable with they will say something. The family and friends who are over often bring up memories with the boys or try to offer an outlet, be it visiting them to talk or just going to play sports whenever they want. The boys respect and are grateful for the offers and support from everyone, yet at the same time, they would rather not have the memory brought up so often. They just want to be kids and move on. They know they never will, but for all of them, dwelling on or bringing up the memory in support isn't always helpful.

Brett, being the youngest, has become scared of life and his possible death. He will shy away from talking about the death, but talking about Landon he is okay with. He also starts to spend a lot more time alone in his room with his music. Friends came over to visit and that breaks him out of his shell, but he starts to find that he likes being alone to figure out his thoughts. He even will escape the friends who sit around playing video games at his place to just go to his room and listen to music. He isn't depressed in the sense that there is something wrong, but he isn't happy and is scared. Even as a young kid, Brett took life more seriously than most of his age. He didn't want to hear about the fairy-tale heaven that is told to kids, nor did he want to believe there was nothing after you die.

Damon, already a great young athlete in his own right, has always been compared to his oldest brother in everything he did. He was okay with the comparisons, as Landon was a great role model and big brother to him. While hanging out with his friends and texting them the past few days, he decided he wanted to start his own path, and what better way to do so than start now as a way to honour Landon? While his friends are over and family members are coming and going in the house, he sits downstairs with his hockey stick. He plays around with it, annoying others and just playing around like a teenager. Last night he was looking at his stick and thinking of Landon and playing hockey together, and he decided to pay homage to Landon on his hockey stick by taping it the same way his brother did. One strip of white tape at the heel of the blade and one strip of white at the toe. He fell asleep with the stick lying down beside the bed, along with his hockey gloves on them, as if he was holding the stick still.

Whenever he can, Damon talks to his family about the loss of Landon. Not the questions of *Where is Landon now? Is he in heaven or hell?* Instead, he wants to know more about his brother's life. He enjoys hearing the stories from all ages of Landon's life; it makes him feel comfortable when thinking of his family's loss. Damon was never a quiet kid but is polite, and even though he speaks a lot he always waits his turn and tries to be friends with everyone. This is something that Landon showed him indirectly. Landon told him that girls like a guy who listens but has a mind of his own and doesn't always follow the norm. He is more the centre of attention than Landon ever wanted to be but is still willing to let others shine.

★ ★ ★

Michelle wakes up Sunday morning and eats brunch with her family, and they talk about life and where she is at. They make it about her, but not in a mourning or heartbreaking manner. They keep the conversation more on how she feels and what questions she may have about her own life and what she wants. Her parents often act around her friends like modern-day hippies—heck, rumours even circulated that they grew pot. She never saw them as that type of hippie, just more like the ones who are in love with nature and freedom in the spiritual sense.

As she sits there at the table eating her scrambled eggs and banana-nut muffin, still tired from the long night, Michelle's eyes drift off to pictures on the fridge. "Mom, why are we so lost in all these memories?" she asks as she takes a bite of her muffin.

Her mom, who is sitting across from her at the kitchen table, looks confused before noticing that Michelle is looking at pictures on the fridge. "It's what life is built on. The good and the bad, it is how we remember everything," her mother tells her. "Sometimes we put on rose-coloured glasses to remember good times as better and shitty times as good times. As well, we may forget moments in the memory to make them better. You just have to find the balance when you remember him."

Michelle admits, "I have been thinking a lot at night, memories flowing through me one after the other, often blending in. I was even thinking of the future and the memories I won't be able to create with him." She takes a sip of her orange juice. "I just don't know how to move on. I don't even know if I want to. Just promise me that you guys will be patient with me, let me have my space but still always be there next to me." She and her mother share a smile together.

Her dad, who has been reading the news on his tablet all morning, looks up from the e-mails and Yahoo news. "We will always be there for you. You just have to be there for yourself as well." He gives her a smart smile, she smiles back, and they all continue on with their own morning routine.

Michelle finishes her brunch and takes her dish and glass to the sink and rinses them off. "Thanks," she says as she walks by the kitchen table. Both parents nod and smile as she walks by. They know she was thanking her mom for the food, but the undertone was clearly there in her voice that it's also for the encouraging words they gave her.

She heads back up to her room to tackle some homework and maybe clean, trying to distract herself from the constant thoughts and reminders of Landon. She turns on her iPod and the sound of "This Is the Remix" by Girl Talk fills the room. Michelle smiles and begins to dance a little as she starts cleaning up her room. The yearbooks and notebooks are picked up and put away on their shelf. She flips through them as she is putting them away. She moves on from them to making her bed and setting up her pillows all neat and orderly. As she is finishing up straightening the covers, she lies down to rest even though she is not tired and woke up only an hour or so ago.

She stares up at the ceiling, no thought in her head, just the image of the ceiling above her. Only the sound of "Damini" by USS from her iPod fills her mind. Her eyes shift around the rooms, ceiling and walls as she lies there. She wants to get up and do something but doesn't want to move away from the relaxing feeling she is enjoying, which is something she hasn't had in the past week. Time slowly ticks away as she listens to the music and stares off at the ceiling. Slowly, random thoughts pop into her head. Nothing that serious or concerning about Landon or life in general. Thoughts like *I should paint my room. Should I cut my hair? Oh my gawd, I didn't know I had '80s metal on my iPod. Who put this song on my iPod? I haven't heard from sis in a while. I wonder if she will be home for Christmas.*

After deciding on nothing and thinking lightly on all topics that come to mind, she finally gets the motivation to move from her bed. She rolls over and gets up again for the day. She brushes her hair back from her face; she runs her fingers through it, making it look naturally beautiful. Even though the chances of anyone seeing it is slim to none today, as she has no plans as of yet to leave the house. She gets up and strolls over to the patio doors and opens the curtains, letting some light in. She then walks over to her desk and pulls the chair out to sit on it. She sits and pulls the chair close to the desk. She wants to start on her homework, but she is quickly distracted by the world outside her patio windows.

The view is clean and clear, the pine and birch trees shivering slightly in the wind. The sun is shining down on the overnight frost still lingering on some of the buildings and trees. Off in the distance, just past the gravel road, she can see a moose grazing on some grain seed that must have spilled from a farmer's truck. She marvels at the majestic beast. She wants to tell her dad that there is a moose outside their yard, as it would make his day. She's not sure if he has a tag to hunt it or if it is still moose season even. However, she just wants to watch this animal from a distance and decides to sit there and enjoy it.

After a few minutes, the moose must have heard something and goes off into the bush to hide from whatever noise it may have heard.

Michelle has already distracted herself from the moose by opening up her laptop and jumping on Facebook. She has dozens of messages in her inbox from friends who are trying to offer condolences and whatnot. Her homepage and her wall is plastered with stupid pictures and humour cards from her friends, not to mention all the people still talking about Landon. They offer up quick one-liners or short memories of him, and others quickly respond. These she tries to skip over, but she finds herself looking at all of them and laughing and sighing as she tries not to get to down from it.

She answers some of the messages in her inbox, as they are from family and friends who aren't near her but want to be. Some of the messages are from boys who are trying to offer a shoulder to cry on, something she wishes would just stop. She thinks of deleting them from her friends list but holds off for now.

★ ★ ★

Later that night, Michelle is hanging out in the basement watching television as she texts with her friends. All of them are talking about school on Monday and how awkward it feels to be going back there without Landon. Some of the friends are making jokes and trying to stay light on the subject, but some are still dwelling and emotional. Michelle can handle both, even if it brings up emotions or laughter. It helps that she is alone at her place so no one is seeing her physical reactions to the conversations.

As she watches *Empire Records* on the television, she sprawls out on the couch with a blanket. She finds herself in the characters in the movie. She relates to each of them in a small way in how she sees herself at this moment as well as how she sees herself in the past and for the future. She has seen the movie a few times before, as it was Landon's favourite movie and he made her watch it. She can be quietly heard quoting lines from the movie and giggling with the humour on screen. She dozes off to the movie playing in the background.

She wakes up to her mom shutting the television off. She asks her mom in a confused and groggy voice, "What time is it?"

With a laugh and a smile, her mom says, "It's almost midnight. You have been asleep for the past three hours or so."

"Why didn't you wake me up?" Michelle asks.

"You looked comfy, and I didn't know if you had been sleeping a lot lately, so I let you rest," her mom says as she walks past, giving Michelle a loving pat on the head before heading back upstairs.

Michelle lies there for a moment staring at the wall, trying to focus enough to wake up but not so much that she can't fall back asleep for the rest of the night. She sits up on the couch, the blanket hanging off her legs as her cell falls to the floor. She picks up the phone and sees there are over 20 missed texts and a couple of voicemails, not to mention a few more than normal Facebook messages in her inbox. *How out was I?* she asks herself quietly as she rubs her hands on her face to wake up. She quickly replies to the more pressing texts that are sure she has done something stupid.

# Day 6
## Monday

As classes resume after Landon's death, the school brings in a few counsellors to help any kids who may need to talk about their emotions and how they are dealing with the loss. Parents push their kids to go back to school, believing it's the best way for them to deal with the pain and find comfort with their friends. The community is being strong for one another; it's good to see people come together, even if it takes a tragedy to make it happen.

The school's single hallway fills up with students of all ages coming in off of the buses. The older students who drive to school stroll in slowly to their lockers and homerooms. The atmosphere is a dull roar mixed with the chit-chat of the everyday life that they all are going through as well as the quiet talk about Landon and the funeral. Trying to blend the two together seamlessly seems to be what the older students are doing. The younger ones are going on about their day, talking about homework, sports and video games, and making fun of each other because so and so likes so and so. To the younger ones, it is another school day with small occasions of talk of the death. The older kids are still taking it one day at a time and treading lightly around each other, be it with casual banter to distract them or gossiping quietly behind each other's back.

The younger grades are in their classrooms learning their subjects and focusing on the tasks at hand. The teachers do their best to stay away from the topic of Landon or death. But the kids want to ask a question whenever it comes to their minds, usually in English and social studies classes. The teachers talk openly about it but still allow for the children to explore within their own minds what they are trying to understand and feel about the entire situation. For most of the kids, this is their first death to deal with. Some have lost grandmas and grandpas or a pet in their young lives, but losing someone this young makes them want to know more. Religion comes up a little from some of the younger ones who are a part of Sunday school at the local Lutheran church. The teachers stay away from religion but speak about it when it's brought up by the students. No matter the struggle to understand it all, the young students are more than willing to get back to work and learn and find out their answers later. They play with youthful exuberance during their breaks and don't let the drama get to them. The rest of their day is filled with casual schoolwork and a movie in the afternoon before they head home.

The middle-year students up to about grade 8 are looking to rebel and question everything. They are close friends with Landon's brothers and are having an awkward time being around Brett and Damon, as they don't know how to act and talk around them. They try to keep it light and away from the subject, but it still came up in conversations. They are in their classrooms going about the day with their assignments as their teachers try their best to keep them focused. They are asking questions and bringing up concerns of irrelevance, basically to kill time during the day so they don't have to do work. The teachers are comforting and lenient, as they know it is just a phase the kids are going through, yet it's important maintain some sort of control in the classrooms.

Brett and his friends are not rabble-rousers or bad kids, but they are still kids and are trying to come to an understanding. Brett is filled with questions and pain, but his friends help him by keeping a smile on his face with their juvenile stupidity, and at the breaks they let him get some aggression out by playing football. The students in the middle years are also trying to find out what they can do to help Brett and the rest of the family, as they want to help in any way but don't want to overstep a boundary. The afternoon is spent doing art projects while a movie plays in the background. Some of the students have sports after school or have to get back to the farm and help out with anything they can, which usually is garden work.

Damon, on the edge between the middle-school and high school years, finds more sarcasm in this social setting with friends and teachers. He isn't trying to be rebellious; instead, he's just found a different way to deal with his emotions. He's not really letting many into his thoughts, but in short moments he gives glimpses of hope and solitude with himself. The conversations around Damon are mainly of the social scene into which they are all trying to fit. Some are trying to be real close to Damon, while others quietly go their own way while still being respectful. The girls, most of whom already liked Damon, are now passing him notes and wanting to show that they care and are there for him. He questions their intentions, but at the same time has no issues with a girl or girls wanting to be around him. Maybe he can even make out with one or two of them. Today, though, it is just notes being passed between friends in the classes and texting each other all through the night after school.

Landon's old classmates take the morning to talk to one of the counsellors about his death, with the plan to take the last hour off to go get done what they have to do for the funeral. They take the morning group session as a way to not do schoolwork, and the afternoon as an excuse to help the family get certain things ready. Landon would have done the same thing to get out of schoolwork. He could miss half a class, and the teachers never gave him shit about it. He was the golden boy of the school, but he never acted like he was king shit, as most would in his situation. Oftentimes Landon would wander the school just to kill time, and he never got into the trouble that other kids would doing the same thing. He had a knack for never getting caught like the rest; even when the teachers would question him on his whereabouts, he always had a response that seemed plausible.

The high school students have decided that they have to take control of their own destiny. The loss of Landon has made them all look within to see what really is important to them. Some it is just the simple life, while others are planning to go on and do big things. Today they sit in their classrooms doing as little work as possible but focusing in on the conversations, be it with each other or with whatever the teacher is speaking about. They still joke about day-to-day issues, but sometimes stop short when they realize it would have been better with Landon.

Michelle and her friends are separated from the group within the group when they all gather during breaks. It isn't that no one wants to talk to Michelle, it's just that she prefers to be away from the scene and not the centre of attention. Some of the older students bring Michelle into the conversations, making her feel welcome.

Ethan is the constant smart-ass and yet still stays level-headed, even though his mind is racing, trying to come to terms still with the loss of Landon. Renee and Shane are looked to by the other high school students as well as the younger ones for guidance and acceptance in this time of sorrow as they move on with their lives. They have to be the strongest outside of the family for the rest to feel strong enough to continue. They talk about the funeral and what if anything they can do to help out, whether at the farm, the burial or the funeral service. Not to mention how they could honour Landon throughout the year at the school, especially during the athletic events that Landon performed in and loved.

The male athletes decide that they will take Landon's jersey with them on the road as well as frame his home jerseys up in the gym in which Landon became a local star. Volleyball season is already in full swing, and with early-morning practices restarting next week, there won't be a lot of time to let the season come to them. So they feel the need to make the season a memorable one and play hard and as a team, just as Landon did when he played alongside them. They also take a vote and decide that Gord and Ethan will take on the role as captains in honour of Landon and the way he led with a level head, always wearing his heart on his sleeve.

The girl's volleyball team decides to get headbands with Landon's number on it as a way of honouring him. Their leaders, Renee and Michelle, take it upon themselves to find ways to keep the girls motivated and honour Landon all season long. Even though Michelle is in grade 9, her volleyball skills are on par with most seniors in the school and the division they play in. Landon always teased her that she still had a long way to go before she was even somewhat as good as he was. That pissed her off and motivated her to be better.

The older students are sitting around in class talking about memories from school involving Landon. They get on a track of talking about the dance last year after the guys made it to provincials and finished fourth—the highest the school has ever placed in provincials. Shane remembers how they got a local DJ in to play music on a Friday night. Kids from grades 8 to 12 showed up for the dance, as well as students from other schools. It wasn't a big dance party but one of the bigger ones for the school in many years.

The story eventually advances to the end of the dance, which was around midnight in the school gym with about a hundred high school kids in attendance, all leaving by the time midnight struck. Gord and Max organized a party for later that night at Gord's parents' farm in the garage. They asked the DJ if he would be willing to come out and play for the party for a few extra dollars. Max adds in to the story that it ended up being a couple hundred, but they gathered enough money up from their friends to make it work. The party was well attended, but the majority of the attendees didn't last long into the cold November night. By the time two in the morning came along, most had gone home. The DJ stayed around and played songs for the remaining kids for a little while longer.

Ethan asked the DJ if he would play a country song they could dance to, and the DJ obliged, putting on Carrie Underwood's "Last Name." Not the exact song that Ethan had in mind, but it was a good country song to grind to. Ethan got Chantal up to dance, as Michelle dragged Landon up to dance as well and a few others joined them, making the dance floor full of only about 10 people. The dancers stayed out on the dance floor for a few more country and rock songs, stopping only to grab their drinks.

By now there were only six people left at the party. The DJ told those left standing that this would be his last song. The kids thanked him for staying so long, and the DJ put on one last slow song for them to dance to. Michelle and Landon were together, Ethan and Chantal were snuggled up on the dance floor, and even Shane had himself a partner with Renee as the DJ plays Dierks Bentley's "Come a Little Closer." As the song was nearing its end, Shane and Renee walked out together, leaving the two couples alone in the garage with the music. The song ended with Michelle's head resting on Landon's shoulder as they slowly swayed to the beat.

Other students start to ask Shane and Renee questions about the night, trying to find out what else happened other than a dance. Rumours are out there, but neither will say more than it was a nice dance on a cold night. Even in a time of remembering Landon and telling stories of good times, his friends find time to humour each other and laugh. They aren't doing it intentionally to numb the pain, but it helps them remember the good times that life has to offer even in a time of loss and grief.

The high school students take time among themselves in their afternoon English class to talk with their favourite teacher about what has happened and how to move on from it. They like her for her honesty and casual approach to being an authority figure. Not to mention, the boys have no problem looking at her. She allows them to ask anything and speak freely. She knows they will be going through this for more than just one week; some may never fully come to terms with it. She knows that she must help guide them down a path that will let them be comfortable with the subject and never feel regret for living a full life while Landon only got to live a short one.

The senior class asks if they can work on things throughout the year to honour Landon at the graduation ceremony as well as at the school in general—from fundraising to athletics to academics, they are motivated to do more. Even the rebel kids, the so-called bad seeds, are willing to step up and do what they can. They share stories of Landon, his family and school activities in general, which brings on laughter and tears. Some of these tears are of joy while some are of pain as the emotions of even casual conversations bring up greater emotions that some may not have been expecting.

★ ★ ★

Chantal and Ethan become closer after Landon's death. They were close friends for many years, both hiding that they wanted more from the friendship. They are a quiet couple, often sneaking kisses when alone and trying to make sense of their loss. At school, the two can often be seen comforting each other as they hold hands while walking the hallway of the school. Ethan allows Chantal into his life and his most intimate thoughts, but can never tell her everything, as he doesn't know how to trust or deal with some of his thoughts himself. Certain thoughts of death, life and the inevitability of the uncertain he keeps to himself in fear of scaring her off or scaring himself.

Chantal is also struggling with keeping her feelings in check, as she has fallen in love with her long-time friend at such a tough time in both of their lives. She is also there for Michelle and her needs, be it in person or by text and phone conversations. Michelle is very compassionate toward Chantal and her relationship with Ethan and makes sure to not overreact when her friend talks about their relationship even though every word brings sadness to Michelle. The two of them have a great give-and-take and understanding of each other's needs. Their friendship is stronger than ever as they both help one another move on and find happiness in their day-to-day lives.

Ethan and Michelle talk a lot after Landon's death. It is during this time that they often have moments of confiding in each other about their loss, talking about the stuff that keeps them up at night. Ethan spends most of his free time with Chantal. They share a lot of their time with their friends and find comfort in talking with their peers about the loss.

For the most part, the students at the school all get along, but being a normal high school there are cliques that don't always mesh well. They gossip about Ethan and Chantal as well as Michelle and Landon even in his passing. Teenagers can be cruel to friends and frenemies alike. Just because there is a death, that doesn't mean everyone stops being themselves; it usually just brings out the real *them*. Some are compassionate and understanding, while others became more indignant and insufferable. Ethan just lets it slide when he hears the whispers and rumours in the school. Chantal and Michelle are looked at as selfish and attention-seeking by some. Both allegations are far from the truth. Chantal only seeks attention from Ethan, while Michelle finds comfort within herself and doesn't want to be looked at differently than the rest.

Ethan isn't sure where his life is headed, and he doesn't know how he is going to get there either. He thinks the farm would be an easy thing to do, as he grew up with it in his blood, but getting an education and making his own life seems a lot more fun. He also wanted to make sure that Chantal will be happy with his choice for his life and theirs as well. Ethan knows that he and Chantal are in love, but always has thoughts in the back of his mind whether it will work if they chose different paths after high school.

He thinks about his future a lot and where it will lead him. He is scared to venture out on his own but wants his own path at the same time. Ethan remembers discussions with Landon about travelling and seeing things that aren't the same every day. They talked about going past the wheat fields and parties at the moon tower and finding stories at new lakes, new hockey rinks and even the bright lights of random cities, big and small. Ethan already knows that he is going to miss out on the opportunity to see the world with his brother, but when he does venture out, Landon will be there with him in his heart and mind.

★ ★ ★

The school day ends as the students rush away from the classrooms and into the crisp autumn afternoon, heading onto the bus to get home and get on with the rest of their day. Some of the older kids stick around and hang out by the cars, eventually moving the cars toward the outdoor basketball court. They sit around listening to music and playing on the playground. The girls take to the swings while the boys to the basketball court. It is completely casual and short-lived. The conversations are light-hearted and even somewhat about schoolwork.

Ethan and Chantal are hanging out near his car, talking about finding time to be alone, trying to hide their affection from the rest even though it is obvious, as most high school young love isn't hidden all that well. The kids eventually head off to their respective homes for supper and to work on homework, or at least tell their parents they are working on it. The texting and phone calls continue between the friends, be it casual joking or deep conversations about the future.

Their parents are going about their day-to-day lives; some are in contact with Justine and Kevin to see how everything is going and to also talk farming. The day has been a full one for everyone, but it is just one of many they are going to have to go through. Remembering

Landon and moving on with him in their memories is what they have to work on and not let it get them down when they feel as though life has gotten too tough.

★ ★ ★

Michelle sits up in her room. The music is on quietly in the background as she goes over her homework. She can't help but drift off in her mind with the songs and think about Landon, her future and life in general.

She thinks of the conversations at school among friends as well as the teachers and the counsellors. She can't help but overanalyze the stories and conversations of life and death today. She questions religion and the belief of what happens after death. She debates in her mind the path in which she wants her life to go and how she can help others as well as herself.

She can't stay up as late as she did the night before. She is already tired from that, and her mind is burned out from the conversations earlier today. She turns her iPod down and crashes on her bed to the sound of Colbie Caillat's "I Never Told You."

# Day 7

## Tuesday

Some friends of Michelle's have been approaching her since the passing of Landon and talking religiously and spiritually with her. Michelle is polite to them, as they are her friends and she knows they don't mean harm, yet at the same time Michelle isn't a big believer in the Lord or the Bible. She has read the Bible over time and remembers and understands the gist of it. They try to convince her to go to some church services on Sundays and even help with some bake sales and such, but she politely refuses the offers.

Michelle has learned things from the Bible but doesn't necessarily believe it as a whole. However, there is one thing that has stuck with her: The Bible says that God is in each and every one of us, and that we shouldn't believe in a false god, so we should believe in ourselves and the goodness of others, as we ourselves and everyone else are our own gods. Placing an almighty power over everyone seems to be a bit glorious in the whole scheme of things to Michelle. She does struggle with her own demons and life situations, and she knows that her strength and understanding comes from within as well as from her friends and family, but she doesn't feel that an almighty power that she can't see or hear is going to save her or guide her.

She keeps these thoughts close to her and only lets out glimpses of her most intimate thoughts to her friends and family, letting them in on the parts she knows they can handle. She is just like Landon in many ways—ways that neither of them even knew in their short time together. Some of these thoughts they both shared but not always with each other.

At school, Michelle finds that some of the students are talking behind her back about her relationship with Landon. The ones who are talking aren't always in with the crowd Michelle hangs with. There isn't a lot talking, but in whispers it seems like everyone. When there are roughly a hundred kids from kindergarten to grade 12 in a school, it doesn't take long before it becomes a distraction and an annoyance. She overhears in the hallway around the senior lockers from some of the girls, "She seems to be looking for attention" followed by "She was dating Landon for what, a day?" Being on the outside of the cool-kids crew, they don't know much more than rumours they have heard at parties in the past. That, however, doesn't mean much when teenagers want to start rumours and break down the ones who seem to be bigger than the rest in the high school society.

A few rumours came about from the jealous ones in the school. The rumours didn't start right away after the death, but once everyone was back in school, the students got back to being teenagers. The main rumour that did stick with the kids and was a constant murmur in small groups of kids—and it even got into some of the adults' conversations— was one about how Landon took advantage of the situation of a vulnerable Michelle and even got her to give up her virginity to him. The alleged event date varies; some think it was during the summer at the lake, while others think it happened at a party a couple weeks before his death.

It's all just lies, as Michelle and Landon never even kissed until that day he asked her out, minutes before he died in the car crash. Michelle remains strong and never confronts the girls or the rumours. At home, however, the gossip creeps into her thoughts and gets her upset, but she tries to not let it get to her then either.

Michelle maintains her innocence and virginity; still, some who aren't in her main peer group are quick to look at her as if she is a slut. Shane shoots down the rumours among his athletic buddies from outside of the school. Even though most guys would love to be the man and say that they were the first to be with Michelle, Shane knows nothing happened between Landon and Michelle as long as they were friends.

Sex among teenagers is the X factor to everything from relationship status to conversations about it, as well as social leprosy. Michelle pays no attention to those who talk about her sex life or lack thereof. She knows that she will eventually have sex but is in no rush to do so, especially now with Landon gone. Michelle has even mentioned to her girlfriends that she isn't sure if she wants to have sex while in school. She rarely gives in to peer pressure unless it is something she's already comfortable doing, like pulling the power of rural houses at Halloween or jumping off the bridge into the river in the summer.

Chantal, Amanda, Renee, Carmen and Brittney all offer their support and also try to shut down these rumours, as they know the true story. Chantal hears lots of the rumours and knows the pain it causes to those around Landon's family, not just Michelle. Chantal, while being very close to Ethan, gets the angle from the family and how they feel bad for Michelle and all she has to go through just to live her life after the loss of a true friend. The family isn't worried if what they hear is true. They know these are rumours, and that is life as it is.

Even with all the rumours, Michelle battles through with a smile on her face and the truth in her heart. The only thing that troubles Michelle is the memory of Landon. What is he missing in life, and what really happens to us after we die? The nights are long and very lonely; even with the love and guidance of her friends and family when needed, she still finds it tough. Especially when she doesn't tell them about all her thoughts she is having after his passing.

She tries and tries to let some people into her thoughts. Shane and Ethan found out about her feelings of the future and memories of Landon. Michelle told Chantal of her feelings of religion and love and wanting to escape her present situation. Her parents listened to her talk about her fear of never being more than what she is today, and her ideas on her future and that she doesn't know where she is going in life. Amanda learned of Michelle's mindless random thoughts in her dreams, often ideas so far out there that neither could remember them the next day—just like most dreams. She let these people into her life with the stuff that they would understand the best and have the best advice with.

What Michelle wishes she could tell everyone is that she is scared—scared of life and scared of death. She lies awake late at night with her music playing in her earphones; songs by the Tragically Hip ring through her ears and resonate in her thoughts. She finds patience and understanding in their lyrics, just as Landon once did. Every song speaks to her at night with a new story to tell, making her more and more comfortable in her thoughts no matter how frightening or satisfying they may be.

Death is easily distracted in her thoughts by these songs, but it is a thought that truly never goes away. She finds religion in these songs, not religion like those who make you pay and worship a God who may or may not exist or any of the other religions that are often mistaken as truth but to her are nothing more than the original fairy tale. Michelle wants to find her truth, and is finding more and more truths in her life through the lyrics of the Hip.

★ ★ ★

Carmen and Brittney, while being out-of-towners compared to the rest of the main group of friends Landon left behind, talk only of the good that they know about Michelle as well as the memory of Landon. They don't believe in the rumours and try to set the stories straight as best they can. They may be seen as bitches or stuck-up to some people, but those who know the two understand that they are great girls who can be bitchy at times. Most teenage girls are like that. Both of them talk with Landon's friends and family to make sure they know what is being said among their friends about Landon and his accident.

The girls only knew Landon for a few years, mainly through his days of hockey and the parties he would attend throughout the years in their town. Even in just that short time, they grew close and feel that they got to know Landon well. Landon was never much a talker, especially about himself, and as for rumours, he never paid any attention to them. If he heard a rumour of any nature, he would ask those involved if it was true, and no matter if the answer was a lie or the truth he would believe their word over the rumour. He often told the girls that even when you hear things from others about someone, you should take it with a grain of salt until you find the truth. The pursuit, when done right, to find the truth is better than truth itself. Sometimes finding the truth brings out the wrong in all of us. The attempts that we each make to find the truth in the world is what matters.

Landon oftentimes would be sitting around a fire at the moon-tower parties or the lake; while everyone else was drinking and being young and crazy, he would be staring in a trance into the fire. He would join in with some conversations now and then, but most times he would be lost in thought among the flames in the fire. The girls often came and sat by his side to see if he was okay or if he needed a pop or some food. He always declined their offers as they knew he would, but they asked anyway. Sometimes when they came and sat by him in their young drunken state of mind, they would cozy up to him and talk to him about their lives, the good and the bad. Landon never shied away from philosophizing with those who seemed to want to hear his thoughts.

The girls always told him about their relationships. The details sometimes came out in full, and Landon would always shake his head and tell them that they didn't have to tell him all the details. He often told the girls that they needed to look at themselves and see what they wanted from their lives. It didn't matter how young you were, your decisions to act on impulse affected future decisions. He never told them to stop leading guys on or getting drunk for the hell of it, never told them to only have sex with those they love or to be a better daughter for their parents. He would only tell them that it was best that they choose their story and be sure that their story is being told by them and not a friend or someone who pretends to be a friend. The girls often forgot most of what he said as the night went on, but every now and then they would remember it days, weeks or months later. Only now, though, have they taken into account the conversations around those campfires with Landon, as they deal with life's struggles and being better people to themselves and those close to them.

Renee, the oldest of the group of girls who were closest to Landon, is somewhat lost at school without him. She misses the smart-ass sarcastic comments he would throw out every now and then in class or in the hall. She hates hearing people run down Landon's memory through the bashing of Michelle and what may or may not have been between them. She wants to snap and tell them all to shut up, but she knows that will only spark more fires within the idiots, especially as most know that Landon and Renee had a history together, albeit a brief one.

She remembers the days back when the two of them dated, even though it was only for a short time. They knew it wasn't anything more than a junior-high thing. They barely hung out together, held hands or even kissed. But they were together for what being together holds when you are in junior high in a small-town school. She is happy that Michelle is the one he eventually chose to be his girlfriend, and it took him long enough to ask her. Her feelings are hurt by the rumours that are being spread by the assholes jealous of others' popularity and happiness.

Now, Renee is the president of the SRC at the school, and at the time of his passing Landon was the vice-president. The two worked together a lot on trying to make the school a fun place to be, though most of their ideas got turned down over and over again by the school board and the principal. That never stopped them trying.

Always a loud one within the walls of the school, Renee could be heard loud and clear, figuratively and literally, in most day-to-day activities. Landon and Renee would often talk about the state of certain things in the school, be it milk and Vico for the students, the use of personal vehicles to and from the school, or the organization of fundraising for different school events and class functions. Landon even came up with a plan for how the graduating class could get more money from the school for grade decorations and then use the extra money on alcohol for the party. This came from the guy who never drank, planning an event many months ahead of time for those who do enjoy alcohol while not of legal age—an event that Landon will now be unable to attend. He will be there in spirit, though, and in the minds of his friends.

★ ★ ★

The night before the funeral, there are a few family members and friends at both farms, mainly split up, with the older crowd up at the grandparents' farm and the younger crowd and middle-aged parents at

Kevin and Justine's. Both places are just quiet social gatherings talking about Landon, the weather, farming, sports and family events that some family members may have missed lately. The grandparents' gathering shuts down early in the evening and everyone goes home to sleep, while down at Kevin's there are still a fair amount of people. Matt and Robyn, Liam and Jaclyn, and their cousins Trent, Scott and Emma are all upstairs with Justine and Kevin. They are sharing stories and laughs over drinks in the living room.

Meanwhile, downstairs, the three boys have some friends over. Most have already left by now, as it is late in the evening, but those with a driver's licence and a car hang around. Brett and Damon are staying up late tonight with their brother and his friends. Renee, Michelle, Chantal, Shane, Max, Johnny, Gord and Jen are staying late, sitting around watching movies and laughing at anything and everything they can think of just to distract themselves from the moment, even though they all look at each other to see if it is okay to laugh. Even though Ethan's brothers are younger and not really supposed to hear some of the words being said, tonight it isn't worried about. They need this just as much as the rest of them do.

Stories come up of hockey games and road trips with Landon, or how he got away with so much at school. They all talk about how Landon is always there to drive someone home and how he still manages to always be one of the last people to leave a party. They also share the annoying stuff that can still make them laugh, things Landon did to them over the years. How on road trips he would drive away slowly if you were outside the vehicle peeing, or the way his spitball and paper-clip fights with someone in class always ended up hitting the girls around them. As the night wears on, they all start to realize that there are a lot of little moments and sayings of Landon's that they are going to miss.

It is getting late and they all decide it would be a good time to leave, as the funeral is going to be here early in the morning. Chantal gives Ethan a real long goodnight kiss as they say goodbye, surprising both of them as well as Michelle and Shane, who are still around as they share that moment. Family members all take off as well, some a bit earlier and some as the kids are leaving, all of them heading off to their respective places of rest for the night. Trent and Scott leave with Matt and Robyn and stay at their place, as both are slightly intoxicated, and there's no room for them at Kevin and Justine's.

★ ★ ★

The lobby of the skating rink is decorated with pictures and signs for Landon, just as if it was a big game and the students made them for him to get pumped up. Trophies that he won are lined up along a table as you walk in, along with a white-lace guestbook with a picture of Landon beside it, wearing his skates in the house with a hockey stick in his hand. Currently there are no flowers in the arena, but soon there will be many brought in for decoration and many more brought in to pay respect to the deceased.

The entire building is empty at the moment other than the decorations for the funeral and the chairs on the gravel surface where the ice would be in the winter. This is the same ice Landon played on as a kid with excitement and then later on as a teenager just for fun. Landon and his team won the league on that ice. They came back from a three-goal deficit to win by five in the final game thanks to Landon, Bernie in net, and Rob, who shadowed the other team's best player. In a few hours, this place will be filled with friends and family, and many tears will be shed for this young man who lies before them, gone too soon. But for now, all is silent, as the darkness is all that is seeing Landon's gifts and accomplishments.

★ ★ ★

Up in her room after a phone conversation with Shane and some texting with Chantal, Michelle decides to sit out on the balcony by her bedroom and listen to her music. The first song from her iPod is "Another Midnight" by the Tragically Hip. The music is soft and quiet out in the night air, just loud enough to fill the mood.

Michelle sits on her chair wrapped up in a blanket looking up at the stars, thinking of Landon, missing him even more with every new star she sees in the sky. Her heart is always going to be with Landon no matter who she is with, but she isn't sure how she will know who will be the one. With Landon, there was an age difference and not knowing where he would have gone after high school—but she knew it was right and they would have made it work.

She sits for a few hours that night in the brisk autumn air, the frost on the ground becoming noticeable to the naked eye. The sound of the water off in the distance soothes her mind into the thoughts she wants to think about and even the ones she doesn't but that she knows will come up once her mind started wandering. Animals often walk near her house, as she lives in a bit of a wilderness area. Deer, raccoons and other small woodland creatures walk through the yard without paying attention to the people as if everything is cool and no harm is meant.

Michelle watches a deer stand out near the trampoline and then approach the water fountain, taking a few sips from it. She smiles as she thinks of the innocence the deer possesses and the freedom it enjoys even though it is hunting season. The deer perks up as it hears a sound from the house; it is just a creak from the chair Michelle is sitting on, but it's loud enough to make the deer decide that it's time to move on into the nearby forest. Michelle whispers a soft goodnight into the autumn breeze.

Michelle sits back in the chair, her eyes gazing up into the night sky filled with stars and some soft night clouds, the moon giving off a nice soft glow that opens up the night to be enjoyed. Her mind wanders to thoughts of the night when she was last out there. Thinking of Landon and his death, she ponders with wonder what life would be like today if Landon was around. Would they be talking about life after Landon's graduation? Would they be having sex, or would they wait until it was right? What would they have exchanged for gifts over Christmas? She thinks of the little things, and even the intricate things like what it would be like to feel his arms around her. Would it be the same as when Shane holds her in his arms? What about hearing his voice at school in conversations, or seeing him lead the school sports teams to a higher level?

The thought of Landon being in a better place, as many religious or spiritual people tell her now and then, gets in her thoughts late at night and doesn't sit well. She has trouble believing that after death a part of you, your soul, goes to heaven. Your soul, which is something that is not seen, but can leave your body and go to heaven if you have been good, or if you are bad it goes to hell. Who decides whether you are good or bad in life? Michelle fights with these thoughts among her other thoughts of the good memories and what could have been with Landon. She falls into a slight depression at night when she is dealing with these thoughts. Tonight is worse than most nights.

Michelle tries to distract herself by singing parts of the songs she is listening to, but that doesn't always help her; it often just delays the inevitable thoughts. She sings along with "Emergency" by the Tragically Hip, and the song drives home the insecurity and confusion she is dealing with in her mind. She slowly drifts back into her thoughts of life and death, and thinking about what really happens when one dies. Her eyes are not sparkling with wonder as they once were. Now they are sparkly thanks to tears that fill them up. A few teardrops trickle down her face, and she doesn't wipe them away because only she herself and the night sky know the tears are there.

She questions everything from religion to politics to media in her search for answers about death and life. She stays calm with her thoughts, never fighting to make any one thought sound more right than the other. The song "Inevitability of Death" by the Tragically Hip comes on, and she takes a deep breath as her mind races with thoughts of mortality. She wonders if and when we die, are we truly remembered by those we share our lives with, or are the memories taken out of context and expanded and decomposed as time goes on, until eventually the memory of you is forgotten? Unless you are of worth to the media—then you are prolonged forever in society for those who remember you or not.

Michelle tosses and turns and tries to get comfortable in her chair as she fumbles around with her thoughts. She is chilled from the night air and can't figure out if she should sleep or not. She misses Landon, the one she is in love with. That scares her. She is afraid she won't be able to love anyone, with her heart truly being meant for Landon. She knows they weren't Romeo and Juliet, or any other star-crossed lovers whose time came to an end too soon. "If I Die Young" by the Band Perry plays on her iPod, leaving her with more thoughts of what she should do, thoughts of heartache and hope. She looks up at the night sky searching for answers in the stars, hoping a moment will come true and help settle her mind.

Michelle drifts into thoughts of death and the significance of our lives in the grand scheme of things. She deals with issues in her mind that for the most part drop by unannounced, that most people shouldn't even think about, no matter what their age. Michelle is a simple girl with big dreams, and now she is filled with fear and the unknown as she dreams when asleep and while awake is lost in thought.

She quietly whispers into the wind, hoping only her and the trees are listening as she contemplates the depth of every spoken thought: *I am not afraid of death ... I think. I don't know if I want to be buried or cremated, six feet deep or on a fireplace mantel. The thing that scares me is what comes next.*

These thoughts paralyze Michelle with fear of the unknown. She fights them off with more thoughts of fear, distracting one set of fearful insights with other fearful insights. She wonders if there is life out there past what we know on this planet and in the universe. Is it like the movies in any way, or are we believing in a false prophecy within the various movies of life not from this planet, just like we believe in a false prophecy that is of a higher power creating all that we see on earth and beyond? That includes any and all of the gods and the subsequent religions and beliefs that tear this world apart.

Michelle hopes that the movies are the truth and not the words written in a book hundreds of years ago. She believes that most of it is just rumours anyway, along with groups of people trying to lead others into their group. It is a clash of high school cliques with the power to control your deepest and darkest fears with promises of a brighter day when you are no longer on this earth.

Michelle looks at her watch and sees that it is 1:37 a.m. She has been outside with her thoughts for well over three hours, and she should get to bed. Before she heads in, she looks up into the stars in the night sky and thanks them for listening along to the thoughts in her head. She then whispers a sombre goodnight to Landon into the night air, in the hope that if there is life after death, he heard it. She has to believe that one day she will see him again, so that she doesn't feel sad for herself and for him in death. She is conflicted by thoughts on religion and what happens after one dies. She finds her comfort in the hope that this isn't the end of it all when we pass away, but still she fears that there is nothing after our last breath.

# Day 8

*Wednesday*

The morning sun wakes everyone up from their dreams. Some wake up with tears in their eyes, some wake up still feeling the effects of the night before. Some wake up and don't want to roll out of bed, while others get right up and start their day as soon as they can. The school is closed for the day; a lot of adults took the day off from work as well to attend the funeral.

Michelle wakes up on this morning with tears in her eyes, but she can't stay in bed—she must get up and start her day. She stands in the bathroom in front of the sink and mirror as she brushes her teeth. Her mind is stressed and overflowing with thoughts. She tries to think of the song on the radio, but it's not working to fully distract her from the stress. She stops brushing her teeth for second, holding her toothbrush in one hand as she leans on the other hand on the sink. She looks into the mirror, hating how she looks, wondering about her struggles and her own death. Inside she is sad and confused, but she fights on as she drops the brush in the sink.

She wets her hands in the running water and brushes her hair away from the front of her face with her hands. She takes a deep breath and looks over at her iPod. The song has changed, and it hits Michelle harder than a song has done before. She takes another deep breath and looks away and back into the mirror, her eyes searching in the reflection for some answers. She searches for these answers as Jewel sings "Standing Still" from the iPod.

On the desk in the bedroom is a piece of paper, and on it she has written what she would like to say at the funeral, as well as a special note that she wants to place with Landon in his casket so that only he can read, if it is ever to be read. Every word written on the paper is heartfelt and will always stay with Michelle in her heart as the note lies with Landon for eternity.

Justine and Kevin are awake, lying in bed looking up at the ceiling. Silence fills the room. The two share a loving sad glance as they turn and embrace one another, something that at times isn't easy to do. The tension comes and goes when they are alone, but right now they realize that they have to be strong for each other and their kids.

"I love you," Kevin tells his wife as they gaze into each other's eyes.

She replies, tired and honestly, "I love you too. I can't do this without you."

"I will always be there for you," he tells her as he leans in and kisses her on her forehead. They lie in bed holding on tight, not wanting to let go but knowing they have to let go today, but they will never forget their love for their son. Kevin and Justine embrace in a loving kiss just before they toss the blankets aside and get out of bed, both trying to make today no different from any other day in their actions. They both know it will never be just another day but are too scared to let that in yet.

Brett wakes up not wanting to roll out of bed. He stares at his walls, thoughts of sadness and loneliness filling his head. He doesn't cry, he just stares at the wall with empty eyes. He reaches for his iPod and puts the earphones in his ears and turns the music on. Songs of rage and energy play in his ears. He lies there filled with thoughts in his head underneath the loud thump of "The Prisoner" by Fozzy. He tries to distract himself from thoughts of the funeral and Landon, but no matter what he thinks of, they slowly creep back into his mind. He fights the emotions as he lies there alone, unknowingly letting a few tears trickle from his eyes.

Damon wakes up slowly, confused and still a bit tired. He rolls out of bed and walks to the bathroom, not even sure if he wants to be up or not. All he knows is he has to make it to the bathroom, as he has to piss like a racehorse. No thoughts of the day are running through his head yet. He finishes up in the bathroom and heads back to bed and lies down on the covers, his head face down and deep in the pillow. He rolls over as it hits him. He takes a few deep breaths as he looks up at the ceiling. "I can't believe it is today already. Fuck, this sucks," he says as he tenses up and wants to scream and let it all out, but he only releases a long, deep, frustration-filled sigh.

Ethan wakes up from a bad dream, sweaty, only to realize that the reality he has woken up to is much worse, and it won't be better for a long time. He has tears in his eyes, and thoughts of sadness fill his mind, mixed with thoughts of Chantal and what she means to him. He wipes the tears from his eyes and goes to his closet and puts on some sweatpants and a Saskatchewan Roughriders T-shirt. He slips on his moose slippers and heads upstairs, where his parents are sitting around the table drinking coffee and talking quietly about the things they have to get done today.

The radio is on in the background with the sound of the radio DJ's voice giving the weather report and farm report. His mom looks up from her coffee. "Good morning," she says to him. She sees he is still groggy and shuffling on his way past his parents to the fridge, where he grabs some orange juice.

His father asks, "Are your brothers up yet?"

Ethan finishes taking a swig of orange juice from the jug and replies with boredom and fatigue in his voice, "Far as I know they are both up, but pretty sure they are just lying in bed." He takes another swig from the jug before getting a glass and sits at the table with his parents. The three of them sit around the kitchen table drinking coffee and orange juice. They share a quiet moment, no one saying anything that their eyes and body language can't say.

Finally Ethan breaks the ice. "So, what is going to happen today? Do I have anything to do?"

His mother looks at him, still lost in thought and trying to not get overwhelmed by the day just yet. "You will have some stuff to do, I just can't think of what right at this moment."

"I really don't like that the funeral is today," Ethan replies.

"None of us does. You think we haven't thought about it?" his father says with pain and intensity. They let the conversation fade away about the day's events and the frustration that is on the verge of breaking down the family on a day that is meant to celebrate a life taken away too soon. Before the rest of the boys come upstairs, they regain their strength, keeping their emotions of frustration and sorrow in check and not letting a teardrop fall, even though their thoughts and conversation about missing Landon and his funeral may lead them that way. There are only a few hours before they have to leave for the funeral, and none of them is truly ready for the day. Still, they will put on a brave face for those attending.

★ ★ ★

Matt and Robyn wake up with Robyn in Matt's arms. They are lying close to each other, spooning. Matt blows intentionally on the back of Robyn's neck; the air tickles her neck and she gives a little shrug. Matt leans in and gives her a gentle kiss on the back of her head and whispers, "I love you, Babe."

She turns her head to look at him smiling and gives him a quick kiss on the lips. "I love you too."

They lie there in bed for a few more minutes, looking lovingly into each other's eyes, both trying not to dwell on the day's events. Their eyes search for answers and hope in each other's, but their own confusion and emotional strain blocks that. They finally get up from bed and go start their day. Matt heads into the washroom as Robyn makes her way to the kitchen to find something to make for breakfast. She stands there at the fridge staring at the leftovers and drinks and realizes that she can't do this. She isn't strong enough. She slowly begins to sob and break down. Her hand slides down the fridge door, slowly shutting it as she sits down beside it. Her hands cover her face as the tears flow.

Matt finishes up in the washroom and makes his way to the kitchen to see Robyn crying on the floor. He gets down beside her and brings her into his embrace. "What's wrong?" he asks, unsure what has changed in the few minutes they were apart.

"I don't think I can do this today, or ever," she says as her voice cracks with emotion, trying to get out every word, her body shaking, trying to calm herself down in his arms. "I am not ready for this. We shouldn't have to be going through this."

Matt holds her close, trying to reassure her that she will be okay and everything isn't as bad as it may seem.

★ ★ ★

A long black limo pulls into Kevin and Justine's yard to take the family to the funeral. Ethan looks out the kitchen window as the limo pulls up to the driveway. "Holy shit! Burt Reynolds is here!" he says with excitement, hoping to lighten the mood. Everyone laughs at the comment. The family slowly finishes getting ready to leave, putting the final touches on their outfits and making sure they are in their Sunday best. The family members who had been staying there have already left for the funeral, leaving only the five of them to make their way to the rink.

The boys are all dressed in black suits, each with a different colour of tie—not to set each apart, but as a way to remember Landon. Brett is wearing a blue tie symbolizing Landon's favourite colour and teams, the Edmonton Oilers, Dallas Cowboys and Michigan Wolverines. Damon is wearing an orange tie that symbolizes Landon's randomness and the calmness with which he lived every day. Ethan is wearing a red tie symbolizing the love that he and his brothers have for their brother, even if he is no longer with them. Kevin is wearing a black suit with a grey shirt highlighted by a white tie. His wife, Justine, is wearing a long black dress with subtle black outlines of roses in the design along with a black overcoat.

They all get into the limo sent from the funeral home and head off to the rink. The driver has some classical music quietly playing. The family isn't sure what composer it is—all they know is they want something else to be played. Justine politely asks over the music "Can you change the music to something more current? It's not like we are going to a funeral or anything." Everyone is shocked and brought to laughter by the comment.

The driver turns the stereo over to the local radio station, where songs like "Coming Home" by City and Colour, "Times Like These" by Kid Rock and "We Rode In Trucks" by Luke Bryan play on their way to the funeral proceedings. The family sits in the vehicle talking about sports, farming and school as they pull up to the rink. There is pain in their voices, as they know they are going to lay their loved one to rest. It is a much-needed distraction for them, but they try to maintain normalcy even in such a heart-rending moment.

There is already a good amount of vehicles in the parking lot and on the schoolyard field. There hasn't been this many vehicles parked around the hockey rink in many years, not since the heyday of the senior men's hockey team and the midget teams who went to provincials every winter, which was about 15 years ago. There are two spots reserved near the front-door entrance. One is for the limo and the other is for the hearse, which is already there.

Family and friends alike are heading inside for the funeral, some showing their emotional grief while a select few have a laugh as they walk in. Kevin and his family get out of the vehicle and are greeted by family members they haven't seen in a few years who are just arriving at the same time. Pleasantries are exchanged as the family makes its way inside.

Inside the rink, people are lined up and dressed in black formal attire for the most part. Some, however, are dressed in a clean black polo shirt and black jeans, which seems to work for most of the younger guys in attendance. There is chatter among the guests, all offering sympathy and retelling the story of the accident as they wait to sign the guestbook. Some young children are running around in their Sunday best clothes as their parents look on, making sure that they don't get hurt or wreck anything.

Music is playing from the sound booth in the arena, the music that Landon's friends picked out to play instead of the depressing organ music that is normally heard. The music sets the mood for the funeral, making sure that everyone remembers that they are here for a young man who died too soon, and to remember the precious moments they had with him and those they love from here on. The sound of Staind's "So Far Away" gently fills the rink, winding among the casual conversations of those in attendance.

There are probably around 200 people in attendance for the funeral. For such a small farming community, the turnout is a large one. The mix of young and old, family and friends is a happy sight for the family, a sign that their son and brother was truly loved and will be missed. The lobby is filled with many adults who are standing around conversing about farming and catching up with long-lost friends and family members. The younger generation and those who were close friends of Landon are mingling with their friends while surrounded by the adults.

Michelle and Emma are sitting at the guestbook welcoming people, trying to be kind and bring some laughter as the people arrive. Many of the guests share memories of Landon as they see his picture on the table and others placed in the lobby. Some of these memories bring on sadness but no tears; Michelle and Emma fight them off as more guests come in. Scott, Trent, Shane and Renee are ushers to help people make their way to their seats, making sure certain ones make it to the reserved seats.

Out on the gravel rink, which is covered by plywood, Landon's casket sits along the goal line where the hockey net would be. Above it is the lobby. The lights from inside shine out dimly onto the seats for the funeral. The casket is surrounded by framed pictures of Landon from high school and each of his jerseys from the various sports he played, as well as pictures of him with his family and his classmates. Flowers are lined up behind the pictures. The rink smells of lilacs and roses along with the autumn farm air that creeps in from the doors that are left open to allow the building to breathe and keep those in attendance cool.

There are signs hanging along the boards with "Rest in Peace Landon" written on them, and each person is allowed to write a personal message to Landon and his family. Some messages are short and sweet, like "You will be missed" and "Gone but not forgotten," or the longer ones about memories or lyrics that remind them of Landon. "Long Time Running" by the Tragically Hip plays as people find their way to their seats or take their turn going up to the open casket where Landon rests peacefully.

Landon is dressed in a black suit with a blue kerchief in his pocket and a blue tie to go with his black shirt. On his head is his favourite Oilers hat, the same one he was wearing when the accident took place. Some people say a quick prayer as they look in, others shed more tears and whisper how they are eternally saddened by his death. Some just go up to take one last look to remember him and see that he is at peace. Some don't even go up to take a look, as seeing him like that isn't how they would rather remember him; they want to remember the boy who ran around this very rink with his stick in his hand calling out for his mom by her first name, or how he would sit around at the lake cooking marshmallows and having water fights. Those who knew what today was supposed to be go up and quietly wish him a happy birthday.

All the mourners have finally arrived and are sitting in their seats, awaiting the arrival of the family members and the preacher. "Who You'd Be Today" by Kenny Chesney finishes playing as those in attendance wait for the funeral to get underway. The front rows are currently empty but will soon be filled up as the family members and pallbearers enter for the funeral proceedings. The preacher makes his way out from the side of the rink toward the podium, which is just to the side of the casket and the elaborate arrangement around it, as Enya's "A Day Without Rain" plays.

The preacher stands before the congregation "Will everyone please rise?" he asks as he looks to the player benches. Walking in from the home player's box are the pallbearers: Warren, Gord, Max, Shane, Scott, Trent, Liam and Matt, followed shortly by Jaclyn, Devry, Ty, Robyn, Grandma, Grandpa, Brett, Damon, Ethan, Kevin and Justine. They all have on a brave face, politely smiling at some guests as they pass by. A few head nods of thanks are shared between them and those in attendance. The kids are heartbreaking to watch, even though they try to walk to their seats without tears in their eyes. They make little or no eye contact with anyone as they pass by, only looking at the casket or the floor before them.

The pallbearers sit on the front right side and the family on the front left. Behind the family side of the seating are other family members who have come in from all across the prairie provinces and beyond. On the other side, the rows behind the pallbearers are reserved for Landon's classmates, his closest of friends, and those who he played sports with. Eventually the rest of the seats are filled with casual friends and those from the area who have known the family and Landon their entire lives, including the farmer who found Landon in the ditch that day. He is there with his wife and two kids.

The song ends as the family members take their seats. The preacher stands before them. "Welcome, everyone, and thank you for coming here on this very emotional day. I can tell that the young man who we are gathered here for today is loved. I can tell this by the generosity and tears shed by the many in attendance today, from the family and friends who came from far away to those who were around him in the community."

He pauses as he opens up his Bible, taking his eyes off the congregation for a moment. "I knew Landon like most of you. The athletic skill he possessed, the subtle smile and inviting eyes that wanted you to know more about him. He was a kind and gentle person who you could count on for help or even a smart-ass remark." The crowd chuckles as the preacher makes the observation.

"I had the pleasure of knowing Landon through the community," the preacher continues. "I baptised him and saw him through his confirmation into the Church. The community lost more than a young man today; we lost a young man who wanted more out of life, someone who never stopped believing in himself or the goodness of others. I know from knowing Landon and his family, Kevin and Justine as well as their kids Brett, Damon and Ethan, that they don't want to have today be a sad day. It is a time for remembering Landon's life and rejoicing in it. His sense of humour was always on display. He wouldn't want his friends and family to be sad today. He would want us to remember the good times and laugh as if he was still with us."

He looks down at the Bible. "I would like to read from John 5:24: 'I tell you the truth, whoever hears my word and believes him who sent me has eternal life and will not be condemned; he has crossed over from death to life.' This message is true today, as God has taken his child to him and into eternal life. We must believe and know that Landon is up there with God, looking down upon us."

The preacher looks out into the congregation and sees cheerless and unimpressed faces. He knew that it would be a tough funeral service to preside over. When speaking of a young life taken away too early, there is a fine line for the preacher to walk. He knows that the church isn't for everyone in attendance, but they are polite and respect the process. However, he can't get away from his beliefs and teachings. He decides to change the atmosphere of the room and bring up someone who knew Landon well. "Matt, may I ask you to come up to the podium and say a few words on behalf of the family?"

Matt is slightly slouching in his chair with Robyn next to him. The two have been holding hands the entire sermon but have made very little eye contact. Matt slowly gets up from his chair; he exhales deeply as he is getting up. He leans over and gives Robyn a cute church kiss before walking to the podium. He has a slight quiver in his lip from the sorrow and nervousness as he hears "Angels" by Robbie Williams playing softly in the background. The preacher gives him a supportive embrace before he stands alone in front of the congregation. He takes out a piece of paper that he prepared with the help of Robyn in the days leading up to the funeral.

Matt stands at the podium looking down at the paper, trying to gain enough composure to speak in front of the audience. He is not one for speeches, especially in front of a large crowd—maybe a locker room if need be, but even then it is not his style. Robyn looks at him and gives him a smile as her eyes fill with tears, as she knows the loving words that Matt is about to say. He shoots a delicate smile from his finely quivering mouth and then takes his hands and puts them together like he is about to pray. He puts his hands over his mouth, taking a couple of deep breaths. He looks out into the audience and begins his speech.

"I would like to thank everyone on behalf of the family for coming out today for Landon's funeral. Landon's family I know is very appreciative of all the support that has been shown during this difficult time." He pauses for a quick second to scan the audience before looking back down at the paper to continue on with the words that he is struggling to even look at, never mind say.

"I am not one for giving speeches, so bear with me. Landon was my nephew; he was almost like a little brother to me. Watching him grow up and being able to be a part of that meant a lot to me. I never knew what to do or expect about being an uncle. I was young when Kevin and Justine had Landon. I still remember when Kevin came into the dressing room at hockey when he was coaching my team. It was in an old barn of a building at a tournament. He brought in blue gum cigars for the entire team. I think the adults got real ones, not sure though. Back then, I wasn't focused on that. I do recall winning that game though, and I'm pretty sure we won the tournament as well." Matt looks up at his family in the front row and gives Kevin a smile.

"We all know of Landon's athletic ability, and the love he had for sports. That I am pretty sure is as much a part of the family as ketchup is on every meal." The crowd quietly chuckles at the comment. "Landon grew up with skates on his feet or a ball glove on his hand. He loved to just play; he played with kids older than him and was always accepted. He just wanted to be a part of the game. Sometimes he was even better than the older kids. He always played the game for the right reasons, and always played for his teammates. He hated to lose, but he was never a poor loser. He must have gotten that from his mother. Right, Kevin?" The family and the rest of the crowd laugh at the comment, knowing that when Kevin played sports back in the day he lost his cool on occasion. Kevin and Matt look at each other and share a smile as Kevin shakes his head at his little brother.

"Landon loved his teams, be it the Oilers, Wolverines or Cowboys. Oh, and the Eskimos—not sure how he snuck through and became a fan of them in Rider Nation. I may have had an affect on that, but I am sure Landon knew the difference between championships and, well, the Riders."

The crowd slightly boos the notion of cheering for the Eskimos. Matt smiles back at them with a bit of a chuckle. "He knew the history of the teams and the sports. We would talk for hours, sometimes very late, about who should be traded and why or about players long forgotten but for random factoids that he always seemed to be full of. We used to go through my old hockey-card collection, often making fantasy trades. Pretty sure that is how the Maple Leafs and their fans do it as well."

Another burst of laughter arises from the crowd, most of whom are Leaf fans or closet Leaf fans depending on how well they are doing that season. Matt pauses to laugh with them and gain some composure before the tough stuff comes up.

"Landon never seemed to be in a bad mood. I know he had moments when he was frustrated or needed advice, but name someone who doesn't. He often came to me or Robyn and asked for advice. We did our best to help him with whatever it may be. Be it schoolwork—that part was Robyn, pretty sure we all know why there—his teen love interests or just dealing with family. He was a level-headed kid and went with the flow. I know he wasn't perfect, and I am not trying to make him out to be that way. But I wish I was more like him. He showed me things about me that I didn't know about myself, even though he didn't know he was doing so. He showed me that I can be a mature adult when needed. That I can believe in myself and those close to me. How I can love the little things as much as the big picture." Matt pauses as tears fill his eyes.

"I just thought of this and it actually isn't on my paper, but I have to tell you a story about Landon and my dad, back from when Landon was maybe four or five," Matt says. "It was sometime in the spring and most of us were at my parents' place for supper. After supper, the women were in the kitchen cleaning up and such. The men were in the living room relaxing, watching the news. Landon and I were playing football outside and just came back in as it was getting dark. My father called Landon into the living room. So we both go in there. I sit on the couch next to Kevin, while Landon was called over to my dad and sat on his lap. My dad asked him if he ever heard of holy Moses. Landon looked confused and said no. So my father began to tell him a not-so-innocent saying for a five-year-old. *Holy Moses, happy land. Baby shit in mother's hand. Mother went out to get a switch. When mother came back. Baby called her a son of a bitch.*"

The crowd gasps and laughs at the story. The family is in tears, both from laughing as they know the story as well as the tears of loss. Matt stands there wiping away tears as he laughs; he barely could get through saying it without crying and laughing. The crowd slowly quiets, allowing Matt to continue with the emotional speech.

"I saw Landon moments before his last moments. We stopped at the corner at the highway and talked for a few minutes. He was so excited. He was shy about it, but so happy. He said he had just asked out Michelle. Sorry, Michelle, I am not trying to make this worse for you." Matt looks at Michelle, as she is in tears and in the arms of Chantal. She looks at him and gives him a painful smile that it is okay. "I knew he liked her for a while but he was afraid of asking her out for reasons that I still don't understand. Not sure what took him so long. He was excited for his senior year of high school. He had the girl, he had the year planned for what he wanted to accomplish for sports. He was even planning on going to college to play sports mainly—academics, well that was just sort of there. He was a dreamer and full of big ideas."

Matt pauses and looks out at Landon's friends before he continues reading. "Landon loved his friends. He was really close and loved hanging out with his close friends Michelle, Renee, Max, Shane, Warren to name a few. I have known all of them their entire life; I watched them grow alongside Landon. I know they will miss and never forget him. They all have a tight bond as friends, which I believe comes from this community we are in today. In a day and time of remembering Landon and his memory, we cannot forget about those still here. His friends and his brothers need each other and all of us now to help them get through this. I could tell you all stories of the parties at the moon tower, school activities and family fun. However, I don't want to bore you all with stories that we can all share in the future when we speak of Landon."

He pauses from reading the touching words to gather his composure as he fights through the speech. He stands there and looks around the arena, seeing the faces of all who knew Landon as well as all the memories posted around to pay respect to him. He looks down at the end of the arena into the darkness, unsure if it is the nerves or what but he sees a couple of dimly lit figures skating at the far end. He stares off into the darkness with emotional strain in his eyes and face as he watches what he thinks he sees. The two figures stop and pick up the puck before skating off into the darkness. He regains his focus and wipes the tears from his face. He takes a nervous exhale trying to gain composure and begins to speak again to the audience, who are all sitting in silence as diverse emotions can be seen in everyone.

"I am going to try to get through this last part as best I can, so bear with me. We held the funeral today at the rink because, well, where else would Landon want to be? I am going to miss the early mornings of World Juniors, Saturdays of college football and 'Hockey Night in Canada,' card games at the lake, his laugh and smile."

Matt begins to choke up with emotion and steps away from the podium to gain poise to continue. He steps back and continues to speak, still fighting to get words out. "Our family is not exactly the biggest supporter or believer in church. Personally, I do not know where Landon is today. If he is by chance watching down on us, I hope he sees all the love he gave and we have for him. If heaven only exists in those who still are alive, then we must never forget the memories of the loved ones we lose in death, because if we forget about them, then they may not have a place to go. I will always remember Landon, my nephew, the older brother, the doting son, the compassionate friend, the smart-ass, the quiet leader and now the angel."

Matt's body is shaking and the tears are falling from his eyes as he finishes his last trembling words. He steps away from the podium and walks slowly over to his nephew's casket and stands over it. Looking down at his fallen friend, he whispers, "I love you, and I will never forget you."

He steps away from the casket still unable to gain control. Robyn stands up with tears falling down her cheeks as she listened to the loving words from her man. She walks to him and embraces him and walks him back to his family and his seat. He gives Justine a hug and a kiss, as the two cry into each other. "Thank you for that," she whispers through her tears.

Kevin gives his little brother a manly hug, holding him tighter than ever before. "Thanks," Kevin tells him as they embrace. Matt then goes over to his nephews and gives them each a quick hug, as they all have tears on their heartbroken faces. Before sitting down next to Robyn, he gives her a quick kiss and hugs her again as they sit down by each other's side holding hands.

The preacher walks back up to the podium. "Thanks, Matt, for your kind and loving words. Your words and honesty mean a lot to everyone here." He pauses to see who is next to speak. "Would Landon's hockey team like to come up and share a few words?" The hockey team gets up from their seats as "Only God Knows Why" by Kid Rock plays softly in the background. Led by their captain, Nathan, all 17 members rise up wearing their uniforms. Some of the guys can't hide their emotions as tears are noticeably in their eyes, while some are trying to maintain some strength although they are emotional wrecks inside.

At the podium, Nathan stands before the audience with the team around him in solidarity. "Landon was a friend and a teammate for all of us. All of us up here have played with and against Landon our entire life. As a teammate or foe, he was always a leader and showed sportsmanship in all aspects of his game and life. We will always have Landon in our thoughts when we step on the ice, as well as when tackling life outside the rink. His scoring touch and leadership will be missed this year, but as a team we will play every game hard in hopes of doing him proud and bringing a championship home. We would like to thank Kevin and Justine and the rest of the family for allowing us to speak today. We have something for the family and if Kevin, Justine, and the boys could come up we would like to present it to them now." Kevin and Justine are touched and slightly surprised by the gesture.

The family gets up and walks slowly up to Nathan and the team. Standing next to Nathan, they look at the young man as he begins to speak again. "This year on our jerseys, there will be a patch on the shoulder with Landon's initials and number on it." All the players currently have it on their jerseys as they stand before the crowd. It is a black circle with white numbers and letters in it. "As well, we would like to present you with Landon's jersey with the patch on it and let you know that Landon will always be with us. I hope we can make him and your family proud this year."

He hands Kevin and Justine the framed white jersey with black and gold stripes on the sleeve. They give Nathan a thankful embrace and then place the jersey in front of the casket. Kevin and Justine then walk down the line of teammates, giving each young man a handshake and a quick kind word. They all make their way back to their seats as the preacher returns to the podium.

"I would like to ask Michelle to come up and say a few words on behalf of Landon's friends," the preacher says as he looks out into the audience at Michelle, who is full of nerves and is visibly shaken next to her friends. She gets up from her chair and makes her way gingerly up to the podium to speak to everyone. Her nerves are a mess and she is scared of opening up. The sound of Jewel's "Hands" plays softly in the background as Michelle collects herself and slowly makes her way up to the podium.

The hurt and sorrow in Michelle's eyes and body are noticed by everyone. She tries to hide as much as possible while in front of everyone there. She takes a moment and stands a foot or so in front of the casket, looking with loving sad eyes at the boyfriend and close friend she lost on what was to be a glorious day. She whispers to him, "I love you, Landon." She pulls out a note that she has written for him. She kisses the note gently and steps forward and with tender innocence rests her hand with the note in it on Landon's chest where his heart would be. She then slips the note into his pocket, the whole while looking with childlike and poignant eyes into his closed eyes. A tear falls from her eye and onto Landon's unknowing cheek.

She turns around and looks out at Landon's family and his friends; her lip is trembling as she tries to gain composure. She knows she can't do this alone, so she gives a gesture with her sad eyes and nervous hand toward Renee and Chantal for them to come up, as she needs them to get through this. The two girls, their eyes overflowing with tears, make their way up to Michelle to offer her support. They embrace in a three-way hug in front of the casket, each whispering kind words and encouragement to one another. Those in attendance are also having a hard time keeping their tears and sorrow in as they watch the three young women help each other through this tough time.

At the podium, Michelle stands bravely as tears trickle down her face, and her lip quivers as she tries to say the words she wishes she never had to say. Renee and Chantal stand behind her as she begins to speak. Michelle's voice cracks and weeps of sorrow as she begins to get the first few words out. "I would like to thank Kevin and Justine for asking me to speak today on behalf of Landon's friends."

She takes a tissue and wipes her eyes, and then she takes a deep breath, trying to find a smile to get her through this moment. She finds it as she looks out and sees Brett smiling back at her, a comforting smile on such a cheerless face. Michelle stands there for a short instant locked in a moment with Landon's youngest brother. She gathers herself from that moment and continues on with her loving words of sadness and loss.

"Landon had countless friends who could have been chosen to speak today. It is an honour to speak about a great person and a true friend today. I wish I didn't have to be at a funeral, though, to be doing so. We all as Landon's friends have our own memories of him and stories. Most of which aren't exactly funeral friendly." She looks up and chuckles with a sombre smile, hoping to have the crowd help her along with their own laughter.

"The day that Landon died seemed to be just like any other day at the school. The news hit us all hard and fast as it got passed along through friends. It hit me really hard. That day was a happy one for me and for Landon. He had just asked me out only moments before the fateful accident." Michelle's face is filled with emotion as tears fall from her grave eyes; she is unable to get through the words. Chantal and Renee stand beside her with arms around her, offering as much comfort as they can. She stands there shaking between her two friends. She can barely look up, knowing that if she sees the family she will break down even more. She gathers her composure through some deep breathing and steps back up to talk.

"We are all better people because of knowing Landon and having him in our lives. He touched all of us in different ways, even in ways we may not realize until we are old and grey. I know myself and my close friends have had a few conversations about Landon and how much he meant to us. Landon's idiosyncrasies made him different from most, but he was always one of us. He was quiet and a great listener. However, if you ever left yourself open for a smart-ass one-liner, an innuendo-filled rebuttal, he was quick to remind you that he was there. Even if the one-liner was directed at you, you knew it was comical and would make you laugh at yourself. Landon was great at laughing at himself. He never took himself too seriously, but he knew when to have those serious moments."

She pauses and looks out into the audience as they sit there in silence, trying to remain in control of their own emotions as much as possible. They know that she needs a brave face to look at while up there, but that doesn't stop tears from falling from many listening to Michelle speak of her friend.

"You may be thinking right now about some of those moments. The times he made you laugh, or when you got to hear his quiet little laugh. The comments he would make in class, the locker room or at home. He was never afraid to lighten the mood. The little moments spent with Landon mean more now than ever, as they will always seem greater in memory—as they should be, as we always have Landon in our hearts and thoughts. If you were to see Landon's room, you would see trophies and a history of his achievements all over the place. He won many trophies as MVP or just a tournament win, but he also has his friends pictures up on a bulletin board, which I am sure he thought were just as important as any trophy. Well, any trophy other than the Stanley Cup, that is."

The crowd laughs tenderly at the hockey comment. Michelle even gets to break out of her anguish to laugh innocently with them.

"We all can agree that Landon was all about sports, and it was very easy to see from an early age, from what I have heard from my family and others. How he grew up roaming this very rink with a hockey stick in his hand and calling out for Justine—not mom—whenever he needed candy or a rink burger. Even on a Saturday night in the winter, Landon would not show up to a party until he watched 'Hockey Night in Canada,' unless the Flames were the late game. Then he would pass on that. Hockey was his religion, it seemed; he knew the game inside and out, and loved everything about it. He played basically every sport available to him, and watched as many as he could. It wasn't just hockey and his love for the Edmonton Oilers; he also religiously followed the CFL, NFL and college football, especially the Michigan Wolverines, the college he wanted to play for. He played baseball and loved watching the game as well. If we can ever love and respect something in life as much as Landon did his teams and the sports he loved, we should be so lucky."

Michelle stands up there finally gaining some composure among all the pain. She begins to speak again, her voice trembling and breaking from time to time as every word comes out. Some parts are better than others, but she battles through them for Landon, her friends and his family.

"If there was one thing that Landon did that all of us as his friends were a part of at some point, it was his road trips. These ranged from trips to the city for food and shopping, or for sporting events and concerts. Some, actually a lot, were also booze cruises on the weekend, as he was always the sober one and as people needed rides home he would take them, but often it would be the long way home as they all never wanted the party to end. I am not sure how he managed to always be up for it, but he was. He always had music for the road trips, be it burned CDs of his favourite songs at the moment or a long list of songs on his iPod. It was a given that certain artists would be played: the Tragically Hip, Stone Temple Pilots and Brad Paisley, to name a few. Even the songs today that you are hearing before, during and after the funeral are all from his iPod that we, his friends, went through and decided would best remember him. These songs are what he and us, his friends, would want to hear during this time of sadness and loss in hope to find some comfort, healing and understanding on a day when his memory may not be so easily celebrated as we mourn."

Michelle, fighting through her heartache, stops to gather herself, as she has trouble finding the composure to speak her next few words. She is comforted by Chantal and Renee, as they embrace her in a loving hug.

"I would like to thank Chantal and Renee for their support up here with me today. They are also good friends of Landon's and the family. Today is such a tough day for us all. I can't go on without mentioning that today would have been Landon's 18th birthday. This celebration of his life is funny in a way if you know Landon. He never celebrated his birthday; he never made a big deal about turning 16, 18 or even looking forward to turning 21. He felt that birthdays were best when you were a child. I have had talks with Justine over the years and just recently actually about Landon's birthdays. She told me he could remember all of the parties thrown for him as a kid. Not only that, though, Landon could recall who got him what present and what year. That was Landon—even if it seemed like he didn't care or wasn't paying attention, he always did."

Michelle looks back at the coffin and Landon's lonely body and whispers, "Happy birthday, Landon, I miss you." Without even asking or expecting it, the entire crowd collectively breaks out into singing "Happy Birthday" to Landon. Justine is in the front row looking up at Michelle with her eyes overflowing with tears as Kevin holds her close to him. She shoots Michelle the saddest of joyful smiles, her lip trembling as she thanks her for everything. Michelle smiles back at Justine as the crowd finishes up the song.

"Before I leave the stage today, I would like to leave you with a poem that I wrote inspired by songs that remind me of Landon." Every word trembles from her quivering heartbroken lips as the raw emotion touches all in attendance, as the innocence in the words coming from such a beautiful and brave young woman in such a sensitive and sympathetic time.

"Lay a whisper on my pillow
For they might wake me from this sleep
Pick a flower and hold your breath
It's a vain pursuit but it helps me to sleep
A tuneless moonlight
No dress rehearsals this is our life
I just shouldn't think any more tonight 'cause
Hearing your name the memories come back again
I had the photo album spread out on the bedroom floor
Off to a time and place now lost on our imagination
In an epic too small to be tragic
Well I'm terrified of these four walls
I just want to feel safe in my own skin; I just want to be happy again
I will gather myself around my faith
This ain't over, no not here, not while I still need you
So I'll be holding my breath until the end
The morning rain clouds up my window
You took your coat off and stood in the rain
I want to photograph you with my mind
I'm sick of sight without a sense of feeling
And all I remember is sitting beside you
She says it's cold outside and hands me my raincoat
I love you even when I don't even know I'm doing it
Somebody showed me I was the last to know
And I like the way you like me the best
Those words touch me too deeply
The first step you take is the longest stride

And all the roads we have to walk are windy
Like God's representatives on earth
Falling further from just what we are
Nothing ever stops these thoughts and the pain attached to them
It's just not the same because of this
Well I can't help but be scared of it all sometimes
Gonna make it all right but not right now
Breathing is the hardest to do
It's a sad day, bourbons all around
Last chance for one last dance
My soul slides away
Gone like it was destined
Through half-squinted eyes becoming a mirage
I ponder the endlessness of the stars
Until we're talking in whispers again."

All those in attendance that day have tears in their eyes as they listen to Michelle read the poem. Michelle's eyes are also flowing with tears both sad and blissful as she speaks the words that make her remember Landon. She stands at the podium with everyone looking back at her offering comfort and condolences with their tear-filled eyes. She offers a smile back from her quivering lip and steps away from the podium with Chantal and Renee by her side as they head to their seats.

Kevin, Justine and the entire family each give Michelle a huge hug and tell her thanks. Justine and Kevin whisper to her as they embrace, "Landon was lucky to be your boyfriend, and you will always be a part of the family. Thanks for being so brave today."

Back in her seat, Michelle sits up strong, her eyes the saddest they have ever been. Her hands are shaking but she holds them together to hide the nervousness. She sits there as the preacher steps back up to speak again. "Thanks, Michelle, for your kind and honest words about such a great friend. You and all of Landon's friends were lucky to have him a part of your lives, just as he was to have all of you in his life and here to remember him today."

Then, just before the lights go out and the rink sits in almost complete darkness, he says, "I would like you all to now direct your attention to the video screens for a special video presentation that Landon's family and friends have put together."

Two projector screens are hung from a bar going across the rink behind the casket. As the video starts with the lights out in the building, a lone light shines on Landon's coffin. After a moment of silence, they all sit in the dark with their own thoughts patiently waiting for the video to start. The projectors whir and the sound of Nickelback's "Photograph" fills the darkness. Soon, pictures and videos appear to accompany the music being played. The song ends and blends into "Dirt Road Anthem" by Jason Aldean. The songs are spliced and mixed into a medley, blending in perfectly with the pictures on the screens. Laughter along with *oohs* and *aaawws* break some of the silence in the audience as they all sit and watch. Sarah McLachlan's "I Will Remember You" plays the video out, until only McLachlan's angelic voice and the light shining on the casket remain. The crowd sits in the dark, emotions shining through.

The lights are turned back on and slowly regain their glow. It is like a quiet reminder to those who have Landon's memories in their hearts that even though he may not be with them anymore, his memories and life will not be forgotten if they let him back into their hearts. The preacher makes his way back to the podium. "I would like to thank the family and Landon's friends who took the time and effort to put together the montage to honour Landon."

He pauses as he looks down at his Bible before speaking to the congregation again. "Originally, I had planned to recite the universal verses from the Bible in the hope of consoling and healing the hearts of those in attendance. Instead, I would like to take a page from Michelle's touching poem and unite ideas from verses and make them into one that fits the moment."

He had made a note of what he wanted to say as he was watching Michelle speak and during the montage that played. He begins to read the note, hoping it conveys to the family and friends that Landon is in heaven and it is a better place for his presence. "To everything there is a season, and a time for every purpose under heaven. A time to be born and a time to die. For whether we live, we live unto the Lord; and whether we die, we die unto the Lord. Blessed are they that mourn;

for they shall be comforted. Be joyful in hope, patient in affliction, faithful in prayer. Wait for the Lord; be strong and take heart and wait for the Lord."

The preacher stops his speech and looks out at those in attendance and smiles at Landon's family and close friends before he gets right back into his speech. "You all should believe in the memories you have of Landon and never forget him, as he is with the Lord looking down on all of us. He is up there watching and remembering all of us, rejoicing in seeing all of his friends and family grow into the people that they will become."

He closes his Bible and holds it close to his chest as he looks out at everyone. "May Landon's memory last forever, and may we see him in another light when we are taken from this earth to be with him. He is with God and watching down on us, smiling, seeing all his friends and family show love for him. The family and I would like to invite those of you who want to join us at the burial site to follow us to the cemetery shortly after we leave here. After that, there will be a social lunch gathering at the local hall, which you are all welcome to come to."

The funeral ends as the family is the first to leave, passing by Landon's coffin followed by the pallbearers, and then the family and friends soon follow, going side to side by row as everyone passes by the coffin. As they walk by the coffin and the arrangement at the front of the rink, some say a private and quiet word to Landon, while others are too emotional to even look over at the coffin as they wipe tears from their face.

Michelle stays in her seat, letting everyone go ahead of her. As people pass by her, they offer their condolences and awkward glances. She sits there politely in her chair. The sadness hasn't left her face, but hope and patience are slowly seen in her teary eyes. She stays in her seat for many lonely minutes sitting content, looking at Landon's coffin. Her mind is a mess, but she has a quiet conversation in her head with Landon. She tells him of her love for him, how beautiful and proud the funeral was and that she will never forget him—and one day, if there is a day to meet again, she will wait patiently for it.

A few minutes pass as people are standing in the waiting room glancing out toward Michelle with concerned eyes. Without even looking up at them, she notices the awkward emotion on their faces looking out at her. Matt and Robyn walk out to Michelle in the empty rink. They sit on either side, neither one saying anything to her. They know that right now words aren't what she wants. Robyn holds on to Michelle's left hand as Matt leans forward, resting his head on his hands clenched together as if he was praying.

The three of them sit in the dark arena sharing a quiet conversation. "I loved him. I know I am young, but I believe that he was the one for me," Michelle tells them as they stare at the coffin.

"Landon knew you were the one for him. He talked about you a lot. The last conversation we had, he couldn't stop blushing and talking about you," Matt tells her as he turns and looks her directly in her young, loving, tear-filled eyes. "He will always be there with you, loving you and guiding you into the great things you go on to do with your life."

Robyn adds, "He will always be with you. And he will always love you." The two embrace in a tender hug while they shed tears on each other's shoulder.

The three of them rise up from their chairs and walk solemnly by Landon. Matt and Robyn are holding hands as they pass, with Michelle following them. Michelle blows a kiss to Landon as they pass by. "I will never forget you. I love you," she says innocently in a hushed tone as her eyes tear up. She doesn't let a tear fall as she wipes them away and blows one last kiss to Landon as they leave the rink.

★ ★ ★

The coffin is loaded into the hearse and leads the procession to the cemetery out in the rural area near the town. It is followed by the family and close friends of Landon. Not everyone is going to the burial. Some have gone to visit among themselves at people's houses in the community until the lunch social takes place.

They arrive at the cemetery where the final resting place for Landon has been prepared. It's next to his great-grandma and great-grandpa, who died long before Landon and his brothers even knew them. Behind his burial plot is a gravesite of another young man who died in the community over 25 years ago. Sadly, his family moved away and his gravesite and his stories have been forgotten by most in the area. Michelle arrives with Matt and Robyn at the cemetery as the sound of "Heaven Is a Better Place Today" by the Tragically Hip plays from the speakers of their car.

The preacher begins the burial proceedings with the coffin above the open grave, and the family members gather closely around the preacher and the coffin, with his classmates and close friends right there among the family members. Michelle stands to the left of Matt and Robyn, while her friends Shane, Amanda and Renee stand just behind her. Justine, Kevin and their sons stand next to the gravesite with his parents.

The cold air adds to the chill everyone is feeling as an autumn wind blows gently through them. The family stands tall, trying to stay proud of their son in his final resting place even though their faces are full of heartache. Justine is shaking and can't control the tears as they fall from her sorrow-filled eyes. Kevin holds her hand tight and brings her close to him, hoping to help his loving wife at this moment. He stands there, tears slowly trickling from his eyes as he listens to the preacher. Their kids can't even look up; they just stare at their shoes. Their eyes are filled with tears that constantly fall at their feet, each tear sadder than the one before. The rest of the family stands around them quietly and patiently as the preacher speaks. There isn't a smile on any of the faces, as it truly is hitting home now as they see Landon's casket at the gravesite.

In Michelle's right hand is a rose. Her hands grips the rose ever so gently but firmly enough so that it will not drop. When the casket is lowered, she and others will place their roses on the casket. The colours of the roses are red and white, signifying the innocence and love that is lost. The preacher reads scripture from the Bible as everyone stands in silence in the bitter chilly autumn air. Their heads are bowed in respect to the departed, holding each other close for support in this time of need.

Chantal and Ethan are standing next to each other as they hold each other's hand, trying to be strong as tears fall from their eyes as they look at the casket. The preacher is continuing on with his sermon as the cool air circulates around them in a brisk autumn breeze. Friends and family with roses slowly come up one by one and place the flowers on the casket before it is lowered.

Michelle, Robyn, Matt, and Landon's brothers all wait until everyone has placed a rose on the casket. Damon and Brett go and place theirs on the casket followed by Matt and Robyn placing theirs. Matt, who had been holding his emotions in check for the most part, starts to cry harder than he has since the death of his nephew. He and Robyn embrace in an affectionate consoling hug as they step back with the crowd. Justine and Kevin try to comfort them as Matt and Robyn themselves try to comfort Justine and Kevin, who are shedding tears through strong sad eyes.

Ethan and Chantal follow shortly after as they place their roses on the casket. Ethan, who has remained strong with his emotions up until now, stands at the casket and sheds tears over his rose before setting it down. He kneels down beside the casket and quietly whispers, "I will never forget you, Landon. You were the best big brother we could ever ask for."

Kevin and Justine step forward and place their hands on his back to comfort him. When he gets up, his face is covered in tears and sorrow. He hugs his mom and dad harder than ever before. "I love you guys," he says as his parents embrace him.

Michelle steps forward with her rose, and her footsteps are soft and scared. She tries to put a smile on her face as she kisses the rose, but her nerves hold her back from the smile. Michelle gives it a gentle loving kiss with quivering lips before placing the rose on top of all the other roses on the casket. She stands there for a moment that seems like forever before turning to Kevin and Justine. She gives them a heartfelt and caring hug before heading back to be with her friends.

The service ends as the casket is lowered into the ground with the sound of "Gone Away" by the Offspring and Emily Armstrong playing in the background. Everyone begins to slowly head back to their vehicles, some walking hand in hand with loved ones, some walking alone even among the crowd. They all leave the cemetery in a timely and orderly fashion as they head back into town to the lunch that is being served.

At the hall in town, people have slowly been arriving for the lunch. Conversations and togetherness is shared as people stand around or sit in groups at tables during this time of need. The preacher says grace so that everyone can begin to eat the vast amount of food that has been prepared by some of the women from the church group. Everyone is sitting around the tables in many assortments of groups.

One table is of Landon's close friends. This includes Michelle, Chantal, Shane, Ethan, Renee, Amanda and a couple others who come and go from the table. The conversation is light and respectful as they sit there and enjoy some snacks and sandwiches.

"You did a great job up there, Michelle," Ethan tells her as the two sit across from each other at the table. She smiles back, being modest, as she doesn't want today to be about anything more than Landon's memory.

"I really liked your poem and the honesty in your speech," Amanda adds politely as she sits next to Michelle. Shane takes the opportunity to steal a pickle from her plate, and she doesn't even notice or care.

"Thanks, guys. Any one of you would have said great things about Landon and what he meant to you," Michelle replies, smiling at her friends but trying to only be a part of the group and not the focal point.

"Michelle," Jaclyn says as she walks by to her seat, which is at the table behind her. "Landon would have loved the speech. You have all been great friends to him and the family. Thanks." She sets her plate of food down before giving some of the teenagers, including Michelle, a gentle thanking hug as they remain seated. She picks up her plate, walks to her seat, and joins in the conversation going on behind the teenagers.

At Jaclyn's table are Landon's aunts and uncles as well as some cousins. They can hear the kids at the table next to them talk about recent events at school and at parties. They stay out of the conversation and keep to their own discussions about family. Some of it is whispers about who is there and how they may be avoiding certain people.

During lunch, people walk around and converse among other

groups, young with old, friends with family, everyone reconnecting with one another as well as talking about the weather and farming in the community. Laughter is all around in the hall as conversations became light-hearted among the sadness of the day. Stories are being shared of Landon and random memories of the past, especially at the tables of friends and young family members. They speak of the parties in the area, from the big bonfires at the moon tower to house parties at Renee's to the pre-grad and grad party sites.

The two tables have basically turned into one as the conversations have joined and chairs are turned or people have turned sideways to the table behind them. They all invite each other into the conversations as family and close friends share stories.

"There are so many party stories that you may or may not know," Shane tells the family as they chuckle. "Landon was always the last to leave the party. He always said it was because he wanted to say he shut the place down. We all knew it was because he knew he had to always take one of us drunks home." They all laugh, knowing how true that was to Landon.

"Oh, trust me, Landon didn't just party with you guys," Trent chimes in. "When his family would come out to visit us, we always took him out to places his parents still don't know about."

"Oh really, like what?" Justine asks with a hint of laughter in her tone as she glares over at Trent.

"Well, remember when we always came home late from the movies or the hockey game?" Trent retorts, taking a sip of his coffee and still feeling it a bit from the night before. "We would often go to a local pub and try to set him up with some cougar, or just go to a small house party for a few hours before we came home." Trent starts laughing with his brother Scott, as they were the culprits in this. The rest soon follow suit.

"Don't worry, Landon never did anything bad. He wouldn't even give the cougars a chance." Scott assures them. Looking at the kids, he gives them a wink that the family can't see. The teens laugh as they are let in on the joke.

"You boys were always an influence on him, usually good but sometimes I guess not so much," Justine says as she looks at them, shaking her head and smiling. Kevin sits there beside his wife with a smile on his face hearing the stories of his son.

"I have to know, who or where did Landon learn to be so dry, sarcastic and great with one-liners?" Shane asks the family.

"That would have to be from his grandpa or father, if anyone in the family. Also, when he was growing up, some of his great-aunts were always full of stories and lines. So I am sure they played a part in that as well," Justine tells Shane and the rest in the little group they've got going on.

"I think all the men in this family have that trait in them. Sometimes it is cute and playful. Then there are times you wish they would stop," Robyn says as she looks over at Matt with a smirk. He smiles back, knowing full well that he is slightly in trouble for some comment he made recently.

"At the lake, I remember many nights around the campfire with a party going on around, he would always just sit and listen to the fire and watch it crackle, while still knowing what was going on around him. I never knew how he did it," Ethan mentions.

"Trust me, us girls always wondered it as well, how he would know who was hitting on us or whatever," Renee adds. "He would just sit there, and then quietly out of nowhere he would slip in a one-liner. Without even looking at those he commented to, still looking at the fire."

"Not to get too sentimental, but I always loved his bunny hugs when they smelled like campfire," Michelle says with a gentle laugh. "I think he enjoyed pestering me with comments and tickling and schoolyard flirting." The mood remains upbeat even though Michelle brings in some tender comments. They all laugh with her as she tells them of these moments.

"You know that means that he liked you and was protecting you from the jerks that are out there," Justine tells her with a comforting smile. "Trust me, that I know is a family trait." Just as she says that, Kevin tickles her ribs and armpit, making her squirm away frustrated, but she knew it was coming.

"You mean like this?" he says, knowing full well it is. The teenagers laugh with them as they see that they still have the ability to be carefree and love each other fully even in this dark time.

"I couldn't even tell you the number of times he saved me from hooking up with some ass clown at a party," Renee says as she looks at the girls. They all sit there smiling and nodding in agreement, as they were also thankful for that.

"Usually parties at my place or the ones at the moon tower. He would be just sitting around playing Kaiser or watching the fire. Then out of nowhere he would ask a guy which girl he was with. Not sure how, but he heard the entire time that the guy would be saying my name wrong and I never knew it because I was too drunk. He almost got beat up a few times, but his boys would always stand up for him and no harm was usually done." Renee pauses to take a sip of her Dr. Pepper as the conversation is taken over by Max.

"Hey, Renee, is a hard name to say, or in your case, remember that it *is* your name," Max says, almost making Renee spit out her drink as she tries to hold back a laugh. She sets the drink down and gives him a slap. Everyone in their group is laughing at the teenagers.

"I hope you guys never forget him, even when you are partying and move on from here," Jaclyn tells them. "It is these types of moments that fade away without knowing it, so if you can hang on to them in some way it will help Landon to still be a part of your life." She looks at the teenagers with sincere eyes and a blissful tone in her voice, hoping that they take in what she is saying. They all know she is right. The boys, on the other hand, are trying not to get caught ogling her as she talks.

Moving in closer to the table, Kevin says, "Some of you guys may remember coming over and playing football at the house, but using different rules, considering there was usually only three or four of us playing. The rules and how the game was played was created by Landon. Roof was in play and was how you could pass to yourself. There was no out of bounds, but you could only score between the spruce trees and the house at either end. No kick-offs, just throwing the ball, which had to be caught to be returned." He chuckles for a bit as the guys nod their head, remembering times playing with Kevin and Landon in the backyard.

"He would often play by himself out there, playing it off the roof and trying to make highlight diving catches," Ethan adds to his father's story. "I never understood why when I was younger. Now I get it."

"Oh, running through the spruce to score a touchdown or running around the crab-apple trees and using the apples as distractions by throwing them at each other," Shane adds as he bursts out in full laughter, looking at his arms as if he was still scarred by the spruce trees and crab apples.

"Speaking of, I have to know, how did you ever run so fast in those pig-shit-smelling shit-kickers you wore?" Shane asks Kevin.

"I'd tell you, but you are just too slow to figure it out," Kevin replies with the smart-ass smirk that you would expect from him.

"He has been full of shit his entire life, don't let him trick you," Matt retorts to his brother with a smile on his face. They share a laugh at the smart-ass remarks that gets laughs from the rest.

Trent chimes in, "I remember one time out on the farm when we came out and took the yellow three-wheeler out for a spin, and I guess Landon just figured out that if you loosened a screw on the handles it went a hell of a lot faster. So knowing this, we decided to see if we could jump the driveway." He is laughing the entire time he is spitting out the words. "We did jump the driveway, I will say that. Now did we land safely on the bike? Uhm, *no*," he says as he shakes his head while laughing. "I ended up flying off the back and landing hard on acorns. Landon landed with the bike but bounced off, ripping his pants and skidding under the trees. The bike, on the other hand, well, it ran through the trees and into the garden—thankfully not into eyesight of Justine in the kitchen."

"Oh, I saw it," she replies. "It was your mom who said not to get too mad until we see how you two ended up. And, well, other than some scrapes and ripped pants, it wasn't too bad. Plus the story you two cooked up was priceless. Something about getting stuck in the culvert and the bike was in the garden because you were hiding it from the neighbour kids." Justine laughs as she tells the story, the rest of the family and friends laughing with her. The tears are falling from their eyes, however now they are from laughter and good memories.

"Landon was afraid of heights—well, falling more so than being up high, I guess you could say," Scott brings up as he sits there laughing.

"This one summer he was visiting and we went on this roller coaster and he was technically supposed to sit in the middle as he was the smallest, but we got him to sit on the edge. So as the ride was winding over some water below, we would lean into him, making him think he was going to fall out. I swear he was going to shit himself. He was a trouper, though, and never got pissed. He was scared but he barely let it show—but me and Trent could see it on his face."

"I remember that trip," Ethan says. "He was so scared. I was too small to go on the ride. You two bugged him the entire time that he was so lucky he didn't fall into the water, because there were alligators and piranhas in there. That even had me scared a bit. Mom, Dad, do you remember the time we went to some fair on the coast?" Ethan asks his parents.

"Oh, you mean the one were he fainted in the park on our way out to the coast? Then at the park, he puked after going on the fair's version of Disneyland's teacup ride? He came off the ride and straight for the garbage and threw up the hot dog and pop he ate just before he went on the ride. That one?" Kevin replies, trying to keep a straight face as everyone is laughing at the story some already knew while for some it was new to them.

"He was never one for rides. Especially after that," Justine adds.

"No wonder I could never get him to take me on the Ferris wheel at the fairs around here, or any ride for that matter," Michelle says with a chuckle. "I thought he was just afraid of what others might say if they saw us on up there."

"That was part of it as well, trust me," Ethan replies as he looks at Michelle. "He told me after the fair once that he was an idiot for that."

★ ★ ★

After about an hour, Michelle, Renee and Shane head on up to the microphone that is set up at the front of the hall, surrounded by pictures of Landon and the family and various flower arrangements. "May we get everyone's attention for a second?" Renee says loudly into the mic to get everyone's attention over their own conversations.

Michelle steps up to the microphone with a lot less nerves than earlier in the day. "Can we get Kevin and Justine to come and join us up here for a moment?" Landon's parents make their way up to the teenagers with no knowledge of what is coming.

"We would like to thank all of you who helped with this. You may or may not have noticed a hockey helmet being passed along among those in attendance today. We asked everyone to donate whatever they could so that we could make a donation to a charity in Landon's honour. Our math may be a bit off, as we did a quick add before this, not to mention it might be our schooling." That gets a chuckle from the audience as the kids laugh. "Shane, can you bring the helmet to Justine and Kevin? There is roughly $1,110 in there, and I think there is a Bazooka gum and a crumpled up Kit Kat wrapper in there too."

Shane hands Kevin and Justine the hockey helmet with all the stuff inside. The family is surprised and emotional because of the outpouring of respect for their son and the donations made today. They all embrace lovingly as Kevin and Justine tell each of them thanks. Tears are slowly gather in the eyes of the five of them up there. The crowd even shares in this moment as they clap politely and shed their own tears, knowing that even in such a trying time there is still good and hope in the world, especially in this small community.

Kevin gets the mic from Michelle and begins to say a little thank-you speech, even though his wife is better with words and emotions. "I would like to thank everyone for coming out and loving our family and for helping us remember Landon. We thank you for the donation, and we will give it to a great charity in Landon's memory."

Kevin pauses, as he is choking up trying to get through this unexpected speech. He is not much of a speaker at the best of times. "Today is especially tough for us—Landon's birthday, as you all know. So we thank you for helping us all grieve and remember a truly wonderful young man."

He holds onto Justine's hand for support as he slowly gets every word out, taking deep breaths to do so. "I hope that it don't take another one of these moments to get the community, or our family, closer together again. We must give a huge thanks to Renee, Michelle, Shane, Chantal and others of Landon's good friends for being so strong and helping out in any way they could. We never asked them for anything;

they just wanted to respect Landon and do right by him. So I thank you for all coming out, but I have been told by the kitchen that they will be shutting this down shortly. So you are more than welcome to continue talking here for a bit. Thanks again from our entire family."

Kevin finishes off his speech with a smile as he fights off tears and emotion. His wife stands by his side, and they share a quick kiss. The kids stand to the side, smiling and teary-eyed.

The five of them step away from the microphone and head back to their seats to carry on current conversations and start new ones. The crowd slowly begins to disperse, leaving only a few of the closest family members and friends. They all sit around and talk about everything that won't remind them that Landon was put to rest today, but all the stories trigger emotion inside each of them. After an hour or so of sitting around, they begin to load up the flowers and food into some of the vehicles to take back to Kevin and Justine's. The family members all head out to the farm for the rest of the night, while some of the friends head out there for a while but then make their way home.

Ethan and Chantal take Michelle home before they head back to the farm. They try to convince her to come out to the farm and visit, but she assures them that she needs to take some time to be alone right now. It has been a long day for all of them; emotionally and physically, it has drained them. After dropping Michelle off at her home, Ethan and Chantal swing by the moon tower as the sun begins to set. They get out and sit on the hood of the car and watch the sun set.

Ethan holds Chantal in his arms, keeping her warm and embracing her like a loving boyfriend should. They kiss in a quiet moment shared on the hood of the car. Then they leave the moon tower, kicking up dust as they drive away, holding hands. The two young lovers try to move on with their own lives together, with the memory of Landon and how he helped them get together even though he wasn't there.

★ ★ ★

Michelle is back at her place sitting up in her room, her iPod stereo softly playing "Let Me Be Myself" by 3 Doors Down as background music. She has notes from Landon spread out on her bed, her back up against the wall with the pillows giving her support, schoolbooks and yearbooks scattered across the floor. A Kleenex box is next to her on a pillow, as she uses the tissues to wipe the tears away. Her wastebasket is filled with garbage and overflowing with tissues, not to mention that her aim is maybe a bit off.

She goes over the notes that Landon wrote her over the past year at school, some of which are very brief and speak of the class he is in, while in a few Landon wrote about his life and what his plans were—immediate plans of parties and sporting events he wanted to watch or of graduation. Michelle and Landon often wrote to each other at school, since texting wasn't allowed during class time. It gave each of them a physical reminder of something they both wanted but were too afraid to speak of until the day that Landon passed away. Landon's handwriting wasn't the best, and reading some of the letters is a struggle but always worth it for Michelle. The notes were rarely dated, so placing any sort of order on them was not easy, but some did follow a slight storyline from time to time.

She stays up late that night, eventually having to put headphones on and listen to her music that way as she reminisces over the pictures and words that remind her of Landon as well as of what could be of her life. The Arkells' song "Kiss Cam" comes on and Michelle smiles. She quietly sings along as she looks at last year's yearbook.

She gets up from her bed and walks over to the French doors that lead to her balcony. She opens the doors and steps out into the night with a cool breeze gripping her body. While standing outside, she stares up into the sky, amazed and scared by the endlessness that it presents. She heads back in to grab her Winnie the Pooh blanket. She takes it outside and sits in her wicker chair with the yearbook in her hands. She stays out there for half an hour looking over the photos and taking time to enjoy the calmness in the scenery around her.

The wind flowing through the trees, the faint whisper of water on the river passing by in the distance, and the harmony of the wild animal sounds in the forest that surround her place bring her to an understanding for that moment of life, death and her perspective on the ones she loves. The last song she hears while outside in the serenity of the solitary sounds of nature, which she needed after the worst week of her life so far, is the Tragically Hip's "Now the Struggle Has a Name."

Michelle looks up into the night sky of clouds and stars, hoping to find a sign that Landon is okay wherever he is. She feels conflicted as she struggles to believe in the word of the Bible and what the afterlife is like, if there is one at all. Her eyes are no longer full of tears. There is some remembrance found in them, but she is finding her happiness again among the stars and the memories she has of Landon and of her own life—a life that is blessed with love and support from her family and friends, who she may have taken for granted up until that point in her life.

She walks back into her bedroom and shivers as she gets back into the warmth of her bedroom. She turns to close the door, and as she closes it, the yearbook falls from her hand, landing at her feet. As she bends down to pick it up, a shooting star passes by in the sky outside Michelle's bedroom. She doesn't see the shooting star, but as she stands up with the yearbook in hand, she looks at the starry sky and smiles goodnight to Landon, wherever he may be. "Goodnight, Landon," she says softly into the night sky.

She heads off to the bathroom to brush her teeth and do her facial routine. After finishing, she returns to her bedroom and the mess she made around her bed and on her bed. She switches off the main light in the room and turns on the table light beside the bed. She then takes the mess off her bed and places it in a pile to one side. She climbs between her sheets, which are slightly chilled from the night air that passed through from the balcony. Her pillows are fluffed up after being sat on before. She turns around and turns off the table light, with only the dim light of the stars coming in giving some tender light in the room. Finally she lays her head down to fall asleep for the night. She still has her earphones in, and "Goodbye" by Avril Lavigne helps her slowly drift off into dream land.

She slides her hand underneath her pillow as she does every night as she tries to fall asleep. When she reaches under the pillow, she feels something that isn't normally there. She feels around a bit more and realizes that it is a note that must have slid there from when she was spreading them out around her before. She rolls over to turn the light on and looks at the note in her hand. It is folded up four times. One side has her name written on it in random styles of letters, while the other side has a quick drawing of a smiley face with the tongue sticking out. Michelle looks at the note for a bit, trying to remember it, and then realizes that this was Landon's first note that he ever wrote her at school. She wants to read it, but she can't bring herself to. She doesn't want to put it down among the others or on the nightstand to possibly forget about in the morning.

She reaches over and turns the light off again. She puts her head back down on the pillow to once again try to fall asleep. She slides her hand under the pillow and falls asleep with the comfort of the note in her hand and the memories of Landon in her mind. A small smile shows on her face as she drifts off to sleep with the memory of Landon comforting her.

CPSIA information can be obtained at www.ICGtesting.com
Printed in the USA
LVOW081944200613

339468LV00002B/256/P